Flora Harding began writing over thirty years ago to fund a PhD on the disposal of waste in Elizabethan York (more interesting than you might think!), and she's juggled fact and fiction ever since. Under various pseudonyms Flora has written fiction and non-fiction in a range of genres and has more than seventy-five books under her belt. She is fascinated by the relationship between the past and the present which seems to be at the heart of whatever she is writing.

Flora lives in the wonderfully historic city of York and if she goes out of her front door she can see the city walls and the Minster at the end of her street. She is a keen walker, traveller, cook and card player.

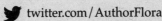 twitter.com/AuthorFlora
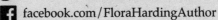 facebook.com/FloraHardingAuthor

Also by Flora Harding

Before the Crown

WITHDRAWN

THE PEOPLE'S PRINCESS

FLORA HARDING

One More Chapter
a division of HarperCollins*Publishers* Ltd
1 London Bridge Street
London SE1 9GF
www.harpercollins.co.uk
HarperCollins*Publishers*
1st Floor, Watermarque Building, Ringsend Road
Dublin 4, Ireland

This paperback edition 2022
1
First published in Great Britain by
HarperCollins*Publishers* 2022
Copyright © Flora Harding 2022
Flora Harding asserts the moral right to
be identified as the author of this work

A catalogue record of this book is available from the British Library

ISBN: 978-0-00-844692-5

This novel is entirely a work of fiction. The names, characters and incidents portrayed in it are the work of the author's imagination. Any resemblance to actual persons, living or dead, events or localities is fictionalised or coincidental.

Printed and bound in the UK using 100% Renewable Electricity
by CPI Group (UK) Ltd

Chapter One

Buckingham Palace, March 1981

The wind is keening round the corner of Buckingham Palace, sending vicious splatters of rain against the window as Diana peers down at The Mall. A few diehard tourists are huddled at the forecourt gates, taking photographs in spite of the weather.

Can they see her? Diana wonders. And if they can, would they guess that the lonely figure at the second-floor window is Lady Di herself; future Princess, future Queen, the girl who finally got the wary Prince of Wales to propose?

Sighing a little, Diana lets the net curtain drop and turns back to the sitting room. Books lie scattered on the sofa and the coffee table is littered with coffee mugs and empty cereal bowls. She takes them into the kitchen, washes them up and puts them neatly on the side. The housemaids would do it, but Diana doesn't mind tidying up. She quite enjoyed being a char for her sister, Sarah, for a while.

And at least it's something to do.

The public assumes she is living with the Queen Mother at Clarence House, but in fact she has been given an apartment on the nursery floor at Buckingham Palace. The idea was to give her some privacy, and, at first, Diana was thrilled. She doesn't care that the rooms, originally intended for nannies and governesses, are smaller than the usual palace rooms. She has her own sitting room, bedroom and bathroom, and the use of the old nursery kitchen. And Charles's apartments are just down the corridor. Well, on the same floor. Barely five minutes away.

It was going to be perfect, a chance for them to get to know each other properly now that their engagement has been formally announced.

At first, Buckingham Palace seemed a haven of peace and security after the frenzy of cameramen that waited outside the entrance to her flat at Coleherne Court. The machine gun rattle of their cameras made her flinch and the massive lenses focused so relentlessly on her left her feeling raw and vulnerable. She couldn't wait to get away from them.

And now...

Diana sighs again and drops onto the sofa, moodily shoving away the books that she is supposed to be reading to understand the role of a royal consort.

Getting engaged to the Prince of Wales was supposed to be more exciting than this, she thinks gloomily.

And it *was* exciting at first, Diana acknowledges to

herself. Standing on the steps in the palace gardens, Charles's hand warm on her shoulder, the great sapphire heavy on her finger, she remembers feeling dizzy with triumph. She might not have an O Level to her name, but she, Diana Spencer, has succeeded in capturing the most eligible bachelor in the world!

Of course, the interview after the formal announcement was a little disconcerting. The reporters asked such thick questions. *Are you in love?* Diana rolls her eyes, remembering. What were they supposed to say to that? They wouldn't be getting married unless they loved each other, would they? True, Charles's answer – 'whatever *in love* means' – was a little strange, but he *does* love her, Diana is sure of it. He's just not an effusive person.

And she loves him. Of course she does. He is amazing. When he proposed at Windsor, he suggested that she think about it while she was in Australia with her mother, but she accepted without hesitating. 'I love you so much,' she told him. 'I love you *so* much.'

And then Charles said, 'Whatever love means.'

Diana frowns, remembering. It's funny that he said it twice, now she comes to think of it. What did *he* mean?

What *does* love mean?

Unease touches the nape of her neck, an icy finger, but she shakes the feeling off irritably as she gets to her feet. She's just bored.

The truth is that life in Buckingham Palace is not the idyll she expected. When the engagement was announced, the press excitement was at such a pitch that life at Coleherne Court became intolerable. Diana spent that night with the Queen Mother at Clarence House. She endured a rather dull evening with the wrinklies – Charles's grandmother, her own grandmother, Lady Fermoy, and the Queen Mother's private secretary – but they went to bed early and Diana was left to wander around Clarence House, idly running her fingers over the statuettes in the Horse Corridor before the Queen Mother's page, a sweet man, invited her into his office for a drink. Diana remembers being so grateful for the company. He had a folding bike in the corner and she seized it to ride up and down the corridor laughing and singing, 'I'm going to marry the Prince of Wales, I'm going to mar-ry the Prince of Wa-les!'

It was such a relief to be safely engaged. No more waiting by the phone. No more wondering will-he-won't-he? Diana has always known that it was her destiny to marry Charles, she just hadn't been sure Charles had known it too.

But now he does, Diana reminds herself. She is living the fairy tale. She has found her prince and she is determined to be the best of princesses and they will live happily ever after, just like they do in the romances she loves to read.

She had hoped that living under the same roof would mean that she and Charles would be able to spend more time together and, well, get to know each other properly before the wedding, but Charles is hardly there. He has a full schedule of engagements.

'I can't just break them, Diana,' he pointed out when she asked if they could do something together. 'Most of them are arranged more than a year in advance and they're planned down to the last minute.'

4

'I never see you,' Diana pouted.

'Sue Hussey will look after you,' Charles said, but she could tell that his attention was already wandering to the papers on his desk. 'She'll show you the ropes. And Oliver will look after you.'

Oliver Everett is her aide, seconded from Charles's office. He is nice, but he has obviously been told to instruct her in her new role and Diana resents the fact that he clearly thinks she is thick. So what if she doesn't know who was married to Edward VII? She doesn't want to spend her time ploughing through deadly history books about previous Princesses of Wales. Oliver has given her a whole pile of books that so far Diana has refused point-blank to read. Honestly, she didn't leave school at sixteen to end up doing homework now!

Not that there is much else to do. Diana wanders back into the kitchen and shakes cornflakes into a bowl before remembering her diet and cramming them back into the packet as best she can. Watching herself on television after that ghastly interview was a shock. That blue suit with its awful pussycat bow was a mistake – she wishes she hadn't let her mother talk her into it – and it made her look so chubby, so pudgy, that Diana had to swallow hard and will herself not to cry in front of the Queen, who was watching with them. She is *determined* to lose weight before the wedding.

So, no more cornflakes. Guiltily, she thinks of the bowl she had earlier. If only she wasn't so hungry. And so bored.

It's ages until *Crossroads* is on.

Wistfully, she remembers her flat and the giggly, gossipy

evenings with the other girls, legs swinging over the side of armchair. The television on, tights drying over radiators, organising dinner parties, planning larks. She misses her days at the nursery, looking after little Patrick Robertson who was such a sweetie – even cleaning Sarah's bathroom. There was no time to be bored then.

She could ring up one of girls now, but, after her great triumph, how can she tell them she misses them, that the chaotic flat now feels like her safe haven and not the palace? Diana can't imagine calling her sisters either. Jane is married to a courtier and completely at ease in this environment. Diana doesn't want to admit to finding it all a bit intimidating, and as for calling Sarah… At one time her eldest sister had hoped to bring Charles up to scratch herself, and there was no way Diana is going to admit that her life is anything less than perfect now that she has succeeded where Sarah failed.

Restless, Diana heads back to her sitting room, only to stand, irresolute. She needs to take some exercise, but the moment she tries to head out of the palace, her personal protection officer sticks to her like a burr. She can't bear it. Only yesterday she tried to go shopping by herself. It meant slipping out without being seen and she felt ridiculously as if she was escaping. She made it as far as her car, parked in the quadrangle, but, before she could put the key in the ignition, he was sliding into the passenger seat, pulling on the seatbelt and demanding to know where she was going.

'Out,' Diana said.

'Not without me, I'm afraid,' he said, not even bothering to sound sorry.

He'd let her walk around the grounds on her own, she concedes, but they are dreary enough at the best of times, let alone in today's weather. Perhaps she should just walk round and round the palace, along those endless corridors? It would be so dull, though...

Unless... Diana's face brightens as she remembers the roller skates she brought with her from the flat. She can't remember why she tossed them into the box of stuff that is still sitting in the bottom of the wardrobe, but they are there, she is sure.

Suddenly energised, she scrabbles through the box until she tugs out the skates with a triumphant laugh.

Why not? Those long, long corridors will be perfect for roller skating. It'll be fun!

Jumping up, she goes to the door of her apartment and looks out. As she thought, there is no one around. Buckingham Palace is always like this. It's not a home, it's an exclusive apartment block; a base for the Royal Family whenever they're doing engagements, but it's not somewhere they *live*. So who is there to care if she skates up and down the corridors?

The courtiers will care, of course. Diana grins as she straps on the skates, imagining their appalled expressions if they caught her whizzing along those red carpets. Let them disapprove, she decides. It's time Buckingham Palace is woken up a bit.

Chapter Two

Diana sets off, long legs pushing smoothly from side to side, the skates soundless on the red carpet that stretches into the distance. In no time at all she is at a corner where she almost collides with a housemaid carrying a pile of bed linen.

'Oops… sorry!' Diana giggles and rolls on, leaving the housemaid to gape after her.

She is roller skating in Buckingham Palace! Diana laughs out loud at the absurdity of it. The naughtiness of it is thrilling, the knowledge of how thoroughly everyone – even Charles, probably – would disapprove if they knew what she was doing. But she feels herself again. She has let herself become 'Shy Di', when she isn't like that at all. She's the fun one, the giggly one, the one who knows what she wants and is always up for a lark.

Enchanted, she speeds past door after closed door, past priceless porcelain vases placed on spindly gilt tables, past marble statues and elaborate clocks. From the walls,

Charles's ancestors stare down with bulging eyes and lugubrious expressions, burdened by their wearisome royalty.

She passes two footmen, who don't quite manage to hide their grins in time as they leap off the carpet, and waves cheerily at them. An older member of staff steps aside for her, stiff with disapproval, so she waggles her fingers at him too, enjoying herself too much to stop. She goes faster and faster, swishing down the long corridors and skidding round corners, until the faces in the endless portraits blur and when she stops at last she is panting and grinning.

She finds herself in front of a portrait of a young woman with a bright, mischievous face. Her dress is cut low to reveal a voluptuous bosom and her hair is dressed in a style Diana associates with the heroines on the front of Barbara Cartland's Regency novels, pulled into a top knot with curls on either side. She must be one of the many royal mistresses, Diana thinks, but when she peers closer, balancing on her skates, the plaque reads: Princess Charlotte of Wales.

So, not a mistress but a princess, just as Diana herself is going to be. Diana has never heard of her before, but then, History has never been her strong subject. Or Maths or English or Geography or indeed any of the other subjects that bored her so much at school, she admits to herself.

Did Charlotte marry a Prince of Wales, as Diana is going to? Was she hidden away before the wedding the way Diana is? Was she bored and lonely, too?

Charlotte doesn't look bored. She looks as if she would

have roller skated around the palace too if she had had the chance.

Diana twirls on her skates and pushes away, feeling obscurely as if she has found a friend.

She means to go and look at Charlotte's portrait again, but the corridors are all the same and she has forgotten where she stopped. It is not until she is walking to the Queen's apartments with Charles – a rare moment when they are alone together – that she sees it again.

'Oh!' she exclaims in delight. She almost says: *There you are!*

'Who was she?' she asks Charles, who has walked on, not realising that she has stopped.

He turns and comes back, looks at the picture. 'That's Princess Charlotte,' he says.

'I know, it says that,' says Diana with a touch of impatience. 'But who *was* she?'

'The Queen who never was,' he tells her. 'It's a sad story, really.'

'Why is she called Princess Charlotte of Wales? Was she married to a Prince of Wales?'

'No, no, she was a princess in her own right.' Charles slips instinctively into lecturing mode. He likes it when she asks questions. 'Her father was the Prince of Wales. He was the eldest son of George III and when his father fell ill, he was made Prince Regent. As in Regent Street, Regent's Park and so on. Actually, he was the one who made this into a palace when he became George IV,' he adds. 'Before that it was Buckingham House.'

Diana isn't interested in the history of Buckingham Palace. 'What do you mean, the Queen who never was?'

'If she had lived, Charlotte would have been Queen. She was the Regent's only child.

He was married to Caroline of Brunswick, but the marriage was a disaster from the start. Charlotte must have been conceived on the wedding night, but that seems to have been the last time they...' Charles stops, clearly remembering Diana's much-vaunted virginity.

'The last time they slept together?' she suggests.

'Yes.' He clears his throat. 'They couldn't bear the sight of each other and there were no other children at all, let alone any sons, so Charlotte was heir to the throne.'

'So why didn't she become Queen?'

'She died very young, and before her father and her grandfather.'

Diana looks at the portrait, at the face brimming with life and humour. 'Oh, poor Charlotte.'

'Yes, it was felt to be a national tragedy. She was extraordinarily popular and the whole country went into mourning when she died. The people really loved her and everyone reacted as if they had lost a member of their family. Even the poorest wore black armbands.' Charles shakes his head. 'It's hard to imagine people carrying on like that nowadays.'

'How sad,' Diana says.

'Her death created a crisis of succession, too,' Charles goes on. 'The Prince Regent had brothers but none of them had legitimate children and they were all getting on a bit. There was a rather unseemly rush to get married! And the upshot was that Victoria was born and became Queen in Charlotte's place.'

He looks at his watch. 'Come on, we don't want to be late for the Queen.'

Diana casts a last glance over her shoulder at the portrait as she follows him down the corridor. 'So, if Charlotte hadn't died, Victoria wouldn't have been born and you wouldn't be here either?'

Charles looks startled. 'No, I suppose I wouldn't.' He looks down at Diana's thoughtful face. 'If you're interested in Charlotte, ask Oliver. He'll know much more about her, I'm sure.'

———

'Princess Charlotte of Wales?' Oliver frowns.

'The Prince of Wales said that you would know more about her.'

'I don't, I'm afraid,' he says slowly. 'But I think I might know someone who does.'

Two days later, he rings Diana up and asks if she would go down to the Prince of Wales's office on the ground floor. 'There's someone here I think you might like to meet.'

A dumpy woman is waiting with Oliver in a meeting room that is blissfully quiet after the constantly ringing phones and air of feverish activity in the offices where the royal wedding is being planned.

'Amelia Bell is an historian,' Oliver explains. 'She's been working in the royal archives at Windsor Castle.'

'Oh?' Puzzled, Diana returns Amelia's firm handshake and smiles. What do the archives at Windsor have to do with her?

'Amelia found a journal belonging to Princess Charlotte of Wales hidden away amongst a whole lot of other papers,' Oliver goes on, and Diana straightens, suddenly alert.

'*Really?*'

'Yes, it was a lucky find,' Amelia tells her. 'It's very rare to come across anything quite that intimate written by a member of the royal family in that period. I've spent the past year transcribing it. Not the easiest task as her spelling was appalling,' she adds with a dry smile. 'It's not ready for publication yet, but if you're interested in her, I could let you read my transcript.' She nods at a dull-looking lever arch file on the table.

'Oh… thank you!' Diana pulls out a chair and sits down, pulling the file towards her. 'I saw her portrait,' she confides. 'I thought she looked interesting… and fun.'

'I believe she was,' Amelia says as Oliver leaves them with a murmured excuse. 'She was certainly reckless and prone to falling in love with the most unsuitable men.'

'Really? We're talking Regency, aren't we? Jane Austen and all that? I didn't think young ladies then had any freedom to behave badly.'

'Most young ladies would have been brought up very strictly, yes, but Charlotte had an unusual upbringing, quite apart from being a princess. Her parents loathed each other and she lived separately from both of them with her own household.'

'Poor thing. She must have been terribly lonely.'

'She was very close to her servants, who were her real family,' Amelia says. 'And she had governesses and tutors, of course, but none of them were in a position to check her. She was heir to the throne, after all. As a result, she was never taught the social graces you would expect. She spoke too frankly and laughed too loudly and strode instead of walking. There was nothing demure about Charlotte!

'And, of course, her parents hardly set her a good example either. Caroline – her mother – was a German princess, but she was coarse and vulgar and the Prince Regent couldn't stand the sight of her. He said she was dirty and that she smelt like ripe cheese – but he was no oil painting either,' Amelia adds wryly. 'He became grotesquely fat and was crippled with gout much of the time. There was open warfare between him and Caroline, who was still the Princess of Wales, and poor Charlotte was stuck in the middle, a weapon used by both parents – though neither of them seemed to care for her at all.'

Poor Charlotte, Diana thinks with sympathy. She knows what it is like to grow up with warring parents.

'Princess Caroline's way of life was scandalous, but she had a lot of sympathy in the country because the Prince Regent treated her so badly,' says Amelia. 'Still, she didn't do well by her daughter. Charlotte was desperate for affection and attention and was easy prey to unscrupulous men like Captain Charles Hesse, who was an officer she often met at her mother's house. Caroline actively encouraged Charlotte in her liaison with Hesse, passing on letters and arranging for them to meet. Once she even locked Charlotte into her bedroom with him and told them to amuse themselves together, which is not what you would expect a careful mother to do, especially when Hesse was said to be her lover too.'

'Eeuww.'

'The whole affair was very unsavoury,' Amelia agrees, seeing Diana's expression of disgust. 'Really, it's extraordinary that Charlotte turned out as well as she did. She might be too impulsive and unconventional for polite society, but she was warm and generous and gave away much of her small allowance to charity. She was certainly very popular with the people. They were tired of the mad old King, George III, and they disliked the Prince Regent for his extravagance and dissolute lifestyle, so Charlotte was their hope for the future and they showed it. She was cheered whenever she went out and her father was pathologically jealous of her popularity! When she died so unexpectedly, it was as if everyone had lost a much-loved member of their own family. There's been nothing like the outpouring of grief then, before or since.'

'I can't believe nobody's heard of her before,' Diana says, frowning.

'At the time people were sure that Charlotte would never be forgotten but...' Amelia shrugs. 'Time moves on,' she says after a moment. 'The people had a young queen in Victoria instead. Personally, I think it's a shame,' she adds with a faintly embarrassed smile. 'It's very unprofessional of me, but I think Charlotte would have been a good queen.'

'Thank you for telling me about her.' Diana rests her hand on the file. 'May I keep this to read?'

'Of course. It's a copy, so please keep it as long as you like.'

Diana clutches the file to her chest as she stands in front of Charlotte's portrait, thinking about what Amelia has told her. The painted face with its alert expression and lips tilted on the verge of a smile gives no hint of what must have been a sad and lonely childhood and no premonition of a tragically early death.

Feeling oddly excited at the prospect of getting to know Charlotte better, Diana carries the file back to her sitting room. Outside, it is raining again, but, for once, she isn't bored and restless. Settling on the sofa instead, she opens the file and starts to read.

Chapter Three

London, December 1813

'The Princess! The Princess!'

Small boys run alongside the carriage, ignoring the footman's glare, shouting and huzzahing until I throw them some coins. They create a ripple of excitement that makes pedestrians stop and turn. Hats are snatched off heads and shaken in the air. Curtseys are bobbed. Everyone smiles and looks cheerful in spite of the press of people and the broken pavements and the general hubbub.

It is gratifying, I have to admit.

It is a soft December day, the kind that comes as an unexpected gift in the middle of winter. The sky is a pale blue and there is just a gentle breeze to waft away the smell of dung and soot that burns the back of the throat and is threaded always through London's air. My dogs, Toby and Puff, put up their noses and sniff with pleasure.

Toby, curled up beside me, is a female in spite of her

name. An elegant Italian greyhound, she was a gift to my father, who does not care for dogs, and he passed her on to me. By the time she had four puppies, it was too late to change her name. Puff, my old pug, contrary and stiff as always, sits in solitary splendour opposite us, ignoring my attempts to coax him to join Mercer, Toby and me.

I have been granted permission to take the air with my dearest friend, Mercer Elphinstone, and we are bound for Hyde Park, though it would be quicker by far for us to walk by the time William the coachman snarls his way up Cockspur Street and Haymarket before turning the carriage, not without difficulty given the crush of vehicles, into Piccadilly. But I may not walk through the streets of London and so we have to sit here while William does his best to manoeuvre the carriage past drays, wagons and carts, through a tangle of curricles and phaetons and barouches and prancing horses, avoiding crossing sweepers, dogs and darting urchins.

'The people love you,' Mercer comments with a smile. She is looking elegant as always in a pelisse and matching hat in the subtlest shade of green. I declare, I have never seen my dear Mercer look anything less than elegant. If I did not admire her so much, I would be scared of her.

I stroke Toby's silky ears. 'It is lucky that they do, as no one else does,' I say. I mean to sound careless, light, but even I can hear the sadness in my voice.

It has been nearly six months since my nurse died and I still miss her so! *She* loved me. Eliza Gagarin fell passionately in love with a Russian count and married him before discovering that he already had a wife, but she put up her chin and refused to be ashamed. I was sorry for her pain, but glad for myself; for Geggy was more of a mother to me than my own has been. Losing her is the greatest grief I have ever known. One day she was fussing around, clicking her tongue at a stain on my dress, the next she had taken to her bed and the strength drained remorselessly out of her.

I carried her over to the window so that she could look out over the gardens to St James's Park and we sat together watching the blackbirds singing. I held her thin hand, trying to warm her flesh with the heat of my will. I tried to joke her into wanting to live, reminding her of all the times I had been naughty and she had been betrayed into a laugh.

I wanted to remind her of her Russian count, but I was afraid to make her think of the great wrong he had done her. She loved him so passionately, though. I envied her that. Love, the idea of a love so strong it overbears all reason, all sense… I yearn for it.

I hoped to find it with Captain Hesse, but it seems I was wrong about that.

It is strange, I know that Geggy is dead, but I look for her still. Mrs Louis is my dresser now, and I like her very well, but every morning when she comes in, I look up expecting to see Geggy instead. It is as if there is a Geggy-shaped hole moving around the house, a space where she should be but isn't.

'It is lucky I have you, Toby,' I say, kissing her nose. 'Puff only cares who feeds him.'

'Come now,' Mercer begins, 'your family—'

'What does my family know of love?' I retort. 'My father

despises me. My mother thinks only of herself and her enmity with the Prince.' I brood on my family. My royal aunts are tedium personified, and as for my uncles… one has been accused of murder, another has ten children by his mistress and all are as fat as figgy puddings and dissolute to boot.

Oh, we are a fine family indeed!

'My dearest grandpapa, yes, *he* loved me, but he is cruelly shut away, and as for the Queen… Well, my grandmother is hardly what you would call a loving figure, is she? Oh, Mercer, if you knew how *tedious* it is at Windsor! In the morning I must do my lessons like a child, and in the afternoon I may ride in the Great Park and in the evening I play cards with my aunts and then we go to bed early and the next day we do it all over again.'

Mercer laughs at my expression. 'Well, you are in London now,' she reminds me.

'Much good it does me! I might as well be a prisoner,' I grumble. 'My father is determined to keep me from society. I am not to go to the theatre or to balls. If I go to the opera I must sit at the back of the box where no one can see me and leave before the end. I may as well be in the nursery still for all the entertainment I am allowed! Any other young lady of seventeen is allowed to escape the school room, but not I. No, I must still sit at my desk for *hours* every day, hemmed about with tutors and governesses with a walk around the gardens if it is not raining, which it usually *is*, and if I'm very lucky an airing in the carriage in the afternoon!'

Worse, I have to listen to the Bishop of Salisbury – the bish*up* as he pronounces it – prosing unctuously on and on and on about my education, for which he is responsible. I call him the Great Up, although never to his face. I mimicked him to Captain Hesse once, and Charles laughed. 'Pompous old fool,' he said.

Oh dear, I wish I had not remembered Charles.

'Besides,' I go on, I am only in London because the Prince wishes to force me into a marriage with the Hereditary Prince of Holland!'

'It is a match that makes sense,' Mercer says gently. 'Now that Bonaparte is in retreat, Britain needs allies against any future threat from France. Lord Castlereagh is planning to create a kingdom of the Netherlands from the old United Provinces and the Austrian Netherlands.' Mercer is always well informed. 'A marriage between you and the Hereditary Prince would cement the alliance and provide Britain with a vital foothold on the Continent. It was the French invasion of the Low Countries that brought Britain into this wretched war,' she reminds me. 'We cannot afford to be in that position again.'

'I know that,' I say irritably. I may not be as clever as Mercer or as au fait with diplomatic manoeuvring, but I am not a fool. I am well aware of how desperately the country has suffered through these long, dreadful years of war.

But... oh, how can I explain to her? 'I know the government wishes the marriage, as my father does but, Mercer, I have not even met him yet! It is barbaric the way they seem determined to force me into marriage with the Prince.'

'My dear Charlotte, I am sure you cannot be forced

against your will. But you must be aware that you cannot marry to please yourself only. Very few of us can do that.'

'Consider what misery resulted from my parents' marriage, Mercer!' I say. 'They met but hours before they were wed. Am I to suffer the same fate? I am utterly in my father's power, and when I marry, I will be in my husband's. Who I wed will be the most important decision of my life, and I am determined that it is one I shall make for myself.'

Mercer draws in a breath as if marshalling her arguments. 'Do you object to the Hereditary Prince himself?'

'I know nothing of him,' I say, 'although I had the pleasure – if you can call it that – of seeing his father dining in his shirtsleeves.'

Mercer looks disapproving, as well she might. 'Where was that?'

'At Sandhurst College, at a celebration for my father's birthday. I was surprised to be invited, but it was such a hot day, I wished I had not gone.' I remember the stickiness of my stays, my vain attempts to cool myself with my fan.

'The men were all shockingly cut. My father drank so much he couldn't speak. My Uncle York tipped back in his chair and fell right over the back. He cut his head on a wine cooler, and had to be bled and sent back to London. The Prince of Orange took off his jacket and his waistcoat and sat brazenly in his shirt.' I shook my head. 'It was *not* an edifying sight.'

'You would not be marrying the father,' Mercer points out. 'I have heard good things about his son.'

'Mercer, not you too!' I say in dismay.

She holds up her hands. 'I suggest only that you agree to meet him and decide for yourself.'

'I already have.' I sit glumly back against the seat. My grandmother would scold me for lolling, but I don't care. 'The Queen came up to Carlton House with some of the aunts last week. When I went in, the Hereditary Prince's portrait was propped up on a chair. They didn't even *try* to be subtle.'

Mercer puts a gloved hand to her mouth to cover her smile at my outrage.

'Of course, my father was there, looming over me and pointing at the portrait. I was invited to give an opinion on him,' I remember with a sigh.

William is muttering with relief as the traffic clears somewhat in Piccadilly and he can urge the horses into a trot towards Hyde Park. The iron wheels rattle over the paved road as we bowl along, leaving the shouting urchins behind.

'What did you say?'

'What could I say? How could I possibly tell what I thought of him from a portrait? In the end I agreed that he was "not ugly" and you would have thought I had expressed the most violent love for him! My father was beaming. Even the Queen managed a smile. Now I have promised to attend a dinner next week where the Hereditary Prince will be present.'

'Well, then,' says Mercer, satisfied. 'You can have no reservations in agreeing only to meet him.'

I shake my head. 'With my father and the entire

government standing behind me and prodding me into his arms? I will be engaged before the first course is removed, and then where will I be?' I demand fretfully.

'My dear Charlotte, I feel sure you are exaggerating. Meet Prince Willem. Decide for yourself if you like him. If you don't, you cannot be forced into a marriage you dislike. But if you do, then there can be no obstacle to your happiness.'

'It is not as easy as that,' I sigh.

Mercer turns her probing gaze on me. 'What is it that makes you anxious?'

I stroke my muff, not looking at her. 'I may have been... indiscreet,' I say at last.

'Indiscreet?' Mercer looks shocked. 'My dear Princess, how?'

I tell her how I fancied myself in love with Captain Charles Hesse. I was only fifteen. Lady de Clifford allowed him to ride beside my carriage sometimes and I met him at my mother's house. I was foolish, but how was I to know that it was so wrong when my mother encouraged the liaison? It is only since Charles was sent to re-join his regiment in Spain that I have realised how unwise I was to write to him quite so passionately.

Uncomfortably, I tell Mercer about the letters. 'I did ask him to burn them, but I am not certain that he has,' I confess, peeping a glance at my friend. 'And then, when I heard he had been injured at the battle of Vitoria, I sent my portrait and a watch to the Marquess of Wellington and asked him to pass them to Captain Hesse and to make sure that he had the best of care...'

I trail off at her expression.

'Charlotte, what possessed you to do such a thing?' she says, appalled, and shame prickles up my cheeks.

'It was foolish, I know, but I *loved* him and my mother welcomed him.' I hang my head. 'He was often with her, but I fear now that she encouraged the affair for the sake of getting me in her power and using me against the Prince.'

It pains me to say it. My mother is a difficult, troublesome woman and if a fraction of the allegations made about her are correct, she has behaved appallingly. But she is still my mother.

'The Princess of Wales has done you a grave disservice,' Mercer says seriously. 'You were young and you were badly advised, Princess, and the letters were bad enough, but why did you then send him gifts? You must have known how improper that was and how damaging it would be if it got out.'

'I did know, but I was angry.' I try to explain. 'You weren't at Sandhurst that day, Mercer. If you had seen them, my father and my uncles and those generals, you would understand. If you had seen their red, sweating faces, heard their bellowing laughter. The shouting and the slurred words. They drank themselves insensible while the soldiers who won that battle were quite forgotten! So many men have died! Others, like Charles, will have to live with terrible injuries. I thought then that he had lost an arm, and although it seems now that it is not as bad as that, at the time I felt... ashamed. So I sent him my portrait and the watch as my way of apologising.'

'Oh, Charlotte...' Mercer sighs. 'Always so impulsive!'

I twist my fingers together inside my muff. 'What can I do? If the Dutch marriage does go ahead but my indiscretion gets out, the alliance will be ruined and so will I! I do not wish to marry Prince Willem, and I do not wish to be ruined either. I can have no peace until my letters and gifts are returned or destroyed.'

'Do not despair,' Mercer says. She thinks for a while, her eyes on the bare trees. Hyde Park is a haven away from the clatter and clanging of the streets, but I can take no pleasure in it today with my mind so full of my problem. 'Captain Hesse is still in Spain? May I confide in my father?' she goes on when I have nodded.

Admiral Keith is a distinguished naval officer. I nod again, reassured. 'What will he do?'

'He will write on your behalf and ask for the letters to be destroyed and the gifts to be returned. If Captain Hesse is a gentleman,' Mercer says, 'he will do as he is asked and you may be easy.'

I hope she is right.

Chapter Four

Buckingham Palace, March 1981

Diana closes the journal slowly. Poor Charlotte, so desperate for love and affection! It doesn't sound as if being a princess was much fun for her.

Diana's understanding of romance and Regency life comes exclusively from Barbara Cartland's novels which she loves, while not being able to stand the author, her stepmother's mother, ghastly, vulgar woman that she is. If she had been asked to imagine the life of a Regency princess, she would have pictured luxury and splendour, a constant round of balls, of gaiety and doting servants and exquisite manners.

But Charlotte seems to have led a dreary existence, torn between her warring parents and cared for by neither of them, treated as little more than a nuisance.

Diana knows how that feels. She had such hopes when she moved into Buckingham Palace, but now that she's here, nobody seems to know what to do with her. Charles is busy with his own engagements, and the Queen so rarely has any time to herself that Diana is reluctant to intrude when she does. The other members of the royal family have their own apartments and are rarely encountered.

Diana has the wedding to plan, of course, but most of that is being done for her. She loves the design the Emanuels have come up with for her wedding dress. It is a fairy-tale fantasy of a dress, and exactly what Diana has dreamed of, although she was horrified when the first measurements were taken. Her waist measures twenty-nine inches! Coming on top of the mortification of those awful engagement pictures, it was enough to make Diana determined to diet.

She's doing her best, but with nothing to do but drift around all day it's hard to take her mind off the hollowness in her stomach. For a building with so many people in it, Buckingham Palace feels eerily empty. Diana imagines the staff in the offices below like a colony of efficient ants, everyone knowing exactly where they're going and what they're doing, while she is up here in her apartment, trying to ignore how hungry she is.

She has even abandoned her roller skates. Some faceless official down in the bowels of the palace has clearly reported her excursions along the corridors because the last time she saw Charles he chided her gently about it. It was 'rather childish', he said. 'Not really appropriate.'

Chastened, Diana put the skates away and ate three bowls of jelly and custard to make herself feel better.

And then felt so bad about *that* that she made herself

throw up. Diana shifts on the sofa, remembering the strange sense of rightness she had felt. Not with her head down the loo, not then, but afterwards, when all disgusting traces of custard and jelly had been flushed away, she sat on the floor and rested her head against the bath and felt... purged.

Peaceful.

The ring of the phone on the table beside the sofa jangles the silence and makes her jump. She's not used to it ringing. Since she moved into the palace, hardly anyone has been in touch. Perhaps they all think she is too grand now, while she is hesitant about letting any of her friends know that she isn't nearly as happy as she should be.

It's Charles. 'Can you come along to my study, Diana?'

'All right,' she says. 'When?'

'Now.' He sounds faintly surprised, as if that should have been obvious.

Diana is tempted to say that she is busy, but she so rarely gets the chance to be alone with her fiancé now.

'I'll be along in a tick,' she promises.

She rushes into the bathroom to pinch some colour into her cheeks and fluff up her hair, suddenly excited at the thought of seeing him. Everyone thinks she just wants to be Princess of Wales, but it's not true. She *loves* Charles. He isn't like the young men she has known. He's a serious person.

She just doesn't know how to reach him.

Next to Charles, Diana always feels a little stupid, a little silly. He loves her, she is sure of it, but sometimes she's afraid that he thinks of her as an adorable little kitten, sweet and pretty and amusing, but to be put aside when serious matters are to be discussed.

Diana is desperate to make him see her as more than that. She wants to be a princess he can be proud of: slim and elegant and sophisticated.

In the mirror, her reflection looks dubiously back at her. It's cold in the palace and she's wearing cords and a patterned jumper over a blouse with a frilled collar. It's a look Diana likes but is it a bit… young? A bit scruffy?

A bit *childish*?

Oh, it's too late to change now. She makes a face at herself in the mirror. Charles hates to be kept waiting.

His apartments are on the same floor as Diana's, but they could hardly be further away. She had hoped they would be closer and imagined cosy evenings curled up on the sofa together, her apartment there really just for propriety's sake. But it hasn't worked out like that.

Diana hurries down the long corridors, past closed door after closed door, each like a hand held up: Keep Out. It would make sense at the palace gates but here, inside, surely there's no need for this lack of welcome?

But then, as she is learning, Buckingham Palace is not a home. It is an office, a workplace, somewhere to spend the night between engagements.

She is out of breath by the time she reaches Charles's apartment and an impassive footman opens the door for her.

'Hellooo!' she calls cheerfully as she goes in.

'Ah, there you are.' Charles appears in the doorway. 'Come in, Diana. We were just discussing you.'

'We?' Diana falters, on her way over for a kiss.

'Edward and Oliver are here,' Charles says, bestowing a perfunctory kiss on her cheek.

'Oh.' Edward is his private secretary, Oliver is ostensibly hers.

Both men stand when she comes in. Diana nods shyly in response to their greetings. They are both kind to her and it's not their fault that whenever she's in with them she feels like a child summoned to talk to the grown-ups.

'We think it's time we introduced you to the public,' Charles says, waving at them all to sit.

'Introduce me?' Diana forgets her inhibitions as her head jerks up in surprise. Surely the last thing she needs is to be introduced to the public! 'Don't the public already know everything there is to know about me?'

Every time she goes out, she is greeted with almost hysterical excitement. It is the strangest feeling to be the object of so much interest. Diana can never decide if she finds it flattering or intimidating. Either way, it is overwhelming. All those avid eyes on her, watching, assessing, judging. What is she wearing? How is she moving? What is she doing? Is she smiling too much or not enough?

Wherever she goes, she is met by cheering crowds. Like Charlotte was, in fact. Everyone seems delighted for and about her, but there's a bit of Diana that worries that they turn away after she has passed and suck their teeth and tell each other that she's looking chubby.

'We're talking about a formal engagement,' Charles says. 'This will be your first official appearance as the future

Princess of Wales. We want to show you off to the best advantage.'

'What does that mean?' she asks.

'A formal occasion. More controlled than the usual hysteria.'

He sounds faintly dismissive, as if the excitement that has surrounded her so far isn't real. Can't he see that she is having an impact already? Diana ducks her head, miffed. The popularity of the monarchy has soared since their engagement was announced. Nobody ever thinks of that.

'There's a gala evening at Goldsmiths' Hall on the ninth,' Edward says, consulting the diary on his lap. 'Raising funds for the Royal Opera House,' he adds in answer to Charles's enquiring look.

'That sounds very suitable.'

They all nod, ignoring Diana. They are talking over her head as if she's a child.

'And Princess Grace of Monaco will be there,' Oliver says. 'She's giving a poetry reading.'

'Really?' Diana perks up at that. 'Oh, I'd love to meet her!'

She has always admired Princess Grace. She wants to be like her, serene and sophisticated. Grace always looks so composed, so elegant and in control, while Diana is floundering.

When she was Charles's girlfriend and hoping to bring him to the point of proposing, she was clear and focused about what she wanted, but since moving into Buckingham Palace all that certainty has evaporated.

'I'm quite sure the Princess will be looking forward to meeting you too,' Oliver says kindly.

'If she's not, she'll be the only person in the world who isn't.' Charles sends Diana a wryly affectionate look that warms her at last and she smiles back gratefully. 'Nobody is interested in *me* anymore!'

'Are we agreed then?' Diplomatically, Edward glosses over this uncomfortable truth. 'The gala on the ninth? I'll set it up,' he says when Charles and Diana nod. 'Black tie, of course.'

Does he think she doesn't know how to dress for a gala? Diana bristles. 'I wasn't thinking of going in my dungarees!'

'Ask Sue Hussey to advise you on a dress,' Charles says. His attention is already wandering back to the papers on his desk. 'She'll know the kind of thing.'

Diana has no intention of asking Lady Hussey for advice. First thing in the morning, she rings the Emanuels. 'I need a dress,' she says.

Chapter Five

Warwick House, Sunday 12 December 1813

'She'd never even *met* him before she married him?' My chambermaid, Anna, makes no secret of listening as I tell my dresser about my conversation with my grandmother the previous day. Ignoring Mrs Louis's frown, she replaces candles in the candelabra and turns, wiping her hands on her apron.

'She survived three storms at sea before landing in England,' I say, trying to keep my head still while Mrs Louis fastens my hair into a topknot and teases out little curls. 'She met the King at St James's Palace, and six hours later they were married.'

I'd asked my grandmother if she had been happy.

'Happy? Pah!' she had said. 'Marriage for us is not about happiness, Charlotte. It is about duty. And your duty is to wed as your papa and the government advise.'

But why can I not have happiness too?

Anna makes a face. 'I'm glad I'm not royal! I'd want to see what a fellow looked like before I had a brush with him.'

'Anna!' Mrs Louis is scandalised. 'You forget yourself!'

Anna's uncle was head coachman in the Carlton House Mews, and as children we played together in the stables and gardens whenever I could escape from my lessons. When I was given my own household at Warwick House, Anna came too, as my chambermaid. Now she keeps me company whenever I am allowed to walk around the gardens, although we both remember the times when we were able to *run*.

'Usually from an 'iding,' Anna always says, grinning.

It is true, we got into a lot of scrapes, each as mischievous as the other.

Mrs Louis would be horrified indeed if she knew just how much I have heard about Anna's dalliance with the handsome groom in the Carlton House stables and I am not so innocent that I think the two of them have been merely flirting.

'Anna is right,' I say. 'That is why I wish to have a good look at the Hereditary Prince before I agree to even discuss a marriage.'

I am invited to dinner at Carlton House this evening. I am to meet Prince Willem in person, and my belly is swooping and swirling with nerves.

I am not ready. I do not wish to marry a stranger. I do not wish to submit to his embraces, to his bed.

Outside, a sooty fog is pressing at the windows, creeping around the panes in search of a way in. It smothers sound and light in an opaque blanket. I hate it when the fog thickens like this, and today it is abnormally thick and black and cold, like a solid, sinister thing trying to force its way in. We turn away from the windows, afraid, sensing that it would take but a chink for it to pour in and suffocate us.

The fog is like the pressure my father and the government are exerting to persuade me into marriage, making me feel as if I cannot breathe and I cannot escape.

Mercer has brought me good reports of the Hereditary Prince. He has a cheerful, amiable countenance, she says. He is said to be a sensible man. According to her, he has distinguished himself as a soldier, fighting against Napoleon. He has been educated in England and speaks excellent English.

With even my dearest friend promoting the marriage, I am afraid I will be unable to hold out for much longer. I feel as if I am standing on a precipice, with my family and the Prime Minister and the government and diplomatists and Mercer and *everybody* crowding in behind me so that I cannot step back or to the side. The only way to go is to step over the edge and I fear that attending the dinner tonight will mean doing just that.

Mrs Louis is under instruction to ensure that I look my best. The candlelight does little to counteract the gloom of the fog, but I look well enough, I suppose. My hair has been cunningly twisted and curled and I am wearing the Turkish belt decorated with diamonds that my father gave me last week in an unusually affectionate mood. My violet satin gown is trimmed with black lace and has been hurriedly mended where it was torn at the sleeve.

'It is at the back so it will not show,' Mrs Louis decides, sucking her teeth. 'It will have to serve.'

She hands me my long gloves and nods approvingly as I work my fingers into them. 'You look very well, Princess. Very well indeed.'

'Thanks to you, dear Louis.'

'Good luck,' Anna mouths at me as I turn to go. I pull a face in response and she grins. I wish I could stay here with her and Mrs Louis.

In the hall, my Lady Companion, Cornelia Knight, is waiting to accompany me, austerely but elegantly dressed as ever in a mulberry-coloured gown. She is peering through the window and clucking about the fog. 'The coachman tells me they can barely see a foot in front of their faces,' she says. 'He hardly dares take the horses out.'

'Take the horses out in this? Of course they must not!'

'You are not suggesting that we do not go?'

I wish I could, but the invitation has been more of an order and my father would never forgive me.

'It is only a step and it is not actually raining, is it?' I say. 'We shall walk.'

Cornelia looks doubtful. 'But to arrive on foot, and you a princess…'

'If I am to be handed over like a parcel to the first convenient prince that comes to hand, I hardly think my dignity counts for much,' I say. 'I do not think it would be good for the horses to go out in this.'

Still, I cannot help shuddering as I step outside. The dank, blank, black fog wraps itself around us and its chill penetrates to the bone. A sturdy footman sets off first, groping his way through the fog, and we creep behind him, resisting the temptation to hang on to his coat tails.

The fog distorts everything. We are barely steps away from Warwick House before it has been swallowed up behind us and I have no sense of which direction we are headed, although I must have walked this path a thousand times.

Cornelia and I cling together and the distance, which would normally take two minutes' walk at most, seems to stretch alarmingly while the fog presses at us, sliding damp fingers down our necks and wrapping itself around our faces like a ghastly scarf. It is disorientating, not being sure where we are going and testing every step in case we fall.

This short journey is like my life, I think.

Carlton House looms up without warning, and we climb the steps from the garden to the terrace gratefully. Perhaps it does feel like creeping in at the back door, but how much worse would it have been to have arrived at the front?

In any case, there are servants there who leap to open the doors and bow us inside, where so many candles are blazing that for a moment Cornelia and I can only stand and blink. We are escorted to an anteroom where we take off our cloaks and walking shoes and put on our slippers. I contemplate the hair Mrs Louis dressed so carefully. The fog has spangled it with damp and it is now dropping sadly. So much for looking my best.

Cornelia tuts at the mud that has splattered the hems of our dresses, but what can we do? The Prime Minister's wife, Lady Liverpool, arrives and must be greeted. Lady

Liverpool fastens her bright eyes on me, well aware of the purpose of the evening.

'Dear Princess, how well that colour becomes you! We are to meet the Hereditary Prince of Orange at last. Such a charming young man, by all accounts.'

She pats her curls into place in front of the mirror. Somehow *her* hair has stayed in place. I exchange a look with Cornelia. Perhaps we should have come in a carriage after all?

Together we walk up the curving staircase, towards the Prince, and I find myself fixating on tiny details: the intricate design of the wrought-iron balustrade; the ticking of the great gold clock; the smell of the wax candles burning so extravagantly in the chandelier that hangs in the stairwell; the coolness of the marble steps through my satin slippers.

Everything here is the opposite of Warwick House. Where Warwick House is dank and meanly proportioned, Carlton House is elaborately decorated and magnificent. It is all gilding and luxury, all colour and gold and brilliance. The size of the rooms is breathtaking and the light is dazzling in contrast to the thick, dark fog outside. And yet it is not a welcoming house. Its splendour is intimidating, designed to make you feel small and insignificant.

Or that is the effect it has on me, anyway.

The Prime Minister is waiting for his wife outside the Crimson Drawing Room. He bows low when he greets me. He is all deference but we know who has the power here, and whose will is likely to prevail in the matter of my marriage.

A burble of conversation comes from inside the room, swelling in sound as the footman throws open the doors and announces us. I enter first and my father comes towards me, oozing geniality. You would suppose me his dearest child. If I had not known his object, I would have been glad to be welcomed so warmly, but he is only like this because he is having his way.

He waits for the Liverpools and Miss Knight to make their bows and curtseys, then draws me aside.

'Come, my dear, let me make you known to the Hereditary Prince,' he says. 'I need hardly remind you that Prince Willem represents one of our most important allies,' he adds sotto voce.

'No, there is no need to remind me,' I agree, but my father ignores me. He is flushed with triumph already, now that I have been manoeuvred here and he has closed the traps. His face is shining and his waistcoat strains over his considerable bulk. He walks straight through the clusters of guests in the drawing room. They part before him and watch me out of the corners of their eyes.

I put my chin up. I refuse to show them all how uncertain I feel. I will treat this prince as I treat everyone else, so when my father presents me, I do not curtsey. I put out my hand like a man and I look Prince Willem in the eye.

All I take in at first is that he is pale with a high forehead and a strangely shiny mouth, although it is clear too that he is surprised at my offer to shake hands.

I don't care. Ladies do not shake hands with men to whom they are only just introduced – but I am not a lady, I think defiantly. I am the heir presumptive and the future Queen of England.

After the tiniest of pauses, he takes my hand. His is faintly damp. It is not a pleasant sensation and, unbidden, I hear Anna's words again. *I'd want to see what a fellow looked like before I had a brush with him.*

Is the man I will 'have a brush with' this man with his red lips and flaccid handshake?

I try to be generous. I dare say he is as nervous as I. He seems very shy, his eyes skittering away from mine.

The portrait did not lie. He is not ugly, he is just... nondescript. There is a curious blankness about him, a lack of interest in me. He is not looking at me as someone he will lie with. If he looks at me at all, it is as a diplomatic asset, not as a woman.

With a pang, I remember Charles Hesse, with his dark, dashing looks. With those hot eyes and that cool mouth. The assured way he smiled. The way he made me feel as if I were a marvellous gift he could not wait to unwrap.

Willem does not make me feel like that at all. I cannot imagine that he ever could.

Chapter Six

The crimson velvet curtains have been closed against the fog and a fire is blazing. My father keeps all his rooms overheated and in spite of the chill outside, it soon feels overheated and stuffy. Willem is soon looking pink and uncomfortable in his uniform. I am glad of my fan which gives me something to do with my hands while Willem and I make stilted small talk about the weather and my father listens openly, nodding in encouragement and exchanging pleased looks with the Queen as if Willem and I are performing dogs who have mastered their first trick.

At last the Queen leads us in to dinner in the Circular Dining Room where more candelabras blaze down the centre of the table, their light gleaming on the gilt plate, on the elaborately wrought dishes, on the silver cutlery and the crystal. Magnificent lampstands, decorated with writhing golden dragons, stand around the edges of the room, guarding sideboards laden with plate. I see Willem's eyes widen slightly, clearly impressed by the opulent display however much he affects nonchalance.

Opulence is something my father does very well.

It is an intimate dinner with only thirty or so people. I am sitting next to Prince Willem, of course, with Lord Liverpool on my other side. My father keeps the best cook, so I am at least assured a good dinner. While an excellent soup à la Reine is being served, I make laborious conversation with the Prince, uncomfortably aware that everyone within earshot is listening.

However, when I ask him about his journey from Spain, he becomes more animated. He likes being at sea, he tells me, and is never in the least seasick.

'Then that is something we share,' I say.

'Have you then had the opportunity to sail?' Willem sounds surprised. 'I understood from the Prince Regent that you have lived a very retired life.'

'That is true, but I have visited Worthing with the King and Queen. I am never happier than when I am by the sea,' I say. 'I can think of few things I would rather do than spend an afternoon sailing on the *Royal Charlotte*.'

It is comforting to remember the way my spirits lift on board the yacht. Just thinking about the tang on the breeze and how the sun dances over the waves, spangling them in a dazzling display, makes me feel better.

If I were married, I would be able to decide for myself when I wished to go to the seaside. There will be no freedom for me without marriage. Am I being foolish in wanting to decide *who* I should marry? It does not feel like such an unreasonable thing to me.

'I like it when it is rough, too,' I tell Willem. 'There is something so invigorating about the wind in your face and the way the ship heels over, is there not?'

His brows lift. 'You are bolder than most ladies of my acquaintance.'

'I dare say that is because I am not a lady,' I remind him. 'I am a princess.'

I lean to one side a little so that the footman can remove the soup plate. I am aware only of a dark-green arm, a glint of a brass button, a sense of bulky gold frogging, but Willem looks up, and something flickers in his face before he sees me watching and he glances away.

Conversation becomes easier as he helps me to dishes set out near us. In truth, I have little appetite but I let him give me some turbot and a piece of partridge pie. I cut them up and then push them around my plate with my fork while Willem tells me about his time in Spain where he was Wellington's aide-de-camp and I try to ignore the way everyone else around the table seems to be watching us and exchanging significant looks.

He talks sensibly and self-deprecatingly, which I am glad of. I do not care for boastful men. I am reassured to see that he drinks sparingly too. Unlike his father, he shows no sign of getting ready to strip down to his shirt.

Perhaps he would not be too bad as a husband? He is by no means as disagreeable as I expected, but I feel nothing for him.

It is strange to sit next to this stranger and imagine being married to him. I peep glances at him from under my lashes while rearranging the food on my plate. Will I be spending the rest of my life with him? Could it be that one day he will be utterly familiar to me? That I'll know the smell of his skin, how his hair grows, the precise way he cuts up his food?

What is he thinking about *me*? Honestly, he seems more interested in the meal. He asks the footman to fetch him the dish of veal in a béchamel sauce from the other end of the table, and then again for some roast capon.

When the first course is removed, I watch as the footmen flick off the first tablecloth, now stained and crumpled, leaving the pristine one below for the second course. I wish it were as easy to dispose of one's foolish mistakes. If only I could whisk Charles Hesse out of my mind, crumple up the messy memories and dispose of them as easily! Then I could start afresh without the constant worry that my letters to him will be published and expose me to ridicule and shame.

The second course is even more splendid than the first: roast quails and lobster salad, a great haunch of venison, roast beef and a saddle of mutton, a jug of oyster sauce. Interspersed between the meat dishes, pies and casseroles are truffles in wine, jellies and little fruit tarts.

I turn politely to Lord Liverpool with his wispy, receding hair and his intelligent, downturned eyes. I know what is coming. He praises the Dutch Prince to the skies and presses every advantage of the match to Britain.

I feel myself being crowded closer and closer to the edge of that precipice.

Monsieur Watier, the Regent's French chef, produces a spectacular centrepiece of Carlton House rendered in pastry, flanked by two towers of caramelised profiteroles and an array of ices. The desserts are usually my favourite part of a meal, but tonight the taste of pineapple in the ice stings my tongue and although I take a spun-sugar basket, most of it ends up as crumbs on my plate.

It is a relief when the Queen rises and I can leave the table with the other ladies., although I am allowed no time for reflection. No sooner have we entered the drawing room, this one just as overheated as the first, than Lady Liverpool advances and demands to know if I am not delighted with Prince Willem's manners.

I have barely managed to fend her off than my grandmother is beckoning. She is dressed as normal in stiff brocade skirts and a turban. She has no time for modern fashions, deeming them scandalously vulgar. I am wearing smart drawers beneath my gown as so many young ladies do now. They are really very comfortable and if I sit in a certain way, the lace trimming at the ankles is tantalisingly exposed. However, even I am not rash enough to sit like that in front of the Queen.

She points me to the space beside her on a delicate gilt sofa covered in crimson damask. She at least does not ask me what I think. She tells me instead: the Prince is everything I could wish for in a husband. It would be folly to refuse him. I must consider myself fortunate that my inclination is even being taken into account.

And so on. I suppose it gives me a chance to drink my tea.

It is a sign of how eager my father is for the match that the men don't linger over port. The doors are thrown open and the Regent surges through, followed by the other men, and the volume of noise in the drawing room seems to multiply tenfold.

My father wastes no time. 'Come into the anteroom, Charlotte,' he says, and I must put down my cup and saucer and follow him into the adjoining room which allows us some privacy.

'Now, tell me at once. What is your impression of the Hereditary Prince?' he asks. 'He is an estimable young man, is he not?' he goes on, without waiting for my answer. 'You seemed to be enjoying yourself vastly over dinner.'

I would hardly say that. But it is true; in person, Prince Willem is not as offensive as I thought he would be.

My father is looking at me expectantly, anticipation becoming impatience as I hesitate.

'You must have formed an opinion,' he says.

What can I say? 'I... I like his manner very well, at least as much as I have seen of him,' I offer at last.

The words seem tepid to me, but the next moment my father has seized my hands and is shaking them up and down.

'Ah, I am delighted to hear it! Delighted! Did I not say that you would like him? You have made me the happiest person in the world, daughter!'

'Oh, but—' I try to interrupt, dismayed, but Lord and Lady Liverpool are peeping around the door.

'Come in, come in,' my father cries joyfully. 'The Princess has agreed!'

'*No*, I didn't mean... I just...' Horrified at the interpretation he has put on my words, I stumble into a protest, but it is too late. The Liverpools are in the room, gushing their approval.

'Dear Princess, what a happy day this is!'

'How fortunate Britain is to have you as its Princess,' the Prime Minister says, beaming as broadly as his Regent.

They congratulate each other on my loyalty, my sense of duty, my exquisite taste, while I stand, appalled at how quickly the matter has spiralled out of control.

Now my father is at the door, beckoning to a footman. 'Ask the Hereditary Prince to join us,' he orders, all smiles.

I am still trying to make myself heard when Willem is at the door. In the odd way you notice details while everything else is tumbling out of control, I see that the footman who announces him is very handsome, and I see Willem take in that fact too as he pauses.

'Sir?'

'Come in, my boy, and let me shake your hand.' I see Willem suppress a wince as my father wrings his hand. 'The best of news. I am happy to say that Princess Charlotte has agreed to the marriage, have you not, my dear?'

'Well, I... I...' I am stammering, the way I always do when I am upset. I cannot catch my breath. This is all happening too fast. I have *not* agreed to anything but no one will listen to me and how can I now wind this back?

Willem is looking almost as overwhelmed as I am. 'Thank you, Sir. Princess, thank you. This is very good news. My father will be delighted, as will all the Dutch people.'

My father is taking my nerveless hand and slapping it into Willem's. 'Bless you both, and may your marriage be as long and happy as the alliance between our two great nations!'

I can feel Willem's rather damp palm beneath mine, both clasped between my father's hot hands.

The Prince hasn't even made a show of asking me himself or waiting for the courtesy of an answer!

'Papa... Sir...' I keep trying to interrupt, but my father ignores me.

'Mind, no word of this must get out yet,' he warns. 'You're to keep mum, both of you, for now. No puffing it off to your ladies, Charlotte.'

Little chance of that!

It seems there needs to be a political settlement in the Netherlands before the engagement can be made public. Lord Liverpool explains that negotiations about the status of the restored House of Orange are a delicate stage.

'We would not wish to pre-empt any decisions with a premature announcement,' he adds in his rolling, well-modulated voice.

Fine words, given that my own decision has been pre-empted! But what can I say? What can I do? I am overwhelmed by a sense of powerlessness.

'We'll leave the two lovebirds to it, eh, Liverpool?' Still beaming, my father heads for the door, making a big show of offering Lady Liverpool ahead of him.

The door is left open, but effectively Willem and I are alone. He bows gravely.

'I will endeavour to make you happy, Princess,' he says.

And so it seems that it is all agreed. I am engaged.

Chapter Seven

Buckingham Palace, March 1981

A t least she's not being asked to marry a man she doesn't know, Diana thinks, closing the journal, her expression thoughtful. Poor Charlotte, hustled into an engagement without even being given the chance to answer for herself.

Then again, how well does *she* know Charles? Diana settles herself more comfortably against the sofa cushions and mentally ticks off the occasions when she and Charles have been completely alone together.

When she realises that it's barely more than ten, she frowns. Can that be right? She counts them off again, more slowly.

Of course, she has seen her fiancé masses of times, but almost always with other people. They go to Bolehyde Manor to stay with the Parker Bowleses, or with Charles and Patti Palmer-Tomkinson, always with his friends and not hers. Even the even rare times they have an evening in, there are always valets and private secretaries and footmen coming in and out.

She and Charles are never alone, which means they have never had the chance to get to know each other properly. If Diana is completely honest with herself, she didn't try and push it before their engagement. She is not an intellectual, to say the least of it – thick as two short planks as she herself says laughingly if it comes up – and she has been intimidated by Charles's more serious interests. She really didn't want to find out that they had nothing to talk about.

But now they are engaged and will be married. They should be learning about each other.

'A grown-up dress,' Diana said firmly when Elizabeth Emanuel asked her what kind of dress she was thinking of. 'Something black and sophisticated.'

The taffeta rustles seductively as she swings her hips in front of the mirror.

She doesn't look like a little girl now.

Evelyn, her dresser, checks the zip at the back is firmly in place and steps back. 'You look beautiful, ma'am.'

'You don't think I look too fat?' she asks and Evelyn shakes her head.

'You need some bosoms for strapless.'

That's true, Diana thinks. She adjusts the wired bodice that is holding her breasts in place. 'Gosh, I hope I don't fall out,' she says with a nervous giggle. The dress is so very low cut that she has decided against a strapless bra that might show.

'No chance of that with the top being so tight,' Evelyn says, running a critical eye over the dress. 'I'm surprised you can breathe!'

It isn't comfortable, but tonight isn't about comfort, Diana reminds herself. Tonight is about making her mark.

The Emanuels have created a gorgeous confection in black taffeta, off the shoulder and daringly low cut, with dramatically wide skirts. Diana is thrilled with it. She has had her hair done and help with her make-up. Diamonds glitter at her ears and against her throat.

Now she looks grown up.

She is determined to dazzle tonight, her first public appearance as the Prince of Wales's fiancée. She wants to start as she means to go on.

But mostly she wants to wow Charles. She wants him to be proud of her, to look at her and see her as a sexy, glamorous woman for once, as a princess who will stand by his side and not as a jolly teenager.

Taking a deep breath, she touches the necklace at her throat. 'Well, this is it.'

'Good luck, ma'am.'

Evelyn hands her a clutch bag and Diana flashes her a smile. 'Thank you for your help, Evelyn. You've been wonderful.'

Excitedly, she sashays down the corridor to Charles's apartments. The bodice is painfully tight and her shoes are already pinching a little, but it will be worth it when Charles sees how sophisticated she can look when she tries.

She has an absurd desire to visit Charlotte's portrait and let her see how she looks, too, but there is no time for that. Everything is planned down to the last minute.

At the apartment, the footman opens the door for her instantly. Diana smiles her thanks, but he doesn't smile back. Evelyn says they're not supposed to. They're supposed to be invisible.

'Charles?' she calls.

'In here.'

Fiddling with one earring to fix it in place, she walks over to his bedroom and pauses in the doorway.

Charles hasn't quite finished dressing. His head is bent as he concentrates on doing up the cufflinks on his immaculate white shirt while his valet folds clothes and looks supercilious in the background.

Diana smiles. 'Hello,' she says, deliberately throaty.

Charles looks up, sees her and his jaw actually drops. For a moment he doesn't say anything. 'Gosh,' is all he can manage at last, half laughing.

Delighted with his reaction, Diana does a twirl and the taffeta whispers as it swirls about her legs. 'What do you think?'

'Well, it's... it's quite... gosh, it's quite revealing, isn't it?'

Over his shoulder, Diana can see his valet's brows go up and she stops on the point of a second spin.

Revealing? She looks down at herself. 'It's a strapless ballgown,' she points out as if he's a simpleton. 'You *said* it was formal. Everybody wears dresses like this.'

'Well, yes, but…' His face screws up the way it does when he's trying to say something difficult.

'But what?' Diana's confidence, always fragile, teeters.

'You're not *everybody* now,' he says carefully.

'Well, no, but—'

'And…' he interrupts her, peering closer at the dress. 'It's not *black*, is it?'

'Of course it's black!' Diana's voice rises. 'What? Am I not allowed to wear black either?'

'I'm afraid royal ladies only wear black when they're in mourning,' Charles says, half-apologetically. 'It's protocol.'

Protocol, protocol, protocol! Diana is sick of it.

'Well, I'm not a royal lady yet, am I?'

He sighs. 'Didn't Sue Hussey explain all this?'

'I didn't talk to her. I thought I could at least choose my own clothes!' Diana is perilously close to tears. 'It never *occurred* to me I couldn't wear black! And now it's too late to change…'

Her voice hitches and Charles hurries to put an around her. 'Come on now, don't worry, Diana. You look marvellous, honestly. You're going to wow everyone!'

That was exactly what she'd wanted to do, but not by doing the wrong thing.

'I'm sorry,' she says in a little voice.

'Don't be silly.' With a final squeeze, he turns away to let his valet help him into his dinner jacket.

It must be so much easier for men, Diana thinks. They never have to think about what to wear. Black tie suits them all, making them look sleek and somehow powerful while the women are fretting about colours and style and length and jewellery and what shoes to wear.

'You look nice,' Diana says dolefully.

He does. He is much more attractive in the flesh than people think. Taller. More solid.

Charles grins at her. '*Nobody* is going to be looking at me with you in that dress!'

He means to cheer her up, but the damage has been done.

Diana is downcast on the way to the Guildhall. She hasn't been in one of the royal limousines before. The seats are very comfortable and it smells clean and plush and of the wax that has been used to polish the wooden trims to a high shine.

Charles's detective sits in the front with the chauffeur; Diana's is following in a separate car, so at least she's spared *his* company for once. The whole operation of getting into the cars is like well-oiled machinery, every cog sliding into place so that the doors are opened at precisely the right moment, closed in just the right way. The limousine pulls out of the palace courtyard on time to the second.

Everyone has clearly done this many times before.

Everyone except Diana. She doesn't have a clue.

'What do I have to do tonight?'

Charles looks at her. 'Hasn't Sue Hussey been through all of that with you?'

Diana's lower lip pushes out in a pout. Charles is always going on about Susan Hussey. Susan will tell you. Susan will advise you. Susan knows everything.

But Diana doesn't want to be told what to do by yet another 'grown-up', especially not one who is so very devoted to Charles. Diana suspects Lady Hussey doesn't think she's good enough to marry the Prince of Wales and the more Diana is told to listen to her, the more determined she is to go her own way.

'Not specifically.'

She watches his jaw tighten, but after a moment he pats her knee. 'Just smile,' he says. 'You'll be fine.'

That isn't much help, Diana thinks, increasingly nervous. Perhaps she should have listened more to Lady Hussey? But it's too late now.

Chapter Eight

D iana stares out of the window as the limousine moves smoothly up The Mall, past Trafalgar Square and along the Strand. This isn't like driving her little Metro. Police on motorbikes ride ahead and behind, blue lights flashing. There is no waiting at traffic lights, no vans cutting them up, no inching forward through a jam.

She and Charles are in a bubble, sliding through the darkness. They're moving too fast for crowds to gather, but she sees people turning to stare at the blue lights, their faces a blur, and she is conscious of a ridiculous twist of envy for them. She imagines them heading for the pub or a wine bar, or going home and putting their feet up in front of the telly. In the flat in Coleherne Court her friends will be gossiping about their day, borrowing something to wear, fretting about a phone that never rings.

For a mad moment, Diana even wonders what would happen if she opened the door and just jumped out.

But the car is already slowing and suddenly the crowds

are pressing on either side. The sound of cheering is so loud that Diana has to fight not to cover her ears.

'Is it always this loud?' she asks Charles tremulously.

'It's louder for you.'

The limousine draws up at precisely the right spot outside the entrance to the Guildhall. The door is opened. Charles gets out into a swell of noise and a barrage of flashing cameras.

'Wait until you get a load of this,' she hears him say.

And now it is her turn. Hardly knowing what she's doing, she gathers up her skirts awkwardly and steps out. She is met by a roar of excitement, and as she straightens, a gasp runs around the crowd before the cheers redouble. The camera shutters are clicking frenziedly.

It seems that her dress has been noticed.

Smiling desperately and resisting the urge to cling to Charles, Diana lets herself be ushered inside to meet some official dressed in a fur-lined robe.

Her mouth is dry and her cheek muscles are already aching with the effort of smiling. She keeps her eyes lowered, only peeping shyly up as faceless figures are presented to her. The force of attention is almost paralysing. She has felt the pressure of the press pack, but this is something else. Countless pairs of eyes are focused on her. Is she holding her bag correctly? Has her mascara smudged? What if her dress slips?

Oh, God, what if her dress slips?

Now she is expected to climb a whole flight of stairs in a long dress. How is she supposed to do this? Diana bites her lip and picks up her skirts, but they're all in a muddle with her bag and now she's flustered. She can't afford to take her eyes off her feet, but she is excruciatingly aware of a television camera at the top of steps, its lens pointing directly down her cleavage.

Why, oh why, did she choose a strapless dress?

They keep moving forward as if on a remorseless escalator and there at last is Princess Grace, looking serene in blue, her hair entwined with pearls. Diana stands stiffly next to her while they smile for the camera. Next to the Princess, Diana feels blowsy and gauche.

Grace's smile is warm as she chats lightly to Charles for the benefit of the cameras. Diana cannot think of a single thing to say.

When the photographers have been ushered away, Grace turns to Diana. 'That is a *wonderful* dress!' she says.

'Thank you. I think it might not be quite…' Diana trails off.

'There's a lot to learn, isn't there? How are you getting on?'

'Fine, I…' To her horror, Diana feels tears prick and her mouth wobbles.

'Come,' Grace says firmly. 'Let's go and freshen up before the performance.' She tucks a hand under Diana's arm and bestows a gracious smile on guests who are hovering. 'Forgive us, we won't be long.'

She steers Diana to the cloakroom that has been set aside for their use and shuts the door. 'Now,' she says kindly. 'Tell me really how you are.'

Diana sinks down onto a stool and covers her face with her hands. 'I don't know what I'm doing!' she confesses. 'I feel so lost. I thought it would be fun, but nobody tells me anything and I've no idea what I'm supposed to do or wear or *anything*! And everybody's always *looking* at me!'

Grace sits beside her and pats her back soothingly. 'It's hard, I know. But you're doing so well, Diana. Yes, everyone's looking at you, but that's because you look beautiful.'

'Really?' Diana asks tearfully.

'Really. Becoming a princess isn't easy – I should know! – and you're very young, so they should be helping you, not leaving you to find your own way. All you can do is be yourself. I think you've done *wonderfully* well to set your own style already.'

Diana drags a tremulous finger under her eyes. 'It's good to know it gets better,' she says.

'Oh, don't worry, it'll get a lot worse,' says Grace in a dry voice. 'But just keep your head high and you'll be fine. Now, dry your eyes,' she finishes with a final pat. 'We must get back.'

Her dress is on the front page of every newspaper the next morning. Diana spreads them out on the coffee table and studies each one critically. One makes her look really fat and she hides it at the bottom of the pile. The others are more flattering. Yes, she looks quite voluptuous, but the dress is wonderful and Diana thinks she looks sophisticated and glamorous. She thinks she looks good.

And it seems the press agrees. The headlines are

universally enthusiastic. *Di's Daring Debut,* proclaims the *Express.* Everyone is talking about her dress. Diana has made her mark and established herself as a fashion icon – just as she wanted.

Pleased, she hurries along to Charles's apartments, hoping for a word or two of praise. Surely when he sees those photographs on the front page and reads the headlines, he will see that she is already making the monarchy more popular. Isn't that more important than some outmoded tradition about colour?

He is shifting through the various newspapers when she goes in. 'Well, you certainly were a hit with the press,' he says, glancing up with a smile, but there is a hint of reserve that puts Diana instantly on the defensive.

'But not with you?' she asks sharply.

'I thought you looked terrific,' he says, then pauses ominously. 'Granny's a *bit* concerned,' he says after a moment.

So concerned, it seems, that Diana is summoned to Clarence House to see Queen Elizabeth, the Queen Mother.

There's no doubt that Clarence House is cosier and more comfortable than Buckingham Palace, but Diana hasn't found it particularly welcoming. After the engagement was officially announced, some faceless courtier decreed that the public would be shocked if it was known that she and Charles were – shock, horror – sleeping under the same roof. The impression should be given that she was spending the engagement under the wing of the nation's favourite grandmother.

So the first night after the thrill of the engagement,

Diana had to have dinner with Queen Elizabeth, her own grandmother, Lady Fermoy, and Sir Martin Gilliat, an old friend of the Queen Mother's. None of them a day under eighty, Diana didn't think.

Conversation was somewhat laboured. They were perfectly correct, but clearly found her uninteresting, and the feeling was mutual. Diana had the strong impression that they would all much rather have been watching *Dad's Army* with their supper on a tray. She was relieved when they all went to bed and she was left to her own devices.

Charles adores his grandmother, but Diana always finds the expression in the famous blue eyes rather cool when they rest on her. Queen Elizabeth is not impressed by Diana, that is obvious. Or it is obvious to Diana, anyway.

The morning after the Guildhall gala, Queen Elizabeth receives Diana in the Garden Room.

The Queen Mother sits straight-backed on a sofa. As she curtseys, Diana can see behind her a photo of the Queen as a young woman with King George VI. What is it like to be old and to look back at your younger, more beautiful self? she wonders.

The Queen Mother gestures her to a chair opposite and Diana sits a little awkwardly. What will *she* look like when she is old? Will she too become a revered national treasure, a cosy icon of the past? Will she watch a son – or daughter – be crowned and learn to take second place? It is impossible to imagine. Diana is only nineteen and she has never been good at thinking about the future. She thinks about what she wants now and she goes for it. She's not a strategist; she doesn't contemplate consequences.

It is soon clear that for all the gracious smiles, she has been summoned for a thorough ticking off. Charles's grandmother has been looking at the front pages too, and she was less than impressed by Diana's dress. The enthusiastic public response means nothing to her.

'Royal ladies *never* wear black except when we're in mourning.'

'I didn't know that until last night,' Diana tries to explain, 'and then it was too late to change.'

'Don't do it again. And who advised you about that common style? Showing most of your bosom! It was vulgar in the extreme.'

Diana cringes. 'It was just an evening dress.'

'An evening dress that exposed indecent amounts of flesh. Good God, what were you thinking?' The Queen Mother flicks a photo on a front page with disgust. 'You were practically falling out of it!' Her lips tighten. 'You're going to be Princess of Wales, Diana, not a showgirl. 'You need to be above reproach. I could not *believe* how much flesh you were flaunting last night. All those bosoms on show for the public to see!'

That was the point of the dress, Diana thinks bitterly but knows there is no point in arguing.

The Queen Mother's withering comments have destroyed all her pleasure in the dress. The rave newspaper headlines are forgotten. Now she feels chubby, not elegant; ignorant instead of sophisticated.

Mortified, she is close to tears when she gets back to her apartments in Buckingham Palace, where she consoles herself by eating five bowls of custard in quick succession.

Afterwards, she rereads the front pages. Charles's grandmother is right. She looks fat and disgusting, with that vast, swelling cleavage, all that pillowy flesh, exposed for the world to mock.

Diana looks at the empty bowl and is revolted by herself. How could she eat all that custard when she was supposed to be slimming? It churns in her stomach along with her self-disgust and when she is finally able to vomit it all up, she feels calmer and cleansed.

She won't make the same mistake again.

Chapter Nine

Warwick House, December 1813

'The word downstairs is that you're to be married to that Dutchman,' Anna says, moving the jug closer to the fire to warm. It was bitterly cold when she woke me, so cold that frost stars the inside of the window panes and my washing water was covered in a film of ice.

I am still huddled under the covers, cradling the cup of chocolate she brought me earlier. The fire is barely warming the room and I'm glad of the warmth of the dogs pressed against my legs.

'It is supposed to be a secret,' I say, remembering my father's strictures.

I'm not really surprised that Anna knows. The servants' halls are always first with the gossip and it is not as if the Regent ever bothers to lower his voice. There must have been any number of footmen who could have overhead what was happening in the anteroom last night. I wouldn't put it past Lord and Lady Liverpool to have been discussing the outcome of the evening with satisfaction on their way home, careless of any coachman or groom who might be listening.

The news could have got to Warwick House any number of ways.

'It's true, then?'

Mrs Louis is laid low with a chill, so Anna is looking after me and with no one to tsk at her impertinence we have fallen back into our easy childhood friendship.

'So it seems.'

She glances at my face. 'You don't sound very 'appy about it.'

'I have been bounced into it,' I remember bitterly. 'I said merely that I liked Prince Willem well enough – meaning that I would be willing to get to know him further – and the next thing I know, I have apparently agreed to marry him!'

'Can't you say you've changed your mind?'

'It is not that easy.' I sigh. With Lord and Lady Liverpool there as delighted witnesses, I cannot even say that I was coerced, although that is how it feels.

I must marry someone and if not the Hereditary Prince, then who? I have been lying awake most of the night, thinking about it, deciding to be sensible. I'm sure that is what Mercer would advise.

If Willem had not been the handsomest or most charming man in the room last night, he had not been the least either, I remind myself.

'What's 'e like then?'

I hardly know. We were both shy, but he had talked

quite sensibly in the end. Indeed, if he had not been there as a prospective bridegroom, I dare say I would have thought him perfectly amiable. He has good manners, that is important.'

Anna considers this. 'He doesn't sound too bad, and it would be a good thing to be married.' She is nothing if not practical. She cannot afford to be otherwise.

'Yes.' I can hear the doubt in my own voice, but I know that it is true. I have been trying to convince myself that when I get to know Willem, it will all go off well.

'I'll miss you though when you're married. Ma'am,' she remembers to add, an afterthought. She is always forgetting that we are Princess and maid now, are no longer girls, smothering our giggles as we wait to jump out on George, grandson to my governess, Lady de Clifford, and our long-suffering playmate for a while.

Caught by surprise one day, he tripped and tumbled to the ground. 'A pretty queen you'll make!' he told me crossly as he brushed straw off his backside.

Oh dear, I was not kind to poor George. I made him slip outside the gates with me so that we could mingle with the crowds incognito, much to his alarm, and once I made him ride a horse he couldn't control, which was badly done of me, I know. But it *was* funny to see him clinging to the mane – until the horse threw him over its head into a bed of roses. I had meant to intercept him before it came to that. I gave him a watch once, *and* a pony, though, and have lent him much money since, so I am not all bad – I hope.

And now I am about to be married and I wish I was a child again.

'You won't miss me, Anna,' I promise. 'You will always have a place with me. I will keep my household together.' My servants are more family to me than anyone, I realise. 'We will just have a more comfortable house – or so I hope!'

Once I am married, the government will have to find me somewhere to live. I will take all my servants with me. It will be pleasant to have a house of my own, to be able to entertain and be entertained, to go out into the world a bit. I have seen so little of the country I will reign over one day. I should like to see more of it than Windsor and Worthing and Weymouth.

If only I did not have to have a husband first.

Or if I must have one, why cannot I have one who makes my heart beat faster, who makes the blood warm in my veins and pleasure flutter in the pit of my belly?

The way Charles Hesse did.

I catch myself up. I mustn't think of Charles.

I have had no word from Mercer's father, although I know that he has written to ask for my letters to be returned. And the portrait. And the watch.

I must have been mad indeed.

It is all very well for Mercer to talk about Charles being a gentleman, but if he were truly a gentleman, would he not have returned everything long ago without being asked?

My great fear is that instead Charles will choose to make the letters public. If he does that, he would not only ruin my marriage and the diplomatic alliance that everyone sets such store by, he would also destroy my standing in the country. No one would cheer my carriage. They would turn away in disgust or pelt it with stones and abuse the way they do the Prince Regent's.

And my father would surely repudiate me, along with my mother who encouraged the whole affair. My disgrace would give him the excuse to divorce her and marry again. He might have a son, and then I would be utterly cast out.

In spite of everything, though, I think I would rather marry Captain Hesse than Prince Willem.

Anna is poking up the fire, still pondering my engagement. She likes the idea of a house.

'Will it be grand like Carlton House?'

I laugh. 'Nowhere is as grand as Carlton House! But it will be much more comfortable than here, I feel sure.'

'Couldn't 'ardly be less,' says Anna glumly. She sleeps up in the attic. If my rooms are cold, I dread to think what her chamber must be like.

'I shall insist on everything of the best,' I say to lighten the atmosphere. 'There will be all the latest conveniences. New carpets throughout for you to brush. A bathing room, of course, with a bath, and a water closet or two.'

'Ooh…' Anna grins, enjoying the game. 'Will you get Mrs Brough one of them new ranges too?'

'Certainly she shall have one,' I say grandly. 'And I shall have my own barouche and your young groom shall run the stables.'

A smile sweeps across Anna's face. 'Lor, that would be summat, wouldn't it?' Then her expression drops. 'But if you marry a Dutchman, won't you have to go to Holland?'

'Go to Holland?' I echo, jolted out of the game. It is the first time the prospect has even occurred to me. 'No, I will not do that,' I decide. 'Recollect, I will be Queen one day. I cannot go and live in another country... no, no, they dare not ask that of me.'

But the thought nags away at me. Surely they would not expect me to live in Holland? They could not ask it of me. I would not easily be able to get home if needed. True, my grandfather lives still, but he is very ill and my father is so corpulent now that an apoplexy is far from out of the question. And if *that* were to happen, though God forbid, I should be Regent. Or I should be after I turn eighteen, which is only a matter of weeks now.

I have a guitar lesson this morning with Mr Vaccari, but my fingers are so cold that I fumble the chords and in the end I ask him to play for me instead. He sits with his head bent over the guitar and I swathe myself in shawls and let the music soothe my churning thoughts.

I must accept this marriage, for what is the alternative? To continue to be shut away here at Warwick House, confined to the schoolroom? Perhaps I have not chosen my husband myself as I wished, but I will make the best of it, I decide.

Even so, when John the footman throws open the door to the drawing room to announce the Prince Regent and the Hereditary Prince of Orange, my heart lurches uncomfortably. I draw a steadying breath and summon a smile as I rise to greet them. I'm glad Cornelia Knight is with me.

My father is in a jovial mood. 'I've brought Prince Willem to see you, Charlotte,' he booms unnecessarily as Willem bows over my hand. 'I'll have a comfortable cose with Miss Knight next door while you two get to know each other. I dare say you have a few matters to sort out.'

He bears Cornelia out and I hear him ordering madeira from John.

I fix a smile to my face and acknowledge Willem's greeting.

Willem clears his throat. 'I am very glad to have the opportunity to speak further to you,' he says punctiliously. 'We were not able to have a proper conversation last night.'

'No, indeed. I had been hoping to do the same. I'm afraid the Prince Regent's announcement took us both rather by surprise.'

Willem doesn't agree. 'Perhaps I was not expecting matters to be agreed so quickly, but it was hardly a surprise when an alliance has been so earnestly sought by our two countries,' he says. His expression is stolid and I suppress a sigh.

It is all very well talking myself into the practical advantages of a marriage, but faced with the reality of his high forehead, limp clasp and shiny lips, my heart fails me. How will I bear it, tied to his man, *bedded* by him?

But I will have to bear it, I remind myself, I have no option. Nobody else seems to think that I have any choice in the matter.

'We should discuss some of the practicalities of the marriage,' Willem says.

Clearly he is not going to try and make love to me. I am relieved and yet a little piqued, too. Could he not try to make some effort to see me as a woman deserving of some affection, if not love?

'That seems sensible,' I say. I sit down on a sofa and draw my shawl around me. Anna has done her best to stir up the fire but it is having little effect on the room. I gesture to the sofa opposite me, but Willem chooses to stand in front of the fire instead, lifting the tails of his coat to warm himself.

'Your government and mine have already had some preliminary discussions,' he begins importantly and I listen in slowly dawning horror as he enumerates what our marriage will entail. There is no intention to unite the thrones, he explains. It has been agreed that our first-born son will inherit the British throne, our second will be King of Holland.

Our sons. I cannot imagine it.

'While our fathers rule still, I will continue my military career as necessary,' Willem goes on, 'and as my wife, you will obviously accompany me.'

I stare at him in disbelief. I am to traipse around the Continent after him, I who will be Queen? He cannot be serious!

He has not finished. 'Naturally, we will divide our time between England and Holland,' he says

'Oh, no,' I say involuntarily and Willem looks affronted.

'But of course you will have to live in Holland,' he says. 'You will need to learn to live as a Dutch queen. You may choose your own ladies-in-waiting, but while you are in Holland, you will think of yourself as a Dutchwoman.'

It is too much. Ever since Anna put the idea in my head, I have been dreading this and now I am like a teacup with a hairline crack, barely visible at first but which spreads, splinters, fissures until it is beyond saving and it splits in two. My throat tightens unbearably until I hear a wail. It is only after a moment that I realise the sound has come from my own mouth.

'No, oh no, oh no, oh no…'

I cannot bear this! I am being hurried into a marriage which will trap me with this humourless man for the rest of my life. I will never have the freedom I have yearned for. I will have to leave everything that is familiar and be bundled off to a strange country where no one knows me or loves me. No wonder my father supports this! He wants only to be rid of me!

Everything I have dreamed of – freedom, passion, happiness – is being snatched away from me. My face has crumpled in distress and the tears come unstoppably now as I howl. I am mortified and yet I cannot stop myself.

Willem looks baffled by my distress.

Cornelia Knight appears in the doorway, looking concerned. 'My dear Princess! What on earth is the matter?'

I cannot speak for sobbing.

My father looms beside her, tutting irritably. 'Come, Willem,' he beckons, ignoring me completely. 'This is women's work. We'll leave them to it.'

'But Sir…!' Cornelia protests involuntarily.

'What?'

'Princess Charlotte is upset…'

'I can see that. I've got eyes, don't I?'

'Do you not wish to comfort her?'

'I haven't got time to deal with weeping women.' My

father brushes her aside. 'We've got a pressing dinner engagement in the City. Come on, Willem.'

Willem bows stiffly to me and sidles past an outraged Cornelia, leaving me to weep bitter tears at my own powerlessness. I will have to leave my country and all that is familiar. I must learn to be a Dutchwoman, although my destiny is to be a British queen. Worst of all, I must be married to a man who clearly cares nothing for me and has not even the courtesy to comfort me in my distress.

Chapter Ten

Warwick House, 7 January 1814

My eighteenth birthday. On what should be a momentous day, I wake with a heavy head. My nose is red and the back of my throat feels raw and tight. So perhaps it is just as well there are no amusements planned to mark the day from which I might be Queen. I do not feel sociable.

Outside, the trees in Carlton Gardens are rigid and glittering with frost and the ground is iron-hard. The temperature at night has not risen above freezing since a great fog just after Christmas smothered London. It ushered in a cold the like of which no one can remember. The horses' hooves skid on the icy cobbles and every breath leaves great clouds hanging in the air.

The cold is penetrating. There is no escape from it. Even those of us fortunate to have a fire to huddle round are permanently chilled, our muscles aching from the effort of not shivering. I worry about the little birds who sit huddled against the bitter air, their feathers fluffed up. I save crumbs from breakfast and scatter them on the windowsill so that they will have at least something to eat. They are becoming quite tame, especially the blackbird with his glossy plumage and bright, curious eyes.

The kitchen is by far the warmest place to be. Mrs Brough, the cook, is indulgent. Just as when I was a child, she lets me sit at the table and feeds me little cakes although I am sure I must be very much in the way. Polly the kitchenmaid is wide-eyed at my presence until I share my cakes with her.

'Don't you be encouraging her now,' Mrs Brough says, tutting. 'Polly's got work to do.'

'Don't mind Mrs Brough,' I say to Polly, holding out a cake, and she creeps closer to take it shyly, although she seems more fascinated by my shawl and is thrilled when I let her finger the fringe.

I would be quite happy to spend my birthday in the warm kitchen but I slipped on the ice getting into my carriage two days ago – the stupidest thing – and now my ankle is swollen and throbbing and I cannot negotiate the stairs. I could not help thinking of Marianne in *Sense and Sensibility* who was rescued by the dashing Mr Willoughby when she sprained *her* ankle. I loved that book. I am like Marianne, I think, or at least I recognise myself in her passionate spirit rather than in Elinor's prudence. But Marianne fell delicately while I sprawled on the cobbles and in place of a handsome gentleman, I had to be picked up by one of the grooms who was quite clearly having difficulty repressing a snigger and was helped inside by my house steward, Mr Thomas, who must be fifty if he is a day and is about as far from a handsome hero as it is possible to be.

Mr Vaccari is coming as normal for my guitar lesson this morning, and then I am to pay a visit to my mother in her new house in Oxford Street. I am not looking forward to it. The last time I saw her, we quarrelled about Charles Hesse. She laughed at my worries about the letters I wrote and pooh-poohed the idea that she should have put me on my guard instead of encouraging the connection. I am prissy and a prude, according to my mother, who can see no reason why I should not flirt with a handsome officer.

That was what I thought at the time, too, but I am a little wiser now, I hope, and can see all too clearly the dangers such flirtations bring. So perhaps I am becoming more like Elinor Dashwood after all.

In fact, my mother talked about Captain Hesse in such a way that I began to wonder whose flirt he had been. When he was caressing me with his eyes, was he also making love to my mother? I dared not ask her outright, not wanting to know the answer.

We parted on stiff terms and I have not seen her since.

I am tempted to send my excuses for this morning. It is true, after all, that I am not well and I can scarcely walk.

But I go, of course I go. She is my mother, after all. I cannot be with her and not realise that she is a very unhappy and unfortunate woman who has made a great many errors and has many faults but has nonetheless been oppressed and cruelly used by the Prince, my father.

My head is aching more than ever by the time I return.

Mrs Brough makes me a concoction of honey and lemon to soothe my sore throat and I sit by the fire, swathed in another Indian shawl. The highlight of the afternoon is a visit from my uncles, Edward, Duke of Kent and Augustus, Duke of Sussex. Like their brother, the Prince Regent, they are corpulent and their stomachs strain against their waistcoats, but unlike my father, they are both genial. They offer congratulations on my birthday, refuse refreshments and sit cautiously on the old furniture.

Uncle Augustus tells me about a ball that the Lord Mayor hosted last night in my honour. It seems that the ballroom was hung with Prince of Wales feathers and the lamps were decorated with my initials. The guests danced until the early hours, according to all reports.

'I am glad they all enjoyed themselves,' I say wryly.

No one has thought to invite me to a ball. My father could have held one to mark such a significant birthday, but he has not acknowledged it in any way.

'Seen the Prince Regent today?' Uncle Edward asks.

'No,' I say, lips thinning in spite of myself. 'I paid a visit to the Princess of Wales this morning, but I have had no word from my father.'

I don't know why I am constantly disappointed in him. Why am I always surprised to discover that he dislikes me?

As if sensing that they are veering into sensitive territory, my uncles exchange glances and change the subject.

'We must congratulate you on your engagement,' Uncle Augustus says. '*Most* suitable.'

'I am glad you approve,' I say, not without an inward sigh.

Uncle Edward nods. 'It is a great thing for the country and for you yourself, Charlotte. You will be glad to be married. I know you have had much to bear.'

I am not sure why my uncles are so keen for me to wed. Marriage is not something any of them have pursued, all being quite content with their mistresses – or so I gather from Anna.

'Once you are married you will find life easier,' Uncle Augustus agrees.

'Will I? Everyone is talking as if everything is settled, but it is not,' I say, frustrated. 'I am very concerned about the prospect of having to live in Holland.'

'A detail.' He waves my worry away. 'It can be dealt with later.'

'But it is important,' I insist. 'Who is to decide? As a wife, I will be subordinate to Prince Willem, I suppose, but as heiress to the throne of a great power, I will be his superior. It cannot be right that until my succession, whenever that may be – and pray God it will not be for a long time – I will be expected to live in the Netherlands? Must I be exiled to another country before I have had a chance to see anything of my own?'

My uncles shift uncomfortably. 'Dash it, Charlotte, exile is putting it too strongly.'

'Exile is how it feels to me.'

There is some hemming and hawing, and they try telling me not to worry my head about it.

I will not let them get away with that. 'But I do worry. I

have been hurried into this engagement and now I am being manoeuvred into agreeing to live abroad which I do not wish at all to do.' I hesitate. 'You must know that my father dislikes me. He has made that very clear,' I say when they make the obligatory spluttering denials. 'I do not scruple to tell you that I fear there is a plot afoot to get me out of the way. If I am in Holland, what protection will there be for the Princess of Wales? I know that it is my popularity with the people that keeps her safe. My mother is not always very wise,' I go on with some difficulty, 'and if my father were to divorce her, there would be little I could do to help her if I am out of the country.'

'Oh, I don't think it would come to that,' says Uncle Augustus, but his eyes slide away from mine.

Uncle Edward is more honest. He pulls a face. 'I wouldn't put it past him, though. He's been ranting about the Princess for years now.'

'What if he were to marry again and have a son?' I ask. 'It would not be hard then for him to repudiate me.'

'Oh, come now…'

'She's right to be concerned,' Uncle Edward interrupts his brother. He thinks for a while. 'I don't see any harm in the occasional visit to Holland with your husband, Charlotte, but you must make it clear that England will always be your principal residence. Dash it, the Prince can't go abroad without the consent of the King and the Privy Council. It should be the same for you as Heiress Presumptive.'

With that I must be content. It is some comfort that my uncles share some of my misgivings, but it is clear they approve of the marriage in principle. They do not care about the deceit and hurry of the whole business, or that I should be bundled into an engagement after knowing Prince Willem for a matter of hours. When they leave, I feel very lonely.

I confess, I change for the evening in a dismal mood. It has not been much of a birthday. Feeling sorry for myself, I am tempted to abandon the day altogether and take to my bed. But Miss Knight is expecting me downstairs, and Mrs Louis seems determined to dress my hair and coax me into an evening gown.

The house seems very quiet as I hop along to drawing room, accompanied by Toby and Puff. And where is John, the footman? Puzzled, I open the door and stop in surprise. For John is inside and the room is full of my servants, all smiling a little nervously. My housekeeper, Mrs Simm, is there. The steward, Mr Thomas. Mrs Brough. Anna, of course, and my page, Peter.

Miss Knight is there too, with Monsieur Sterkey, my French tutor, and Mr Vaccari and his wife, who taught me to play the guitar in the wild Spanish way. Mrs Louis has slipped into the room behind me.

'We thought we would give you a little party to celebrate your birthday,' Cornelia says. 'Perhaps it is not as grand a ball as you would like, but we all wanted to wish you well on your special day. We hope you do not mind.'

My throat feels ridiculously tight and tears prick my eyes. 'There is nothing I would like more,' I say unevenly. 'This is so much better than a grand ball!'

And it is. Peter hands around glasses of wine and they

all toast my health. After the first constraint, Miss Knight suggests some music and Mr and Mrs Vaccari oblige. Before we quite know what is happening, the carpet is rolled up and we are dancing. My ankle makes me ungraceful, but I do not wish to miss out, so I hop around with Mr Thomas and Monsieur Sterkey and bashful John.

Cornelia dances with Peter, Mrs Louis with Mr Thomas. Anna dances with everyone.

It is a happy evening. This is my real family, I realise. These are the people who care about me. Most of them have been at Warwick House for years and have seen me grow up. They know me better than anyone, and as long as I have my household around me, I will never be truly alone.

Chapter Eleven

Buckingham Palace, March 1981

C harles is back, at last. Diana hurries along to his apartments, only to find that he is dressing for a dinner.

'You're not going out *again*?' she says in dismay. 'I thought we could have a quiet evening in for once.'

'Not tonight, I'm afraid,' Charles says, letting his valet help him into his dinner jacket.

'But I hardly ever see you now!'

I'm sorry, Diana, but these engagements have been in the diary for over a year. I can't just break them.' He notes her downcast expression. 'We'll spend some time together this weekend,' he promises.

Diana claps her hands excitedly. 'Really?'

'Really.' Then he spoils it by telling her they're spending the weekend at Bolehyde Manor with the Parker Bowleses.

Diana's face falls ludicrously once more. 'Can't we go somewhere on our own?'

A muscle in Charles's jaw tightens with irritation. 'I'm playing polo on Saturday,' he says, clearly making an effort to sound patient, 'but we'll drop in at Highgrove and see how the redecoration is coming on, just the two of us. All right?'

His equerry is hovering in the background, looking pointedly at his watch. 'Now I'm sorry, but I really must go.'

Disconsolate, Diana wanders back to her apartments along corridors that feel longer and lonelier than ever.

Charles does have obligations, she reminds herself, and yes, of course she can see that he cannot break engagements that have been organised months, if not years, in advance. But surely he could arrange to spend a little more time alone with her?

Weekends are always spent with his friends. They are all older and what Diana thinks of as 'grown-up'. They're perfectly nice to her, but she never feels at ease with them. She doesn't get their jokes and she always feels as if they secretly find her rather boring.

Which is pretty good given that all they ever want to do is ride around the countryside, shooting things. Diana doesn't ride and she doesn't hunt and although she made an effort at Balmoral last year, she doesn't really like slogging across boggy hillsides either. She has dutifully attended polo matches to watch Charles play but would secretly rather be shopping or drifting along the King's Road with a girlfriend.

Diana misses her friends more than she ever thought she would. There is never any question of Charles spending a weekend with her friends. Diana can't imagine what that would be like and she has no intention of suggesting it. Charles's interests are so different to hers. He would be bored by the gossip and the giggling, and her friends would be intimidated by him. It would be awful.

Perhaps things will be different when they're married. Diana finds herself hoping this a lot. In the meantime, she will have to spend another weekend feeling in the way with Camilla Parker Bowles.

Camilla is always there. Even if they stay with other friends, Camilla comes too. Diana doesn't understand why Charles makes such a point of staying on good terms with all his ex-girlfriends. It's not as if Camilla is pretty or elegant or sophisticated. She always strikes Diana as someone who is a little rough around the edges, happier on a horse than at a party. But clearly she shares a sense of humour with Charles, and Diana has learnt to dread the sound of her oddly dirty laugh entwined with Charles's laughter. It always sounds so… *intimate*. Diana may be sharing a room with him, but even she can see that Charles is relaxed with Camilla in a way that he isn't with anyone else.

But Charles isn't marrying Camilla, Diana reminds herself. He is marrying *her*.

Sighing a little, she lets herself into her apartment and startles a maid who has come to tidy up her bedroom.

'Oh, sorry, ma'am,' the maid says. 'I'll come back later.'

Diana picks up one of the soft toys that cover her bed

and tucks it under her arm. 'Don't mind me,' she says, sitting on the dressing table stool.

The truth is, she is starved of someone to talk to and the maid looks friendly. She remembers reading about Princess Charlotte and how close she was to her staff. 'Or am I in your way?'

'No, of course not, ma'am.' After a momentary hesitation, the maid continues to straighten the bed.

'I'm sorry, I don't remember your name,' Diana says.

'Julie, ma'am.'

'How long have you been working here?'

'Nearly a year, ma'am.'

Diana rolls her eyes. 'Could you drop the ma'am? It makes me feel ancient!'

'We're not supposed to.'

'Well, it's just the two of us, and I won't tell if you won't.' She watches Julie rearrange the soft toys neatly against the pillows. 'Do you like working here?'

'Oh, yes, I love it,' says Julie, warming up a bit. 'It's hard work, but we have a laugh too.'

'Really? What about?'

'Oh, you know… some of footmen are real pranksters.'

Diana's laugh is half-believing. 'They always look so serious!'

'That's just for you and the other royals,' Julia says. 'You'd be amazed if you came to one of the gin parties. Everyone lets their hair down. You probably wouldn't recognise anyone.'

Diana thinks a gin party sounds a lot more fun than a

weekend at Bolehyde Manor, watching Charles play polo and seeing his face soften when he looks at Camilla.

'Do you all live here in the palace?'

Julie nods. 'We're all up on the top floor. There's a male wing and a female wing, but we all mix up at night. Nobody shuts their doors and we dance in the corridors.' She bends to pick up one of Diana's jumpers and folds it carefully while she thinks. 'It's too hard to get anyone from outside through security, so I suppose that makes us a tight-knit group. We're all in it together.'

'It must be hard work being at everyone's beck and call.'

'It's an honour,' Julie says firmly. 'I'm not saying it's not hard work, because it is. The hours can be unsociable, too. I don't suppose I'll do it for ever, but for now, I'm having a great time. The pay isn't great, but I've got board and lodging in the centre of London. I wouldn't never be able to live this centrally otherwise.'

'It sounds fun,' Diana says wistfully. She plays with the teddy on her lap, making its arms move up and down. 'More fun than being here.'

'It must be a bit of an adjustment for you, ma'am.'

'A bit. I miss my job. Well, I miss the children really.'

There had been little time to think when she was working at the nursery or looking after little Patrick. Between that and occasionally cleaning for her sister and planning dinner parties and waiting for Charles to ring, she hadn't considered what getting engaged to the Prince of Wales would actually mean.

Now she had nothing to do but think.

Julie looks around the room, which is now a lot tidier. 'Will there be anything else, ma'am?'

'No, I don't think so. Thank you, Julie.' Diana gets to her feet and props the teddy back on the bed with the others.

'Are you going out or would you like me to bring you supper on a tray?'

'I can't have supper.' Diana rubs her growling stomach. 'I'm on a diet.'

'Oh, but you've got a lovely figure, ma'am.'

How can Julie say that? Every time Diana looks in the mirror all she sees is flabby flesh. It's disgusting.

'I have to get into my wedding dress,' she says.

'Still, you should eat something.'

'Well, maybe a snack,' says Diana, weakening.

'Shall I ask the kitchen to send something up?'

'Yes – no,' she says, abruptly changing her mind. 'I'll come and find something.'

There is a tiny pause. 'I'm not sure…'

'I've been wondering where the kitchens are. The kitchen at Althorp was always my favourite place,' Diana says. Princess Charlotte liked the kitchen too, she remembers reading in the journal. She turns to Julie. 'Can you show me the way?'

Oblivious to Julie's discomfort, Diana chats away as she follows the housemaid down the back stairs, fascinated to see how busy the other floors are. There are some startled looks as various members of staff register her presence, but Diana ignores them. She's delighted with the idea of exploring the staff areas, where there is so much more happening than up in the echoing royal apartments.

The buzz in the kitchen falters and trails off into silence when Diana breezes in. 'I just thought I'd come and say hello,' she says, embracing everyone in her smile. 'And to see if there was any more of that delicious cake you sent up yesterday.'

'Certainly, ma'am.' After a moment's pause, a junior chef is sent off and returns with a piece of cake beautifully presented on a plate.

Instead of taking it away, Diana perches on the edge of a table and makes herself at home, just as she had used to do at Althorp. She struggles to find anything to say when she's dining with the Queen, but here in the kitchen, she feels much more at ease and she chats away, flattering them with attention. She can see some sidelong glances being exchanged, but after a few minutes, most of the kitchen staff have relaxed and are laughing with her.

It's the happiest Diana has been since she moved into Buckingham Palace and she accepts another piece of cake so that she can stay a bit longer. She's just getting really comfortable when an older, starchy-looking individual comes in with a tray of glasses and takes in the scene with a disapproving look.

'The Yeoman of Glass and China,' Julie whispers.

'Ma'am, you shouldn't be here,' he says bluntly to Diana. His cold gaze sweeps around the kitchen where the rest of the staff become suddenly busy. 'You're putting people in a difficult position.'

'I just came for a piece of cake.' Diana says defensively. Licking her fork, she smiles at the young chef. 'Absolutely *delish*. Thank you so much.'

'If you want cake, some will be taken up to you,' the Yeoman of Glass and China says crisply. Haughtily, he points at the door. 'Through there is *your* side of the palace. Through here is *my* side.'

Diana jumps up from the table, cheeks burning. She would really like to have some sharp riposte to put the stupid Yeoman in his place, but she can never think of anything. The best she can manage is a farewell smile to the kitchen staff and a saunter towards the door. She keeps up a careless façade until she out of the room, but the Yeoman's disapproval has done its work. She feels shaky and a bit sick.

Alone, she walks back up the silent stairs to her apartment. She doesn't belong here. She doesn't belong in the kitchen. She doesn't belong anywhere here, she thinks miserably.

On top of which, she has eaten two slices of cake when she is supposed to be dieting.

There is only one way Diana knows to feel better, and she heads to the bathroom.

Chapter Twelve

Warwick House, February 1814

No one can remember anything like it. The snow fell incessantly for forty-eight hours and left the city muffled and eerily silent. It just kept on coming out of a heavy sky, a mesmerising, swirling blur of white. Anna and I stood and watched it falling, falling, falling until the Carlton House gardens were shrouded in white, the bushes transformed into mounds and branches of the trees snapping under the weight of the snow.

For three days, we could not go outside. Toby and Puff simply sank into the drifts and were stuck, unable to move. They had to be rescued, Toby shivering and Puff very aggrieved by the indignity of it all. It was amusing to watch them snapping at the snow but I soon tired of being confined indoors and took to pacing around my dressing room until Miss Knight desired me faintly to stop as I was giving her the headache.

But yesterday we woke to streets carpeted in pristine white snow that glittered in the weak winter sunshine. It was soon dirtied by coal dust, although the wind has stayed in the north and there is still no sign of a thaw.

This morning Anna comes in full of news that the Thames has frozen over. 'I heard as there's a fair on the ice,' she says excitedly. 'It's my afternoon off tomorrow. I'm going to have a look.'

'Oh, I wish I could go!'

Mrs Louis shakes her head as she finishes lacing up the flannel bodice that I confess I am glad of at the moment. 'A princess, wandering around a frost fair unattended? Whoever heard of such a thing! You most certainly will not do anything of the kind.'

'Louis, who is the Princess here and who the servant?' I say with dignity, or as much dignity as I can muster given that I am wearing only a flannel bodice and my drawers. 'Who says who can do what?'

Mrs Louis is unimpressed, as I knew she would be. She has known me since I was a babe and came to work with Geggy. 'It's no use putting on airs with me, Princess,' she told me firmly. 'And Anna, you had no business even mentioning the fair. You might have known that she would want to do something reckless like that.'

'I am never allowed to do anything,' I grumble as Anna rolls her eyes behind Mrs Louis's back. 'I do not go to balls. I do not go to Vauxhall. I do not go to masquerades. If I go to the theatre, I have to sit at the back of the box where no one can see me! It is of all things unfair!'

'You are a princess,' my dresser says as if that is the answer to everything. 'You cannot be exposed to the vulgarity of the lower orders. Who knows what kind of diseases you would pick up? I am sure Miss Knight would agree that you must not think of it.' She shakes out my dress and waits for me to duck so that she can drop it over my head. 'Besides,' she adds, clearly reading my mutinous expression, 'you are eighteen now. You should be beyond childish things like wanting to go to a fair.'

She thinks that is the end of the matter. It is not.

I wait until Mrs Louis has finished and then summon Anna back. 'I want to go to the frost fair with you.'

Anna looks dubious. 'How will you manage it?'

'I will go incognito. Remember I did that when we were children? We sneaked out behind the stables and joined the crowd outside Carlton House and nobody knew I was there.'

'We're not children now,' she points out, but I wave aside her doubts. Anna will go with me, I know. She has an adventurous spirit.

'Can you find me some clothes so that I look like you? I will tell Miss Knight that I have the headache and wish to lie down, and that will give her leave to retire herself. I cannot sit inside any longer,' I declare. 'I will run mad otherwise!'

I am not quite sure what Anna tells the laundry maid, but she produces Ellen's best dress for me, and I wear it with thick stockings and sturdy boots. Unlike my gowns, it is made so that she can put it on without the need of a maid, but Anna laces me up over my petticoat. The material is coarse and scratchy, but when I stuff my hair into a plain cap and pull the hood of a heavy cloak over my head, I am sure of not being recognised. What are we royals without our crowns and our regalia? Just like everyone else.

We creep down the servants' stairs and slip past the guards at the Warwick Street entrance. They wave us through, too cold to come out of their sentry boxes and we hurry down to the river and along towards London Bridge, holding onto each other and giggling as our boots slip and skid on the hard ridges of the snow-covered foot pavements.

The wind is bitter and makes my teeth ache, but I still pause to gawp at the Thames, where ships and boats are lurched to one side, trapped in the ice. We can see the frost fair from a distance. It is an extraordinary sight, the river covered in little booths and stalls and people apparently walking on water. I am a little nervous at first in case the ice should crack beneath our feet, but it feels quite solid when we get there and nobody else seems to be bothered by the prospect so I give myself up to the carnival atmosphere.

'Keep a good hold of your money,' Anna tells me. 'All those varmints running around will pick your purse as soon as look at it.'

There is a main thoroughfare from one side of the river to the other which has been named Freezeland Street, and it is crowded with people enjoying the novelty of a fair on the ice. The seagulls have spotted the chance of scraps and are wheeling and squabbling overhead, their harsh noise adding to the hubbub of hawkers crying their ware, ballad singers, beggars on tin whistles and the excited squeals of children. The air smells of roasting meat and hot pies. I sniff appreciatively.

'Let's get something to eat.'

'All right, but let me do the talking,' Anna warns. 'You don't sound like you should be 'ere. Better keep yer voice down.'

I nod obediently, and wait while she negotiates with a rough-looking individual carving slices off a pig roasting on a spit. 'Best Lapland mutton,' he says with a wink.

It is delicious. I lick the grease from my fingers and wonder what the Prince Regent would say if he could see me now, discovering that street food is tastier – and hotter – than the grandest of banquets served at Carlton House.

Afterwards we wander from booth to booth, marvelling at the range of goods on sale: trinkets and toys, gingerbread and gin, books and caricatures, most of them cleverly but cruelly depicting my father. A whole ox is being roasted, and nobody seems worried about the fire on the ice. Pedlars pester us to buy their fairings, wenches are selling oysters and hot apples, the pie men walk up and down shouting 'Hot pies! Hot pies!' There is dancing and nine-pin bowling and boys run in and out of the crowd and kick balls out on the ice.

We watch a Punch and Judy show and I laugh so hard that people start to look and Anna nudges me to be quiet. I cover my mouth with both hands and snort instead, which Anna says is even worse as she manages at last to drag me away.

My cheeks are stinging in the cold, my fingers and toes

are numb, but I listen to the scrape of a fiddle and smell hot punch and taste the gingerbread that we bought after the 'Lapland mutton' and am the happiest I can remember being... oh, in months! I forget about diplomatic alliances and Prince Willem with his shiny mouth and my increasingly desperate attempts to negotiate a clause in the marriage contract that will allow me to choose when I leave or return to England. I don't think about my future learning to be a Dutchwoman. I am just content to be here with the laughter and chatter around me.

I am not so blinded by merriment that I do not see the dark side of the fair. The beggars: an old soldier in his tattered uniform, pulling his legless body across the ice on a wheeled platform; a blind man groping the air; a child with features horribly deformed. I give them all a penny or two. The pickpockets, darting through the crowds, and the thieves snatching a hot apple or a loaf of bread from a stall and running before the stallholder has realised it has gone. The man who lifts his hand and snarlingly swats a woman aside as if she were less than a dog, leaving her splayed on the ice, her lip bloodied and her eye half-closed.

I start towards her without thinking, but Anna's hand closes over my arm. 'Leave it,' she says in a low voice. 'You can do nothing.'

'I can give her a shilling if nothing else.'

'He'll just take it from her.'

'She can hide it,' I say stubbornly.

'It's too much. A penny would do.'

'A shilling,' I insist.

Anna sighs. 'I'll give it to her. If word gets out you're 'anding out shillings, we'll have the whole crowd after us.'

She slips and slides over the ice to the woman and bends down to help her to her feet and press the coin into her hand.

The woman barely acknowledges her, just turns and hurries off in the opposite direction.

'Ungrateful drab,' Anna grumbles, making her way back to me. 'Waste of a good shilling if you ask me.'

'I have just enough left to buy us a ribbon apiece,' I say, dragging her over towards a booth that I have just spotted. 'And one for Ellen too, to thank her for lending me her dress.'

'You don't need to do that. She'd do anything for you – any of the servants would.'

'I want to,' I say. 'Please, Anna. Or I'll just have to talk in my loud voice and buy them myself,' I threaten. 'Look how pretty they are,' I go on, admiring the display of brightly coloured ribbons fluttering in the bitter wind. 'Which one do you like best?' I ask as we get near, forgetting to whisper.

'Shhh!'

I lower my voice to an exaggerated whisper. 'Which do you like best?' I give her my last pennies. 'Go on, one for each of us.

She sighs. 'Thank you kindly, ma'am. I'll have the green and Ellen would look good in the pink.'

'And I'll have the blue.' I hang back while she buys the ribbons, bantering a little with the stallholder. She is good at that.

If I do have to go to Holland, I will take my ribbon with

me. It may not compare to diamonds and pearls, but whenever I wear it, I will think of this moment, standing in the middle of the Thames, amongst the people who will one day be mine, these Londoners with their dogged endurance who have defied the clenching cold to come out and make a carnival on the ice.

Chapter Thirteen

Carlton House, June 1814

L ondon is *en fête*. The Prince Regent has invited our allies to England to celebrate victory at last over Bonaparte. The King of Prussia is here with his entourage, as is Tsar Alexander of Russia. Military leaders are out in force too. The city is full of dashing officers, brass buttons glinting, uniforms looped with gold frogging. Excitement shimmers in the air. The streets have been cleaned and bunting flutters in the sunshine. The whole country is delighted by the end of a war that has dragged on since before I was born. The people are smiling, happy to cheer every glimpse of the glamorous visitors.

Or so I hear. I have not been invited to any of the parties, dinners or reviews that my father has laid on.

He has spared no expense in entertaining his royal guests. Carlton House has been extravagantly redecorated with the aim of impressing the Tsar in particular, but all to no avail as the Russian royals have chosen to stay instead at the Pulteney Hotel where people crowd around the doors and under her window in the hope of catching a glimpse of them. They have become the idols of London, both for the common people who gawk at them as if they are spectacle laid on for their entertainment and even more so for the haut ton who scramble for invitations to events where they will be present and

The Tsar's sister, the Grand Duchess Catherine came to England first, in a poke bonnet with a huge brim that instantly became all the rage. I have been allowed to visit her in private although not to take part in any of the formal events. Catherine tells me that none of the foreign visitors can understand why I am kept in seclusion and I gather they are all annoying my father greatly by continually asking him where I am. She says it with a sly smile and I have to bite my lip to stop myself from laughing out loud at his discomfiture, for I have still not forgiven him for pushing me into the engagement with Prince Willem.

For months, the marriage negotiations have dragged on. To my father's exasperation, I have held out for a clause that will allow me to leave or return to Britain at my pleasure, and that has now been included. Which means that I have no more excuse to prevaricate and I have signed the contract.

So it is done. I will be married at last. But the more I think of the way I was bustled into agreeing to the engagement, the more trapped and resentful I feel.

I have confided in Catherine and she shares my doubts about marrying into the House of Orange. 'It is quite Gothic for you to marry a man you have barely twenty-four-hours' acquaintance with!' she exclaims when I tell her the whole story. 'London is full of Protestant princes at the moment,' she says. 'There must be one who could take your fancy!'

'That is why my father will not allow me to meet any of them,' I say.

'Pah!' Catherine waves an imperious hand. 'Everyone thinks it vastly strange that you do not attend any of the celebrations.'

I sigh. 'He is quite determined on the Orange match,' I say dolefully. 'Nothing must get in the way of that.'

'I suppose from a diplomatic point of view it makes sense,' the Grand Duchess allows, 'but you know, Russia has played a big role in the victory over that monster Bonaparte. Britain would be wise to look further east to consolidate its alliances. Holland now...' She lifts her shoulders and lets them fall in a shrug that would make the Queen comb my hair with a joint-stool were I to try it, but that on the Grand Duchess looks graceful. 'Yes, doubtless it is convenient for you to have a foothold across the North Sea, but strengthening ties with Russia would be sensible too.'

'Perhaps, but your brother is already married,' I point out.

'Ah, yes, but there are others of high rank who you might consider for a husband, are there not?'

'I am afraid I will not be given the choice,' I say glumly. 'Even were I to meet them, I know that my father would never agree to an alternative marriage.'

For all I sound resigned, I am desperate to find a way

out of the Orange match. My mind runs like a rat in the stables, scrabbling for an escape before the dog pounces.

Catherine is a widow. I suppose I should pity her for her husband's death, but the truth is that I envy her. Widowhood has given her all the freedom I lack. It would be unchristian of me to hope for Prince Willem's death, I know, but that is all that could reconcile me to the marriage now.

In the meantime, I am enjoying her company. She is intelligent and charming and I like her exceedingly. She has a dry sense of humour that makes it impossible for me to take offence when she tells me that I am quite *farouche* and walk in a bouncing way like a boy! When my grandmother tells me the same thing, I am irritated, which is perverse of me, I know.

I am determined to be quietly elegant and to perfect a ladylike glide tonight, if only to show the Grand Duchess that I can. For the first time since the celebrations started, I am to go to a grand dinner at Carlton House. I dare say the Prince Regent would keep me from that if he could, but Prince Willem will be there, amongst other high-ranking guests. He has been away on military duties, so this will only be the third time I have seen the man I am to marry. I am not looking forward to our engagement being treated by everyone as a settled thing, but I see no way out.

Still, my spirits rise as I dress for dinner. It is so long since I have had an occasion to prettify myself for, and I am curious to meet the other Russian and Prussian royals at last. Catherine will be there too, and she will be able to tell me who everyone is. I have a new blue silk gown which was meant to bring out the colour of my eyes, though I cannot see much difference. It has a metallic trim around the neckline and I finger it, suddenly unsure. It is fashionable, but my bosom is quite voluptuous, and I wonder if it might be a little *too* low cut.

It is too late to change now, anyway.

Mrs Louis has brushed my hair to a shine and dressed it so that some curls soften my face. I look well enough, though I cannot help noticing that my shoulders are broad and my figure sturdy.

This is my first visit to Carlton House since Cornelia and I groped our way through the smog to meet Prince Willem. This time, the evening is warm and although I could easily walk, a carriage takes me round to Pall Mall and I walk up the steps into the grand entrance, a visitor, as always, to my father's house.

We gather before dinner in the Crimson Drawing Room, which is stiflingly hot as usual. Also as usual, my father barely acknowledges me, but I recognise the Duchess of York, who smiles and waves at me from across the room. I'm surprised she has been persuaded to leave her dogs. She has some forty or fifty of them roaming free around Oatlands and is generally considered eccentric for preferring them to people. But sometimes when I think about my own dear Puff and Toby, and then about some people I know, I think she may have a point. Perhaps she is here to see her brother, King Frederick William of Prussia.

The other guests are flatteringly interested to meet me. Catherine presents me to her brother, Alexander, the Tsar, who is fair and quite as handsome as I have heard. He is very tall – Anna would call him a regular longshanks – and in his green velvet uniform, all laced with gold and decorated with diamonds, he looks magnificent. No wonder my father is so jealous of him! Next to the Tsar, the Prussian King, Frederick William, is squat and blunt, but he speaks kindly to me and tells me that he hopes to visit me at Warwick House.

Before he can say more, my father is bearing down on me with Prince Willem in tow.

Willem bows over my hand. He is not ugly, I find myself thinking as I did before. But he is not attractive either. Indeed, there is something repellent about him that I cannot identify. Perhaps it is the way his lips glisten, or the limpness of his hand, but it is probably more to do with the utter lack of interest in his eyes when they rest on me.

He says that he is happy to hear that I have signed the marriage contract. We make stilted small talk while my father leaves us, satisfied that he has made his point. With every minute, it seems more impossible that I should have to marry this man who so clearly cares nothing for me. Why, oh why, did I sign that contract?

I would rather be talking to anyone else in the room. Many of the other guests seem to know each other, and indeed, a good number of them are related. In any event, they all seem to be enjoying themselves, at least.

A burst of laughter from a group of young men in uniform – all princes, I assume, because only princes would be invited tonight – makes me watch them longingly. I wish I was with them.

As I look, one glances over towards us, catches my eye and smiles.

I have an impression of a humorous expression, of golden good looks, of warmth and vitality.

Willem is still talking, but I am not listening. My eyes have a will of their own, resisting my attempts to look away and relentlessly dragging my attention back to the Prince. He is looking too, and now he is turning, he is coming over... I am abruptly breathless, so much so that I am afraid I might faint. It is the strangest feeling. It is almost as if there are only two of us in this hot, crowded room.

All my senses are alert. I am achingly aware of my own body, of the fabric of my gloves against my skin. The smoothness of the pearls at my throat. The tickle of curls on the nape of my neck.

'Willem.' A clap on the shoulder, a flashing smile. 'Cousin, present me if you please!'

'Frederick!' Willem turns in surprise. 'I did not know you would be here tonight.' But he seems pleased. His eyes light up as they rest on Frederick as if he too can appreciate that reckless smile and those dancing blue eyes.

Introductions are made. He is Prince Frederick, grandson of Frederick William II and nephew of the current King of Prussia. Which makes him a nephew, too, of my dear Duchess of York. He has seen service on the continent and is already a cavalry general in the Prussian army.

All this I absorb in a kind of daze as Frederick bows over my hand, presses his lips to my glove. I swear, I can feel the warmth of his mouth through the kid. When he looks up at me, his eyes are blue and knowing. They seem to say 'I know you'.

My whole body is pulsating, the blood thudding through me, and I am giddy, tumbling, spinning into a vertiginous abyss. I am literally falling in love and am both thrilled and terrified by the sensation.

Everyone must surely recognise what is happening to me, this amazing feeling that is sweeping me out of control. Can they not hear my heart banging painfully against my ribs? Can they not see that I am changed in an instant? But Willem notices nothing amiss. He keeps talking to Frederick, more animatedly than I have ever seen him and certainly with more interest than he has in me, though I have no idea what he is saying.

Frederick chats amicably back, but his eyes are on me. On my mouth. On my bosom. And wherever his gaze rests, I burn.

Chapter Fourteen

My mouth is too dry to eat at dinner. Frederick is seated at the other end of the table to me, but he might as well be opposite me, he so completely takes up my attention. The hubbub of conversation around the table is muted, the other guests blurred. Odd details jump out at me: the carved griffin on the gilt candelabra; the glitter of emeralds in the Queen's ears; the sound of wine being poured and the chink of forks against gilt plates. The occasional snatch of conversation filters through, too, coming and going like waves on the shore at Weymouth.

'...damned horse shot out beneath me...'

'...I said, you must be out of your mind...'

'...ugh, how can he bear this heat?...'

I try not to, I do, but I cannot help looking down the table and every time, Frederick glances up to meet my eyes. His smile is a tangible thing, looping around my heart and binding me to him. It is as if we are having a whole conversation just with our eyes.

I have no idea what I am eating. The Regent's chef, Monsieur Watier, has outdone himself, but I might as well have been served a crust of bread. Every now and then I hear Frederick's shout of laughter. It is an uninhibited sound that shivers over my skin. He is talking to his neighbours, but then he looks back at me, and his smile tells me he is thinking about me, that he cannot wait to get me alone.

I did not know it was possible to feel like this. My infatuation with Charles was a childish thing compared to this. I am raked by hunger to touch him, to press my face into his skin. I imagine him pushing back his chair, coming for me, careless of anyone watching. If he put hands on me, I would shatter into a thousand pieces. I would not be able to resist him.

I would not want to.

Dinner is interminable. Course after course is removed and replaced with ever more elaborate dishes. Monsieur Watier's extraordinary confectionary centrepieces have to be admired. Conversation gets louder, laughter more raucous. Glasses are knocked over. Every now and then a man stumbles to his feet and heads out to avail himself of the chamber pot. Like the other ladies, I suspect, I haven't drunk anything all day so that I can avoid a similar need.

And through it all, my body pulses with awareness of Frederick and the space between us that seems sealed in a silver bubble of silence.

At last – at last! – the Queen signals that the ladies should withdraw and leave the men to their drinking. We retire to the

Great Drawing Room where doubtless my father wishes to impress his guests with the profusion of gilt and extravagant decor. It is beautiful, I know, but it is too much. There is no rest for the senses here: it is all rich fabrics and colour and perfume and gold, gold and more gold – and not enough air. In spite of the warm evening, the windows are as tightly closed as ever and I even find myself longing for my dark, dowdy drawing room in Warwick House where at least I can breathe.

My grandmother's sharp eyes are on me as I make disjointed conversation until tea and coffee are served and the men come in, full of back-slapping jollity and wilted cravats. The Prince Regent is beaming. He loves entertaining and showing off his treasures. There is no sign of Frederick at first and I agonise that something, somehow, has happened to him between the dining room and the drawing room. That he has been kidnapped or taken ill or thrown down the stairs… but no! There he is and the room seems to snap. All at once the colours are brighter, the scents sweeter, the sounds more melodic.

He comes straight over to where I am sitting with the Duchess of York, who greets him fondly. 'Have you met this scamp yet, Charlotte?' she asks me.

'Briefly,' I manage to say.

'Frederick is my nephew, my brother's son,' she says.

'And as you are married to my uncle, and I call you my aunt, then we are in some sense cousins,' I say, my eyes on Frederick, who smiles.

'I count myself quite one of the family already. Would you care for a turn around the room, *Cousin*?'

'Thank you.' I am quite surprised that my knees will hold me as I get to my feet.

The duchess smiles comfortably at us both as Frederick offers me his arm. I lay the tips of my fingers on his sleeve. The texture of his jacket is rough, the strength of the muscles beneath like steel. I can feel his gaze burning into my skin, but I dare not look directly at him. I could not answer for the consequences. I am pulsating with the need to touch him. My mind is full of wild imaginings: that he will press me back against the wall and kiss me passionately; that he will pull me into an anteroom and gather my skirts in his hand to pull them up and touch me where I most long to be touched.

I swallow hard, frightened by the lewdness of my thoughts. What am I thinking? I force myself to untangle my tongue. I even risk a glance at him.

'Are… are you enjoying your stay in London, Prince?'

He looks at my mouth. 'I am now,' he says and he smiles. His smile is confident, intimate, and warmth pools inside me. 'I cannot explain it, but until tonight it all seemed to lack a certain… delight.'

'And yet I hear that no expense has been spared to entertain you all,' I say.

'Oh, there has been entertainment aplenty! Parties, reviews, dinners, more parties, another review, more parties, more dinners… It has been exhausting! Field Marshal Blücher has been saying that where Napoleon has failed to kill him, the Regent's celebrations might very well succeed,' he adds with a droll look that makes me laugh.

'You do not strike me as someone who is easily exhausted,' I tell him.

'No, but I am easily bored and I had little to hold my attention.' His voice drops. 'Until tonight when I turned and saw you, Charlotte. I may call you Charlotte, may I not? Since we are cousins of a kind?'

'You may,' I say, conscious of a trembling inside. My fingers tighten on his sleeve. 'It was the same for me,' I tell him. 'Everything was dull and now it is bright and interesting.'

'Exactly.' Briefly, he covers my hand with his. It is enough. A touch, a promise. 'Why have you not attended all the celebrations? Everyone hoped to meet you.'

My hand falls from his arm at that. 'My father would not permit it,' I say. 'He wishes me to marry.'

'Willem?'

'Yes. But I do not want to,' I burst out. 'It is a marriage *de covenance*, of course, but I cannot do it.' I look up at him. 'I cannot do it now,' I say, knowing that he understands me. I pause. 'How long will you stay in London?'

He makes a face. 'Not long enough. We are leaving on the twenty-first.'

'Of June?' My expression must show my dismay.

'We sail from Portsmouth that day. I am sorry, I have military duties. I cannot stay, much as I might wish it.' He glances around, and we both register at the same time that my father is glowering and my grandmother the Queen is watching us disapprovingly. He lowers his voice. 'I know my uncle the King is planning to call on you. If we may, we hope that we may come as a family – the Hohenzollerns en masse, if you can bear it – and perhaps then we might make a chance to meet again?'

I am aware of my father approaching. 'That would be most pleasant,' I say as I step back from Frederick. 'I will look forward to it.'

My father bears me off and deposits me before Willem like a parcel but I don't care. I am shimmering with excitement. Frederick feels the same as I do. He is coming to see me. We will find a way to be together.

Willem seems surprised and even a little disappointed to find me beside him once more. He has been talking to a member of the Tsar's entourage, a young man with dark hair and exotic black eyes whose name I do not catch. As soon as the Regent's back is turned, I murmur an excuse and drift off to find Catherine.

I am not surprised to find that the Grand Duchess has noticed my excitement. She is not a woman who misses much. 'So,' she says, raising her elegant brows, 'there is a little spark between you and the Prussian Prince?'

A spark? More like a fire, a mighty conflagration. I am transformed. I laugh a little shakily.

'Is it so obvious?'

'To anyone who cares to look.' She studies Frederick across the room. 'He is a very attractive young man. But be careful, my dear Charlotte. Handsome, reckless, young officers rarely make unselfish lovers. A boy like that, he will always put himself first.'

I have turned my back on him so that I am not tempted to look. 'He feels the same,' I say in a fervent undertone. 'It was a *coup de foudre* for us both.'

'Perhaps.' Catherine pulls down the corners of her mouth. 'Perhaps for now, should I say,' she adds, seeing my disappointment at her lack of enthusiasm.

'You said I was wise to retreat from the Orange match,' I protest.

'I did. I do not think it is the right one for you or for Britain,' she says. 'But you need to play your hand wisely, Charlotte.' She taps my arm with her fan. 'You are too impulsive for your own good, too open about how you feel. You are reckless like your Frederick but you will lose everything if you are not careful. It would not do to make an enemy of your own father,' she adds thoughtfully, 'so be discreet. Do not commit yourself to anything until you are sure of what you want.'

I am sure, I think. I want Frederick.

But I respect the Grand Duchess's advice. She is right about me being impulsive, though I am not sure how she has guessed. She knows nothing of my infatuation with Charles Hesse or the letters that I wrote to him. Or, indeed, the watch and the portrait that I sent to Wellington for him. That was a very foolish thing to do.

So I will be discreet, as Catherine advises. I will not gaze moonstruck at Frederick, much as I would like to. But I will not give him up either.

I go home a different girl. It is strange how everything that had seemed so dull and familiar suddenly appears shockingly sharp and clear. The brass on the front door at Warwick House. The pattern of the tiles in the hallway. The smoothness of the banister beneath my hand.

Mrs Louis and Anna are waiting up for me. 'You're all lit

up,' Anna says straight away and I laugh, spread my arms and spin around and around until I am giddy.

'I am in love!'

They help me undress, unfastening ribbons and stays, brushing out my hair, while I tell them dreamily about Frederick, about his smile and his dancing eyes and the way he makes everything bolder and brighter. In my memory, he stood out, shining like a Greek god.

Anna listens avidly. 'What will your pa say?' she asks and I stop, jerked back to reality.

'I will say nothing just yet,' I decide, remembering what Catherine said. I curse the impulse that made me sign the marriage contract, and the timing of it. If only I had met Frederick two days earlier!

One thing is clear. I cannot marry Willem now.

'I must end the engagement,' I say.

Mrs Louis looks worried. 'How?'

'I have no idea,' I admit. 'But it must be done.'

Chapter Fifteen

Warwick House, June 1814

I am in a fret of impatience waiting for the visit of the Prussian royal family. There is a whole day to get through, and then a morning. I drive everyone to distraction, fussing about what I am to wear until my dear Mrs Louis is betrayed into a 'drat you, stand still' as she tries to fasten the ribbon under my bust while I am leaping up at the slightest sound outside.

Anna takes to putting her head round the door and shaking it before I can ask whenever a carriage wheel is heard. Cornelia Knight doesn't approve of what she calls Anna's impudence, and looks sour, but all I care about is that Frederick isn't here yet.

I must find a way to speak to him alone again. I have enlisted Cornelia's help, because in spite of her austere looks, she is a romantic like me and she doesn't like the way my father is pushing me into marrying Prince Willem.

Oh, why don't they come?

I cannot concentrate on anything. I open a book, close it. I walk over to the window and peer out into the street as if I could will Frederick into appearing. I can see carriages passing in bustling Cockspur Street but Warwick Street, narrow and dark, is empty but for a strutting pigeon. I open the harpsichord and pick out a tune. I sit down and immediately get up again.

'Princess…' Cornelia sounds weary, as if she would like to tell me to sit still, drat it, herself.

'I'm sorry,' I say, contrite, and then stiffen because, isn't that the sound of a carriage? I spin round, only just stopping myself rushing to the window in time.

Anna reappears, eyes brimming with excitement. 'I think it's them.'

At last, at last!

Ignoring Cornelia's irritated tsk at Anna, I arrange myself on a sofa and assume a dignified expression, or what I hope is dignified, but it is hard when my heart is springing around in my chest and my ears are booming.

In the hall, there is a murmur of voices. Now there are boots on the stairs. I must remember to breathe. What if Frederick is not as handsome as I remember? What if I have imagined the sense of connection I felt?

Mr Thomas himself opens the door. 'His Majesty the King of Prussia,' he intones, and starts reeling off other titles, but I am already on my feet, scanning the group for Frederick.

There he is! And I have not imagined it. As my eyes meet his, happiness surges through me in a dizzying rush.

Somehow I manage to greet the King and include the rest of my visitors in my smile. As promised, the King has brought the senior members of the Hohenzollern family with him, which is a good thing as it means my feelings for Frederick are not so obvious. Or so I hope.

We speak in a mixture of German, English and French. Luckily, Frederick's English is excellent as my German is not as good as my French.

Oh, it is heaven to see him here, but I cannot ignore everyone else to speak to him, much as I might wish to, and anyway, Frederick keeps a respectful distance as I converse with the King and with other members of the Prussian entourage. Prince August is particularly charming. He is older than Frederick, assured and handsome, with eyes that droop seductively. He makes me laugh and I am able to enjoy a little flirtation with him, but I am always conscious of Frederick, glowing with health and vigour. I study him as covertly as I can while he talks to Cornelia. I hope she likes him.

John the footman brings in tea which means a chance for me to move around the room. When I have served the King and the others, I carry a cup over to Frederick, who rises at my approach.

'Would you care for some tea, Cousin?' I ask demurely.

'Thank you, Cousin.' He smiles back and takes the cup from me, allowing his fingers to brush against mine.

Cornelia cedes me her place on the sofa and moves discreetly away. Frederick sits next to me, turning slightly so that we face each other. It is all I can do not to reach out and touch him, to lay a hand on his knee, to lean into him. I am excruciatingly aware of him: of the curve of his lips, the blueness of his eyes.

'I am very glad you were able to come today,' I say, wondering if he has any idea of how anxiously I have waited for him.

'I would not have missed it for the world,' he says, adding with a humorous glance around, 'I wish only that I had not so many relatives who were also determined not to miss the chance of seeing you.'

I moisten my lips with the tip of my tongue. 'Perhaps you would like to come again when I will not have so many visitors.'

'I would indeed. Tomorrow, perhaps?'

'Tomorrow afternoon you will find me alone,' I agree. 'Except for my companion, Miss Knight, of course,' I add demurely.

'Miss Knight seems a most excellent person. Does she take her duties very seriously?'

'She is a most… understanding… chaperone,' I say.

Frederick smiles. 'Good,' is all he says, and I shiver with anticipation.

We have eight golden days, that is all. We cannot let anyone suspect our passion so I must entertain others and pretend that my life has not changed utterly, but every day we manage a meeting. My whole household is in on the secret. They ensure that no one else is here when Frederick comes, and Miss Knight leaves us to sit and talk. Sometimes I play the harp for him or the guitar, at others we sing duets at the piano. We read poetry together. But most of the time we just dream of what our life together could be.

Cornelia is such a comfort to me! She tells me laughingly that she is half in love with Frederick herself and when he is not there, I never tire of talking about him to her. She enters completely into all my feelings about his superior qualities and has promised to do everything she can to help us. When Frederick leaves, as I fear he must very soon, we will be able to exchange letters through Cornelia.

She understands how desperately I love him. The only person who doesn't is Anna.

'I don't trust 'im,' she says simply.

'How ridiculous! You do not know him,' I snap.

'I've seen 'im and I've seen how he treats the other servants. Toby and Puff don't trust 'im, neither.'

It is true that Puff and Toby have somehow sensed that Frederick does not care for lapdogs, which he freely admitted to me. The first time Frederick put his arm around me, Puff actually growled, which I thought was funny until I saw Frederick's face. Now Anna takes them away whenever he comes, but that does not give her the right to advance an opinion! She is my chambermaid, after all. I do not care what she thinks.

Anna just shrugs when I point that out to her. 'I'm just saying, I wouldn't count on 'im. Prince Frederick's always going to be number one for Prince Frederick.'

I am out of all patience with her!

But it is easy to forget Anna when I am with Frederick. The more we see each other, the more deeply we fall in love and the more determined I am to break my engagement to Prince Willem, which is a dark, threatening cloud looming over the horizon on a summer's day.

Obviously I cannot mention Frederick, but there must be some other way to withdraw from the contract. There *must* be.

Scenting my lack of enthusiasm, the Prince Regent descends, scowling, on Warwick House with Bishop Fisher, the Great Up himself, in tow. My father wants me to relinquish the clause which says that I will not leave the country without his written permission and my own consent, which I thought important to add, and that if I do leave, I may return either as directed by the King or the Prince Regent, or at my own pleasure.

It is the clause I fought so hard to have included in the marriage contract. Now my father wants me to give it up as a *mark of civility* to the House of Orange. Needless to say, I decline, which makes him angrier than ever, but I must stand my ground. My aunt, Princess Mary, has written too, to say that the moment the Tsar and the Prussians have left, my father intends to marry me off to Prince Willem as quickly as possible, no doubt with the aim of hurrying me out of the country.

If this were to happen, not only would my future be ruined, my poor discarded mother would be vulnerable to any plans my father might have to divorce her. She has already suffered slights enough from the visiting sovereigns, barred as she has been from meeting any of them publicly, and humiliated by waiting in four hours for a promised visit from the Tsar who never arrived. She at least had a moment of glory by attending the opera where the Prince Regent was in a box between the Tsar and the King of Prussia. Sweeping in, magnificently attired in black velvet and diamonds, she took her place to a standing ovation from the audience, which must have been a slap indeed to my father.

And so, I do have excuses enough to break the contract, I think. I do not have to tell anyone about Frederick. It will surely be enough that I cannot leave my mother unprotected.

As the celebrations come to an end, the Prussians are the first to leave. I cling to Frederick when he comes to say goodbye.

'My dearest one, I cannot bear to let you go!'

'It will not be for ever, Charlotte,' he assures me, covering my face with kisses. 'We will be together, my darling, I promise.'

I have to believe it.

I don't trust him. I push aside the memory of Anna's words. What does Anna know?

'My supporters believe that I have grounds for resisting the marriage treaty that has been agreed,' I tell Frederick eagerly. 'I must see Prince Willem and tell him why the marriage cannot go ahead. But then I will be free, and I will send word as soon as I can for you to return.'

'Pray God that is soon,' Frederick says. He lifts my hands to his mouth and kisses them fervently. His lips are warm against my skin and when he has gone, I hold the backs of my hands to my cheeks, wanting to remember the sensation of being desired.

Saying goodbye to him is one of the hardest things I

have done, but he leaves me convinced that he feels as passionately as I do, that he loves me, that he will ask my father for my hand.

But first, I must extricate myself from the Orange match.

Chapter Sixteen

Buckingham Palace, March 1981

Diana is lounging in Charles's sitting room. Her feet are dangling over the end of one of the sofas and she is idly leafing through *Country Life* and chatting about how the wedding plans are going.

'We've had so many presents already,' she tells Charles, who is frowning over various bits of paper while his valet moves around in his bedroom, packing for the upcoming trip to Australia. 'I can't tell you how many thank-you letters I wrote today! I thought my wrist was going to fall off.'

'Wait until you start shaking hands on a walkabout,' says Charles with a humorous look.

For once, Diana is feeling relaxed. This is almost how it used to be at the flat. Well, not quite, she amends, looking around the apartment which is decorated in a masculine style and lacks homely touches like coffee tables cluttered with nail polish and odd bits of make-up, half-drunk mugs of coffee or old copies of the *Daily Mail* or *The Standard*, bought largely for their gossip columns. The magazines here are rather weightier than at Coleherne Court where she spent many happy hours like this, flicking through *Vogue* or sometimes *Cosmopolitan*, although Diana has never thought of herself as a 'Cosmo' girl. Her dreams are more traditional and romantic, and all those articles about sex or careers have never appealed to her. *Tatler* is more her style.

Charles's desk is nearly as untidy as the sitting room in the flat, though. It is covered in piles of papers, while his shelves are stuffed with books on a whole range of subjects too deep for Diana's tastes. There are no romance novels with cracked spines here.

But perhaps when they are married and living together, they can meld their styles?

She can imagine being comfortable here, Diana thinks, dropping the magazine onto her chest and watching Charles smoothing his hand thoughtfully over his upper lip while he reads.

Will comfortable be enough, though? She can't help thinking wistfully of Charlotte's passionate affair with the handsome Prince Frederick. Diana is quite envious of Charlotte having found someone so perfect, and being resolute enough to resist the marriage of convenience with the dull Willem. Frederick reminds her of the heroes in the romance novels she loves so much. Barbara Cartland's heroes are like Frederick: they are passionate, handsome, reckless, ready to take a risk.

Diana can't help wishing that her own prince was as

passionate. Charles is fond, affectionate, but he does not yearn for her, not the way she wants him to love her, not the way Frederick and Charlotte love each other.

But he does love her, Diana reminds herself. Why else would he have asked her to marry him?

'It's so nice to be able to be together tonight,' she tells him. 'I wish you weren't going to Australia tomorrow.'

Charles drops the papers onto his desk. 'I'm afraid there isn't much I can do about it. It's been planned for a long time.'

'Oh, I know, it's just… I wish I could come with you then,' she sighs.

'If only it were that easy to change plans at the last minute!'

'I love Australia, too,' she goes on, thinking dreamily about the time she spent with her mother at Mollymook before the official announcement of the engagement. Charles had wanted her to spend those three weeks thinking about his proposal, but she said yes straight away. When he asked her to marry him, it was a dream come true. Why would she have made him wait for her answer? It had been a lovely time though. While the press besieged her stepfather's ranch at Yass, Diana was incognito on the beach at Mollymook, just swimming and surfing and revelling in the knowledge that of all the girlfriends Charles had had, he had chosen her, Diana, to be Princess of Wales.

It had been the last time, she realises, that she walked alone.

'I don't think you'll find it quite like your last trip.' Charles's voice is dry. 'Nobody knew you were there.' He hesitates. 'There'll be plenty of trips after we're married, Diana. You won't be wishing you could come then.'

'At least we'd be together.' Diana allows herself a pout. 'You don't realise how lonely it is living here.'

'You agreed that it was sensible to move in,' he reminds her. 'You couldn't carry on living in that flat with the press camped outside.'

'I know…' Diana swings her legs down and sits up. 'It's just that while there might be no press, there's no one else either! You're always away. The Queen and the Duke of Edinburgh are always busy. Andrew's in the Navy, Edward's at school.

'Anne is around.'

'Anne doesn't like me.'

Charles sighs. 'Of course she likes you! That's a silly thing to say.'

'We've got nothing in common.'

'Perhaps, but it doesn't mean she doesn't like you. You're not still in school, Diana,' he adds impatiently.

Diana shrinks into herself at his tone. The trouble is that most of the time, she feels as if she *is* a schoolgirl compared to everyone else. 'I'm just saying it's lonely when you're not here,' she says.

'Can't you go and have supper with Mummy?'

'Well, I do ring up sometimes and ask if she's on her own, but she so rarely is and I can't help feeling she'd like an evening to herself. She's always very welcoming, but…'

Diana can't explain how shy she feels in front of the Queen. It is difficult not to feel in awe of her, even when it's just the two of you having supper.

Also, Diana doesn't like wading through all the corgis. She can't understand why the Queen likes them so much. Horrid, snappy little dogs.

Charles has moved around his desk and is sitting down to sign a letter. 'Why don't you ask your sisters to come and see you?' he suggests, his attention clearly on the letter.

That's easy for him to say, Diana thinks. Jane is married to a courtier and although she's been helpful, she doesn't understand how out of place Diana feels now. As for Sarah, Diana is reluctant to admit to her elder sister that everything is not absolutely perfect.

'They're busy.'

'Your friends then.'

The trouble is that her friends all have their own lives and the hassle of getting them through security into the palace is off-putting. Besides, Diana's pride won't let her admit just how much she is missing the flat.

It's different for Charles. His friends are used to him being royal. They are a tight-knit group who have welcomed Diana, but they are all so much older Diana inevitably feels like the odd one out who doesn't get the references that have the rest of them shouting with laughter.

Charles pulls another pile of papers towards him. 'Just let me do these, and we'll talk,' he says.

Diana's mouth tightens. She's always relegated to second place, she thinks sulkily. His paperwork, his visits, his plans… all of those have to be done before there's time for *her*. She debates flouncing out, but where would she go? Back to her empty apartment?

Discarding *Country Life*, she picks up the *Sunday Times*

Magazine from the table instead and begins flicking crossly through it. Clearly she is going to have to wait until Charles has finished reading and signing or whatever else he's been doing. At least there are pictures to look at. She skims over pieces about Sheena Easton, Robert Redford and Lenny Henry, skips worthy-looking pieces about an artist and middle-aged playwrights, and is engrossed in 'A Life in the Day of Princess Grace of Monaco' when Charles finally deigns to pay her some attention.

He sits down opposite her. 'Tell me how the wedding plans are going,' he says, but with so much an air of indulging her that Diana stiffens before realising how silly it is to waste their evening together fighting.

The truth is, it's hard to know much about the wedding. So many of the decisions are being made by other people: the service, the ceremony, the food… the palace officials have all this in hand. Someone is dealing with the presents, someone is compiling the guest list and although her opinion is sought, Diana knows that it doesn't really matter what she thinks. Sometimes it feels as if her only real connection to the wedding is the dress, which the Emanuels are making for her. Diana adores the design and is determined to be thin enough to do it justice on the day.

But she can't tell Charles about the dress, because that would be unlucky. Instead she makes him laugh with her description of how Oliver Everett is helping her practise walking with a long train. 'He ties a sheet to me and I have to walk around with it dragging behind me. It's harder than it looks!'

'I can believe that,' says Charles, amused.

Encouraged, Diana settles into the corner of the sofa and curls her legs up beneath her. Suddenly it seems as if there are other little incidents she hasn't found that funny before that she can tell him about. Charles brings her a drink and she chats away, and it begins to feel fine.

As long as she's with Charles, it's all fine.

It is fine until the phone rings. Charles looks at it and then at her. 'Go on, answer it,' she says good-humouredly. 'The switchboard wouldn't put it through unless it was someone important.'

She sees his face light up. 'Hullo, you!' She knows at once that it is Camilla.

'I'm just here with Diana,' she hears him say. Clearly a warning.

It is so obvious that he wants her to go. Diana's throat closes with disappointment. Part of her wants to sit tight and let him talk to Camilla in front of her, but the other half recognises defeat.

She gets to her feet and Charles covers the receiver with his hand to look enquiringly at her.

'I'll leave you to talk together,' she says stiffly and he smiles at her.

'Bless you. I'll see you tomorrow on the way to the airport.'

Because, yes, she has to go out to Heathrow the next day and play the loving fiancée, knowing that the man she is saying goodbye to has spent most of night before talking to his old girlfriend.

Diana is furious, with Charles, with Camilla, with herself. She sits rigidly next to Charles in the car on the way out to Heathrow. He tries to chat, but she refuses to answer. A lot of people in suits are standing around once they get there. Hands have to be shaken, farewells said. Charles kisses her on the cheek and she forces a smile, but then she's glad to retreat while he climbs the steps to the plane. Tears of rage and humiliation sting her eyes as she watches the plane taxi out and then take off.

Everyone thinks that she's upset because Charles is going away for three weeks and she is, but they don't understand that's not what is really making her cry. It's knowing that three weeks away from her won't bother Charles. The one he'll really miss is Camilla.

Chapter Seventeen

Warwick House, 16 June 1814

'**H**is Royal Highness the Hereditary Prince of Orange.'
I get to my feet as Willem is sonorously announced.
This is the moment I have been dreading.

But I have been waiting for it, too, for as long as I am
officially engaged to him, I can make no plans with
Frederick.

I am resolved to be clear with Willem. It is not just a
question of my feelings for Frederick or my concern for my
mother. I have heard disturbing reports that Willem is not
the well-behaved paragon he seems at first glance. He
might have a distinguished military career, but Anna tells
me that it is common knowledge among the grooms that he
likes to disguise himself as a coachman and join them in
boorish drinking sessions.

'And you don't want to know what 'e gets up to after

that,' Anna added darkly. 'It ain't nice. 'E's not fit to lick your boots, and that's a fact.'

I am still cross with Anna about Frederick, but on this we agree.

'The apple falls close to the tree,' I said, remembering how disgusted I was by Willem's father's behaviour. 'The Prince of Orange was so drunk at Sandhurst that he took off his coat and his waistcoat and sat drinking in his shirt!'

Anna's look could only be described as pitying. 'Prince Willem's doing a lot worse than stripping off his waistcoat!'

But she wouldn't tell me exactly what.

Willem is clearly in a jovial mood. He bows punctiliously over my hand and asks me how I do, but does not wait for an answer. He is full of news about his travels around the country. It seems that news of our engagement has leaked out in spite of attempts to keep the marriage negotiations secret, and to my dismay, Willem feels that it is very popular with the people who have greeted him warmly wherever he goes.

'I had a very hearty welcome from my fellow students in Oxford,' he tells me, flicking the tails of his coat out so that he can sit on the sofa opposite me, beaming still with satisfaction. 'Everyone is delighted at the prospect of our marriage.'

I am not delighted, I think. Should it not be my opinion that matters most?

I can hardly bear to look at him. Willem is so different to Frederick! Thin where Frederick is solid, pale while Frederick seems to exist in a golden haze of health and vigour. There is no humour in Willem's face, no warmth in his eyes. I cannot marry a man like Willem, not knowing what it is like to love Frederick.

'Nobody should be discussing it,' I say sharply. 'Not everything has been agreed.'

Willem looks taken aback. For the first time he seems to register the coolness of his reception. 'How is this? I understood that you had signed the marriage contract?'

'I did,' I agree. 'But I have since been under much pressure to relinquish the clause that would allow me to decide when I leave the country,' I say carefully. 'I am not minded to give up the one sanction against being forced to leave England against my will.'

Although I remain always in my father's power, I am not completely friendless in parliament, and for all the show of royalty, parliament is where true power resides. The Prince Regent, a Whig when it suited him to oppose my grandfather, has switched sides and now surrounds himself with Tories. And because my father is now a Tory, the Whigs support his opponents, chiefly my mother. With me they play the long game, knowing that I believe in their cause and that when the time comes that I am Queen, I will stand a true friend to them as they have been to me.

I do not think my mother has a strategy other than doing whatever she feels like whenever she feels like it, but I listen closely to the Whigs, knowing that they have my best interests in mind. So it is that Henry Brougham, my chief adviser, has warned me that the marriage treaty as it stands is not strong enough to prevent me being taken to Holland whether I wish it or no. And if I am obliged to go, my mother would be left unprotected, vulnerable to any plan the Regent might have to start divorce proceedings. He could then marry again and if he were to have a son, I would be left stranded and disinherited in a foreign country.

Where I would be no use to the Whigs, obviously.

I would like to believe that my father would never do this to me, but I cannot help wondering if this is why he is putting so much pressure on me, if this is indeed his plan.

Oh, why could I not have met Frederick before I signed that wretched contract? If only I had held out for a day longer, things would be so different.

But as Anna always says, there is no point in crying over spilt milk. I must hold my nerve. England is a civilised country and this is not the dark ages. I cannot be forced to marry against my will.

I hope.

Willem's bottom lip sticks out. 'But this has been discussed and agreed.'

My belly is fluttering with nerves, but I keep my voice steady. 'What has been agreed is that I have the power to decide whether I live in England or in H-Holland.' In spite of myself, I cannot prevent the old stammer raising its ugly head under the pressure of the moment. 'I must tell you that I will *not* choose to leave this c-country.'

Willem frowns. 'Let me understand you correctly. You are looking for a way to withdraw from an agreement that is in the interest of both our countries? That has been agreed and approved most heartily on both sides?'

'The agreement may be in the interests of England and Holland, but it is not in my interest, and nor is it in the interest of my mother. I am not just the heiress presumptive, I am also a daughter.'

I swallow, take a breath. I have practised this. I must stay calm. I cannot marry Willem feeling as I do, even if the spectre of exile from my own country did not haunt me most horribly, as does the prospect of what might happen to my mother once I am out of the way.

'I do not understand what your mother has to do with our marriage,' Willem says angrily.

'Her story is too well known for you to be ignorant of it, Prince. You must be well aware of the hostility she faces from the Prince Regent, and the fact that it is only her position as mother to the future Queen that protects her.'

'I know that she has squandered her reputation and has brought shame on her family with her behaviour,' Willem retorts and my cheeks burn.

'It is true that my mother is not always wise, but I cannot forget the claims she has on my duty and my attachment,' I say. 'Recent circumstances have led me to believe that if I were to reside out of the k-kingdom, it would be as prejudicial to her interests as to my own. I would be effectively abandoning her to the slights, and perhaps worse, of those who have been hostile to her from the start.'

My heart is hammering, but I won't let myself falter now. I put up my chin instead.

Willem gets to his feet, clearly offended. 'I cannot believe what you are telling me,' he says, pacing over to the window and back. 'To throw away a treaty beneficial to both our countries on an unjustified fear that a woman who has laid herself open to every insult and indignity might be slighted…!'

'That is not the only reason.' I stand too, not wishing to find myself at a disadvantage. I fold my hands together at my waist to stop them shaking. 'I will be Q-Queen one day, and I wish to stay in my own country. You could hardly expect me to feel differently.'

Willem's eyes narrow and he comes up to me. 'Be very careful, Princess,' he says, an ugly look in his face, and he leans threateningly close until Toby utters a low growl that makes him step back. 'It is clear that you are looking for excuses to break our engagement and the contract that you signed, and all I can do is advise you very strongly to think again. I wish you good day,' he finishes in a glacial voice as he stalks over to the door.

'Good day.' My knees are wobbling and the moment he has gone, I sit abruptly. Sensing my distress, Toby presses against my skirts with a little whine and I stroke her soft head. 'Good girl,' I tell her. 'It is lucky that I have you to protect me.'

The door opens and I look up, afraid that Willem might have come back, but it is only Miss Knight. She comes closer, looking worried as she takes in my expression. 'Is it done?'

'It is… but I must write to make absolutely sure that he understands.' I jump up, desperate to get the whole matter resolved. Willem may think that he has frightened me into changing my mind, and I need to make it clear that will not happen. 'I will do it straight away.'

At my writing desk, I pull paper towards me and dip

my pen into the ink, only to stop and think. 'What shall I say?' I ask Cornelia, suddenly uncertain.

She draws up a chair next to mine and after several false starts I produce a letter explaining again my concern for my mother and new circumstances that make it impossible for me to quit England at present or to enter into an engagement that would lead to that happening in the future.

I show it to Cornelia, who corrects my spelling as she reads. 'Very good, Princess,' she says. 'But I advise you to be absolutely clear. Because being a man, you know, he will very likely read only what he wishes to read. You must spell it out so that there is no room for misunderstanding.'

'Very well.' I think for a minute and then add, speaking the words out loud as I write, 'I must consider our engagement from this moment to be totally and for ever at an end.' I glance at Cornelia as I underline the last few words and she nods approvingly.

'I will tell him that he should inform my father of my decision,' I go on, picking up my pen once more.

'Do you think that is right, my dear? He may find that humiliating and you know, gentlemen do hate to be humiliated.'

'Prince Willem can tell me nothing about humiliation,' I snap. Between my mother and my father, I have spent my whole life being humiliated. Let a prince see what it feels like for a change.

Without giving myself time to think, I sign the letter, seal it and yank the bell until John appears.

'See that this is delivered to the Hereditary Prince straight away,' I say, handing him the letter.

'Certainly, Your Royal Highness.'

'So, that is done,' I say to Cornelia when John has gone. It was an uncomfortable interview, but now it feels as if a great weight has been lifted from my shoulders. My engagement is at an end and tomorrow I will see Frederick.

For now, that is all I desire.

Chapter Eighteen

Pulteney Hotel, 21 June 1814

William Coachman grumbles loudly at the traffic as we make our slow way along Piccadilly. The closer we get to the Pulteney, the greater the crush. Everyone, it seems, has come to take their leave of the Tsar and his sister, and those not illustrious enough to say personal farewells are thronging the pavements and gawking at the parade of visitors. Each coming or going produces a ripple of interest, and the noise of chatter and laughter and the sense of bustle and excitement is quite overwhelming.

My carriage is just another one in a series until I am recognised and then a cheer goes up as William forces a way through at last and gets me close enough to the entrance for the groom to jump down and pull out the steps. The cheers are mixed with speculative whispers. By now the world and his dog have heard that I have broken my engagement to the Hereditary Prince, and I keep my chin high as I incline my head to acknowledge the crowd and walk into the hotel with Cornelia Knight beside me.

The lobby is almost as crowded as the pavement. There are a lot of officers in uniform and politicians and fashionable ladies, most in the poke bonnets that Catherine has made all the rage, and the buzz of conversation is loud enough to rattle the chandeliers. But it breaks off as I stride into the hotel, only to resume hurriedly.

I put up my chin and ignore them all as we climb the staircase to the Grand Duchess's suite. I have come to say goodbye to Catherine, not to gratify the curious.

The Grand Duchess receives me with flattering warmth. 'How glad I am to see you, dear Charlotte! You must excuse the state of things,' she says, waving a hand around the apartment which looks in perfectly good order to me and is indeed far more luxurious than Warwick House. 'We are at sixes and sevens today what with packing up and saying our farewells.'

Not that she looks in the slightest bit harried. I can just imagine Anna pointing out that it is her maid who will be doing all the work of packing.

I refuse Catherine's offer for me to remove my bonnet. 'I can see how busy you are. I will not stay long, but I could not let you go without saying farewell.'

'No, indeed! Come, you have time to sit with me for a while, surely?'

She draws me over to a table by the window that looks out over Green Park. It is a restful view and quiet away from the hubbub in Piccadilly. Cornelia takes a seat on one of the sofas to give us some privacy and I see her surreptitiously craning her neck to catch a glimpse of the bathing room which has a porcelain tub with taps, or so we have heard. I would quite like to see it myself: I must make do with a jug and basin in my bedroom.

Catherine sits opposite me in a flurry of skirts, her eyes bright with interest. 'Since we last met you have set all London – all England! – by the ears. How I admire you, Charlotte!'

'I suppose you have heard it all,' I say half-defiantly, drawing off my gloves.

'I have, but not from the mouth of the horse as you say. Is it true? Did you break off the engagement with the Hereditary Prince?'

'I did. Our tempers did not agree,' I say carefully. 'Everything conspired to forebode a sad future had the marriage taken place.'

I would love to tell Catherine about Frederick as I am sure she would understand, but I have just enough discretion to keep my love affair to myself for now. If it were known that I had thrown Willem over for another man, the consequences for Britain's diplomacy would be enormous.

Frederick has gone. He is with the Prussian King and is even now taking ship at Portsmouth. His absence is an ache already. I do not know how I am to bear it, but I must trust in his love and hope that once the Orange match has been struck down, he will be able to write to my father and return.

'I could not accept the terms of the agreement,' I tell Catherine instead.

'And your papa? How has he reacted?'

With a cold rage, made worse by the fact that he cannot move against me while the foreign visitors, all of whom have met me, are in town. I am well aware that he is biding his time.

'He is… not happy,' I admit, pulling a face, and Catherine nods her head understandingly.

'So I should imagine,' she says. 'He will not care for being made to look a fool. You could hardly have chosen a worse time to make your stand, *ma petite*. It is a time of delicate relations in Europe and you know, the Prince Regent has been exposed in front of everyone as a man who can control neither his wife nor his daughter. They say there was a violent debate in parliament and the Prussian princes were there in the public gallery to laugh about it.'

I know. Frederick was watching, and he told me of the way he and his fellow Prussians shook their heads at the outraged scenes below. I admit, I hoped that he would have been more delighted to learn that I was free. The most eligible princess in Europe is back on the market, as it were, and his for the taking. Frederick gazed into my eyes and told me we must wait.

Wait, wait, wait. Oh, I know he is right, but my whole life is waiting!

I sigh inwardly, remembering our last stolen evening two days earlier. He gave me a little ring with a turquoise as a token of his love. A small thing, as he said, but it means everything to me. Anna sniffed at it and opined that Frederick was cheap; I do not know sometimes why I keep her about me. Cornelia is right; she is impertinent. Besides, she does not understand that Frederick could hardly give me a diamond ring without questions being asked.

I look at the ring on my hand. Of course it is cheap. It is a *token*.

I look back at Catherine. 'I did what I had to do,' I tell her. 'I am not ashamed. I will not accept a life of misery if I have had no say in it.'

'Bravo!'

Catherine is clapping her approval when the door opens and the footman announces

Prince Leopold of some German state that I do not catch, and a young man in the all-white uniform of the Russian heavy cavalry enters, hat in his hand. Still thinking about Frederick, and faintly resentful of having my tête-à-tête with the Grand Duchess interrupted, I return my attention to the park outside.

Catherine holds out her hand. 'Prince, how nice to see you!'

'I am sorry to disturb you, Duchess,' the Prince of Wherever-it-is says. 'I came on business. I was hoping to speak to the Tsar about affairs in Germany, but he is temporarily engaged and so I thought to pay a courtesy call and wish you a pleasant journey. But I see you too are occupied. My apologies.'

'Not at all.' Catherine turns to me. 'May I present Prince Leopold of Saxe-Coburg-Saalfeld, Princess? Lieutenant General Officer commanding the heavy cavalry of the Tsar,' she adds. She smiles at the Prince. 'And this, of course, is Princess Charlotte of Wales. Is it possible you have met before?'

'I have not yet had the pleasure,' he says, clicking his heels together and bowing.

I muster a smile and turn a little in my chair to look at him.

This prince is dark where Frederick is all gold. His face is handsome enough, but his eyes are serious where Frederick's gleam with high spirits. His manner is formal, not reckless. I sense coldness, not warmth.

Oh, Frederick! Frederick! How I yearn for him!

Go away, I want to say to this Leopold. *Go away and come back as Frederick.*

'Prince,' I murmur, inclining my head.

'You are not travelling with us tomorrow?' Catherine asks.

'No, I will be staying in England a little longer until my services are required.' His dark eyes rest briefly on my face. 'It is an honour to meet you, Princess, but I must not disturb you further, Duchess.' He bows very correctly and leaves us alone.

'A very handsome young man, do you not agree?' Catherine says, leaning forward when he has gone. 'The Coburgs are all so good-looking and Poldi more so than most. Cultured and intelligent too, which as you know is not always the case with attractive men.'

'Poldi?' I ask, but without much interest. I'm not sure why Catherine is so keen to tell me about him.

'That is what the family call him. We are related – but then the Coburgs are related to everybody!' she goes on with a little laugh. 'It may be a little country, but it has dynastic connections across the Continent. They have a talent for advantageous marriages! Anyway, Poldi has been serving with great gallantry. You must know that he has distinguished himself as a cavalry officer in my brother's service.'

'I am glad to have met him,' I say with a polite smile as I rise myself. 'I should go. You will have many more visitors to wish you farewell. It was a sad crush downstairs.'

'I am just glad you did not meet the Hereditary Prince downstairs. That would have been awkward.'

'What?' I exchange a startled glance with Cornelia who has also risen. 'He is not here today?'

'He may be coming to see the Tsar today. You will not want to meet him,' she adds, seeing my horrified expression.

'No, indeed.' I feel quite agitated at the thought. It would be bad enough to see Willem at all, let alone in front of all those curious spectators. 'That is the last thing I want to do!'

'Do you wish me to send a servant to see if the stairs are clear?'

I hesitate. There are so many people downstairs that it would be easy not to see Willem until it was too late – and how would a servant identify him anyway?

'Are there some backstairs perhaps?'

Cornelia clucks a little. 'Princess, you cannot use the back stairs like a servant! That is below your dignity!'

'It is better than coming face-to-face with the Hereditary Prince,' I say frankly.

'As you wish.' Catherine rings a bell for her servant, who appears from her bedroom looking hot. As I suspected, it is her maid who is harried and at sixes and sevens. Catherine speaks to her in rapid Russian and she replies.

'Yelena will show you the doorway that opens onto the stairs,' she tells me eventually. 'It leads into a little hall beside the main one. You will be able to send a servant out for your carriage from there without being exposed to the crush in the hall – or to meeting anyone you would rather not!'

She kisses me warmly as we say farewell. 'Goodbye, Charlotte, and *bonne chance*! I have so enjoyed getting to know you.'

'And I you,' I say truthfully.

The staircase is dark and narrow and we make our way down cautiously. When we reach the bottom, though, we discover that the small hall is not as empty as Catherine had promised. It seems that several people have come in to avoid the crush in the main hall, including a tall officer in the white uniform of the Russian heavy cavalry. He has his back to me, but at my involuntary exclamation of dismay at seeing the crowds beyond, he turns and I realise it is the Saxe-Coburg prince who paid his respects to the Grand Duchess. What was his name?

'Your Royal Highness,' he exclaims, bowing to me and to Cornelia. 'May I assist you?'

I look again at the crowds. 'Thank you,' I say. 'I am wondering how to get to my carriage…'

'Let me send a servant for the carriage, and I will escort you outside,' he says promptly.

Poldi, that is his name, but I can hardly call him that.

'Thank you,' I say again. 'I would appreciate it.'

He bows again and beckons to a servant. *What is his name?* I mouth to Cornelia while he is issuing orders.

'Leopold,' she whispers back.

Ah, yes, that is it. I remember now.

I must say, for a prince he seems quite efficient, because in no time, it seems, the servant is back to say the carriage is on its way and he is offering me his arm.

'May I have the honour of escorting you to your carriage, Princess?'

'Thank you.' I smile and lay my hand on his arm while Cornelia follows us through the press of people.

I am more concerned with getting out of the crush without seeing Willem than with Leopold, but nonetheless I am aware of the strength of his arm and the competence with which he steers me through the crowd and outside, avoiding the piles of horse dung that no one has had a chance to sweep away between all the carriages arriving and going.

It seems only polite to make some conversation.

'Have you been in London long, Prince Leopold?' I ask a little distractedly, watching where I put my feet.

'Since the beginning of June,' he tells me.

'Why have you not been to call on me?' I pretend to chide him. 'Every other prince has called, it seems, but not you!'

'Please forgive me,' he says with one of his serious looks. 'I had not known whether such visits would be permitted.'

To my relief, William is waiting with the carriage across the street. The groom already has the steps down and the crowd are smiling and pointing, suddenly realising that I am there.

'Gawd bless you, Yer Royal 'Ighness!' a woman calls from somewhere, and there is a ripple of cheering.

'Will you allow me to make up for my omission?' Leopold stands at the door of my carriage.

'Omission?' I echo. I have been smiling at the crowd, climbing up into the carriage, not really listening.

'I may call on you?'

'Oh… certainly. I will hope to see you soon,' I say politely but without much enthusiasm.

I wait for Cornelia to join me and Leopold takes a pace back as the groom puts up the steps and swings up behind us.

'Drive on, William,' I say and nod farewell to the Coburg Prince, putting him out of my mind completely as the carriage moves off towards Hyde Park.

Chapter Nineteen

Mayfair, May 1981

'You've lost so much weight!'

Elizabeth Emanuel sounds worried, but Diana is delighted. Her diet is working.

Or perhaps it isn't the diet so much as the fact that whenever she overeats, she can throw it all up before it can turn to fat. Diana isn't a fool. She knows it's not a sensible way to lose weight, but how many sensible people are facing being on television in front of a hundred million people, which is what they are telling her. All around the world, people will be watching her marry Charles and the one thing Diana is determined not to look is fat.

She wants to look perfect for Charles.

'That's a good thing. I don't want to look fat on my wedding day!'

'You won't look fat, Diana, that's for sure.' Elizabeth frowns down at the tape measure. 'You've lost over two inches from your waist already. We'll need to take new measurements and adjust the bodice… I don't want to cut into the fabric until we know what size you're going to be.'

'It'll be fine,' says Diana confidently. She turns this way and that in front of the mirror. It is only a dummy, but the dress already seems magical to her. The Emanuels have designed exactly what she wanted, a billowy, frothy fantasy of a dress. She adores its ruffles and frills, the puffed sleeves, the embroidered pearls and sequins.

As a little girl at Sandringham, her favourite book was *Cinderella*. At the end was a picture of Cinderella marrying Prince Charming. Diana always loved that page. Cinderella had blonde hair and a gorgeous full-skirted wedding dress decorated with ruffles and bows, not a million miles from the Emanuels's design. Of course, Charles won't be in a powdered wig or a pale-blue satin coat and breeches, but the *feeling* of the wedding will be the same. Diana is determined on it. Charles is her Prince Charming and although she is not exactly Cinderella, she has still come from nowhere to marry the future King.

Charles is determined on St Paul's Cathedral for the wedding. Something to do with the acoustics. Diana would have preferred the more romantic Westminster Abbey, but she has recognised that there are some arguments she will not win.

Instead, she has had long discussions with the Emanuels about climbing those iconic steps and how the dress will show to the best effect.

'The first thing people are going to see is your back,'

David Emanuel pointed out. 'The back view has to be stunning.'

'I want a train.' Diana remembers being firm about that on her first visit. 'And a veil.'

They have delivered on that. The train will be twenty-five feet long, and the veil even longer. When she gets out of the Glass Coach and walks up the cathedral steps with her father, the train will spread out behind her in a glorious romantic display. Of course, walking with all that material dragging behind her will be tricky, but she is practising with a sheet and her bridesmaids will be there to straighten the train and stop the veil pulling the tiara off her head.

When Elizabeth Emanuel has finished revising the measurements, she tells Diana she has something to show her. 'We've been thinking about the whole "something old, something new" tradition and the Royal School of Needlework have sent us some pieces of old material,' she says, very carefully lifting a piece of lace from a felt cloth. 'What do you think of this?'

'Oh, it's beautiful! What is it?'

'It's exquisite, isn't it?' Elizabeth lays it back on the felt. 'It's handmade Carrickmacross lace, once worn by Prince Charles's great-grandmother, Queen Mary, and at least a hundred years old. It's very fragile, but we could stitch it to the bodice as "something old"?'

'I like that idea.' Diana nods enthusiastically. 'And for "something borrowed" I can wear the Spencer tiara. Jane and Sarah wore it to their weddings. It's rather nice, with tulips and stars made out of diamonds. I'll ask my father if I can bring it in for you to see.'

'That sounds wonderful,' Elizabeth agrees. 'Something new isn't a problem. The silk itself will be specially spun at Lullingstone in Dorset, so it doesn't get much newer than that.'

'What about something blue?'

'David and I been thinking about that. What do you say to us sewing a small blue bow into the waistband?'

Diana claps her hands together. 'Perfect!'

Funny, when she's here talking about the dress she knows exactly what she wants and she's confident and in control. She loves coming to the Emanuels's tiny studio in Mayfair with its wonderful smell of new and expensive fabric. She could happily spend all day here discussing threads and buttons, sequins and pearls, hems and seams and ruching and how it will all come together in one beautiful, romantic dress.

It is so much easier to think about that than to think about life at Buckingham Palace. Charles is back from Australia and has chosen to completely ignore her rage at the way he chose to talk to Camilla rather than spend time with his fiancée before he went away for three weeks. So they haven't talked about it, but then again, what is there to say?

While he was away, Diana had an awkward lunch with Camilla. It was Camilla who suggested it. There was a letter from her waiting for Diana the night she moved into Clarence House. Camilla knew Charles was going to Australia before Diana did. She followed up on the invitation after Charles had flown out and although Diana didn't really want to go, she hadn't known how to refuse.

Camilla is always perfectly pleasant, but she knows Charles so much better than Diana does that it's hard not to resent her.

Conversation at the lunch was stilted. Camilla seemed mostly anxious to know whether Diana was planning to hunt when she was at Highgrove.

Diana can't think of anything worse. Careering around the countryside on a horse, getting muddy, seeing some poor creature killed... Oh, she has heard – so many times! – about the need to keep foxes under control, that it's kinder than poison, blah, blah, blah, but hunting is really not her scene.

'I don't think so,' she told Camilla, who looked relieved.

She wishes now that she had had the nerve to ask Camilla how to reach Charles, how to make his face light up when he heard *her* voice or saw *her* come into a room, how to make him laugh.

Diana can't understand it. She had been sweet for Charles, she had been jolly, she had been adoring, and he had liked it, he *had*. But that sense of closeness she thought they had shared feels as if it is slipping through her fingers and she doesn't know how to stop it.

Well, Camilla and Charles can get wet and muddy together, she decides. They won't want her tagging along anyway. Camilla can have him while they're hunting, but that's it. The rest of the time, Charles needs to be thinking about *her*. She is his fiancée, after all.

Diana doesn't like the fact that Charles is still so attached to his old girlfriends. Yes, they are old friends, but he has her now; why does he need Camilla too? They're going to be finalising the guest list for the cathedral and a more exclusive list for the wedding breakfast and Diana has a number of names that she doesn't want on either.

Camilla is one of them, as is her ghastly stepmother Raine's even more ghastly mother Barbara Cartland. Diana is not being upstaged by anyone on her wedding day.

Pushing disagreeable thoughts of Camilla and her step-grandmother away, Diana turns back to the much more enjoyable business of discussing the decoration of the neckline of her wedding dress.

'It's going to be perfect,' she tells Elizabeth Emanuel.

Chapter Twenty

Warwick House, 12 July 1814

The Prussians have gone. The Russians have gone. The bunting is down and London has subsided into customary summer torpor. The haut ton are on their estates, enjoying the country life for a while, and my father, who has been biding his time, exacts his revenge for my rejection of the Orange match.

He descends, scowling, on Warwick House without warning, accompanied as always by Bishop Fisher, the Great Up. Of course I knew that he would not let such a public humiliation of his plans lie, but still I am not prepared for the severity of his anger or the cruelty of his revenge.

I am sitting with Miss Knight when the Prince Regent is announced and he wastes no time on civility.

'Out,' he snarls, jerking his head at Cornelia before she

has even finished her curtsey. 'I wish to speak to the Princess in private.'

There is nothing Cornelia can do other than send me a sympathetic look as she withdraws with the bishop, leaving me alone with my father.

Who wastes no time in tearing me to shreds. I am obstinate, wilful, an embarrassment. I am improper, indelicate, indecent. I am just like my mother, he rages. It is the worst insult he can think of. Like her, I am a curse on his life.

'I will not put up with your reckless, wilful behaviour any longer. You must lay aside this idle nonsense of thinking that you have a will of your own. While I live, and you are unmarried, you must be subject to me, if you be thirty or forty or five-and-forty.' Spittle is gathering at the corners of his mouth and his face is alarmingly red. 'And since you seem determined not to be married, you will do as I say. I am dismissing your attendants and your servants and you will remove to Windsor where you will see no one until I give permission, and let me tell you, that is likely to be a very long time.'

'You cannot deprive me of my household!' I protest without thinking. I expected anger but not cruelty. 'My household are my only friends!'

'Cannot? *Cannot?* I am your father and the Regent and I can do what I damned well like!' he says, making no apology for his language, not that I expected one.

'Without attendants or s-servants I would be utterly alone,' I try, cursing the stammer which comes back whenever I am upset and which only serves to inflame my father.

'You should have thought of the consequences before you behaved in such a foolhardy way.'

'But it is not f-fair!'

'How dare you preach to me of fairness?' My father is pacing around the room, while I stand, chin up and braced for the rage that comes off him like buffeting waves. 'You deliberately humiliated me in front of our allies. Was *that* fair? Every crowned head and general was laughing at me last week. They were vastly amused that I can apparently control neither my wife nor my daughter! And as for diplomatic relations with Holland, God knows if they will ever recover!'

'I am sorry, but—'

'Sorry? What good is sorry now?'

My knees are shaking but I will not let him see how frightened I am. 'You should not have hurried and t-tricked me into an arrangement so contrary to my own interests.'

He turns on me at that. 'How dare you? How *dare* you accuse me of trickery?'

'You would not listen to me. I said only that I liked what I had seen of the Hereditary Prince at that dinner. I did not say I wished to marry him.'

'You signed the damned contract!'

'And then you tried to make me give up the one clause that protected me.' I am as angry as my father now.

'What nonsense is this? What need have you of *protection*?' he spits at me. 'You are a princess of the realm, little though you behave as one! You do not need to be protected.'

'I may be a princess but there is no one to protect my interests – or those of my mother.'

'Do not speak to me of that woman! I curse the day I laid eyes on her. And you, miss, are going to be as bad as her. You are wilful and disobedient and I. Will. Not. Have. It.' His head is lowered, a bull about to charge. 'You, Charlotte, will take the punishment that you deserve. I am sending you to Cranbourne Lodge at Windsor where you will be under the supervision of General Garth. You will not take any of your household with you. I am dispensing with the services of Miss Knight, who has failed so lamentably to keep your headstrong ways in check. Instead, you will be attended by Lady Rosslyn and Lady Ilchester. You will not see any of your friends who lead you astray, especially not Mercer Elphinstone, and you are not to engage in correspondence with them either.'

'So I am to be taken away, deprived of my faithful attendants and servants and surrounded by strangers?' My voice wavers in spite of myself.

'You have brought this on yourself with your heedless, headstrong ways.' My father's temper has burnt itself out into a cold rage. 'You do not have a will of your own or a mind of your own. You may not behave as you wish. You will do as I say, Charlotte, and be grateful I do not punish you further.'

'It would be impossible to punish me more than this!' My throat is clogged with tears of anger and fear and, unable to bear it any longer, I run weeping from the room and up the stairs to my dressing room.

Cornelia hurries after me, her face concerned. She finds me furiously dashing the tears from my cheeks. 'Oh, my dear Princess, what did the Regent say?'

'You are to be dismissed, my faithful Chevalier!' I grasp her hands briefly before storming around my dressing room, unable to stand still. 'The unfairness of it knows no bounds. You, who have been such a loyal and affectionate servant, and whose character and talents should be rewarded by the protection and gratitude of my whole family, instead of this cruel dismissal!'

'But what of you, Princess?' Cornelia asks anxiously.

'Me? Oh, I am to be sent as a prisoner to Windsor, separated from my servants and forbidden correspondence with my friends!' I am weeping with fury and frustration. 'Oh, I am so angry! God grant me patience!'

'Oh, my dear, what will you do?'

'I do not know, but I will not accept this! All I have ever done is to stand up for my own interests. All I've wanted is to do my duty and to hope for some personal happiness. Is that so wrong?'

My expression must be so ravaged that Cornelia comes over to embrace me. 'No, it is not wrong,' she says. 'Have you… have you heard from Prince Frederick?' she asks, lowering her voice in case anyone else hears.

I shake my head. I have had only one short letter from Frederick and there was little lover-like about it, no matter how hard I scanned the lines about his safe arrival and resumption of duties hoping that they might mysteriously mean that he was missing me as much as I have missed him.

I twist the turquoise ring on my finger. If only Frederick were here! If only I could be certain that once he hears of my treatment he will come to my rescue, tell my father that he loves me and wants me for his wife. It is not as if he is a nobody. He is grandson to a great king, nephew to another, in every way suitable. But he must get on a ship and come to England and face my father down for me, and though I wish with all my heart that I could be certain that he will, I am not.

I am alone, and must deal with my father myself.

John the footman is at the door, looking scared and sober. Like everyone else, he must have heard my father ranting.

'Miss Knight, His Royal Highness commands your presence,' he says apologetically.

Cornelia squares her shoulders. 'Thank you, John,' she says with dignity before turning to me and embracing me once more. 'I had better go. Do not despair, Princess. We will think of something.'

No, I will not despair, I think. I catch sight of myself in the mirror and am shocked at how grim and determined I look. I will be Queen, I remind myself. I do not submit tamely to being treated like this. I refuse!

'John!' I call him back just as he is about to close the door after Cornelia. 'Send Anna to me. Straight away!'

Anna comes so quickly she can only have been waiting for my call. 'Bring me my pelisse and bonnet,' I tell her. I have scrubbed the tears from my face, but my anger is still burning bright. 'Quickly now! I will not stay in this place a moment longer.'

Anna runs to fetch them and helps me on with the pelisse. 'Where are you going?'

'To my mother,' I say, yanking the ribbons on my bonnet into a lopsided bow.

'How will you get there?' Anna doesn't waste time trying to dissuade me. 'The stables have orders not to take out any horses for you.'

My lips tighten. 'I will take a hackney cab then.'

'I'd better go with you,' she says instantly.

'No.' I put out a hand to stop her as she turns. 'No, Anna. I fear for what my father would do to you.'

'I ain't afraid of him.'

'You should be. He is vicious when he is crossed and he would swat you like a fly. Besides, it is high summer and light still. What danger can there be?' I am already heading down the servants' stairs. I have no wish to run into the Great Up, still less my father.

'You ain't never been in a cab,' Anna points out, trotting behind me. 'You don't even have any money.'

'What does it matter? My mother's steward can pay the driver.'

She makes one last try. 'At least wait for Miss Knight.'

'No, I must go now!'

'All right then.' Anna nods and straightens my bonnet. 'Good luck!' She puts a finger to her lips as we reach the hall and peeks out of the door. 'Mr Thomas is there,' she whispers. 'I'll draw him away and you run.'

'Oh, there you are, Mr Thomas,' she says, stepping out

into the hall. 'Such a dust-up there's been! The Princess wants to see you in her dressing room right now.'

The minute he has made his stately way up the main staircase, I give Anna a quick hug, dart out of the stairwell and across the hall. For an awful moment I fumble with the door, but then Anna is there, pulling it open and I am running, running over the cobbles and out to the bustle and freedom of Cockspur Street.

Chapter Twenty-One

I'm not sure what I expect – a shout? Soldiers running after me? – but in fact the only witness to my flight is a cat which pauses cleaning itself to stare as I rush along Warwick Street.

The contrast with the busyness of Cockspur Street is so startling that I pause as I reach the end of Warwick Street. My heart is galloping in my chest and I put out a hand to the wall to catch my breath.

It was not like this when I walked to the Frost Fair with Anna. Then, the streets were almost deserted, the pavements so treacherous with ice and packed snow that only the hardiest souls ventured out.

I have never been alone on a busy street like this before. I am always high in a carriage, accompanied by a groom and a coachman at least, isolated from the hustle and bustle.

Now I am insignificant, almost invisible, as carts and carriages, wagons and hackney cabs rumble past, their wheels splattering through the mud and horse droppings. It is a fine afternoon and the pavements are crowded with an extraordinary mixture of strutting gentlemen and respectable-looking people strolling while harried clerks and footmen and maids dodge between them and the hawkers and ballad singers and crossing sweepers to fulfil their errands. It is overwhelming.

The noise is incredible. Dogs slink and snap and snarl at each other. Horses shake their manes and jingle their harnesses while their hooves clop briskly along the street. A coachman blares his horn as he bullies this coach through the throng with his weary passengers. Children cry. A legless soldier sits on the ground across the road, playing a whistle for the odd tossed penny. And bubbling through it all, the sound of people talking, laughing, arguing, bartering, shouting, scolding, teasing, flirting.

Not one of them has even noticed me.

I glance over my shoulder down Warwick Street. There is no sign of pursuit yet, but I must keep moving. I have been so frantic to escape that it is only now that I realise that I have no idea what to do, and I wish that I had let Anna come with me after all. This is all so new and so strange and without my royal carriage and royal attendants I am just a young girl on her own.

But I cannot go back now.

Biting my lip, I turn left and hurry up towards Pall Mall which is even busier than Cockspur Street. I look frantically up and down for a hackney carriage, but although there are plenty manoeuvring expertly through the hubbub, I do not know how to get one to stop. They are all moving too fast and cannot or will not see me waving at them. I wring my hands. Why did I not think before I rushed out? Look where my recklessness has got me, alone and helpless on a London street.

There is a touch on my arm. 'May I help you, miss?'

Startled, I swing round to see a respectable-looking young man addressing me. 'Forgive me,' he says, seeing my surprise. 'I was in my uncle's print shop over there'—he nods across Pall Mall—'when I saw you in some distress. Are you in need of assistance?'

'Thank you, yes,' I say breathlessly. 'I should be very much obliged if you would find a hackney cab for me.'

'Certainly,' he says. 'Where do you wish to go?'

'Oxford Street,' I say with more confidence than I feel. Surely my mother will give me refuge at Connaught House?

As I watch, the young man puts two fingers in his mouth and produces a piercing whistle. To my intense relief, a cab pulls over. Before the jarvey or the young man have a chance to pull down the steps, I have grabbed them myself and scrambled inside.

'Thank you, thank you, Sir,' I tell my rescuer, almost gabbling in relief through the window, and then, to the jarvey, 'Oxford Street, at the gallop, if you please.'

'A gallop?' He looks at me in disbelief. 'You seen the traffic?'

'As fast as you can then. I will give you... three guineas,' I guess wildly, 'if you will only get me there quickly.'

I fall back into the dim interior of the cab as he clicks his horses into action, just in time before we pass the grand porticoed entrance to Carlton House. I cower in the shadows but who, after all, is going to look for Princess Charlotte in a hackney cab? Surely I am safe now?

I don't feel safe. The cab smells of old leather and something sour. My stomach is churning and my heart still thudding so painfully in my throat that I have to gulp to breathe. I am taking a terrible risk. My father's fury will know no bounds when he finds out what I have done, but what choice do I have?

It is too late now, anyway.

I understand now why the jarvey stared at me when I told him to gallop. Our progress is painfully slow, though every moment takes me further from Carlton House. He grumbles loudly at every obstacle: a cart blocking the way, a street sweeper, a dog fight. I find it oddly comforting that he reminds me of William Coachman, but then I remember that if my father has his way, I will no longer see William or Anna or John or Mrs Brough or even my dear Mrs Louis. It is not to be borne.

When we reach Oxford Street at last, the driver shouts down to ask where I want to be dropped and I direct him to Connaught House. Once there, I wait for him to let down the steps and help me out.

'Wait here and you will be paid,' I say and taking a deep breath I tread up to the door.

It is opened by my mother's steward who stares at me in astonishment before belatedly remembering a deep bow. 'Your Royal Highness!'

'Please tell the Princess of Wales that I am here to see her.'

'Her Royal Highness has gone to dine in Blackheath.'

I am dismayed at the news but determined not to show it. 'Send a groom to fetch her home,' I say, pulling off my gloves with a great show of confidence. 'I will wait here. Tell the cook he will oblige me by sending up dinner for when the Princess returns.'

The steward bows again, wisely keeping his thoughts to himself.

'Oh, and pay the driver of the cab,' I add airily. 'I promised him three guineas.'

'Three *guineas*, Your Royal Highness?'

'Is that enough?'

'More than enough, Your Royal Highness,' he says faintly.

'Well, I do not wish to quibble. Pay him as you think fit.'

Alone in my mother's drawing room, I realise that my knees are shaking and I sit abruptly down.

It is nearly two hours before my mother returns. She comes in complaining, waving aside my curtsey irritably. 'Charlotte, what is happening? Why must I be dragged back like this?'

'I have run off.'

'*Run off*?' Her bulbous blue eyes, so like my own, open wide. 'What do you mean? *Wie? Warum?* Why?'

'I cannot endure my father's cruel treatment any longer,' I tell her. I have had time to think about what I will say and I am feeling bullish again. 'His bullying of me is insupportable, Mama! He wishes to force me into the Orange match and because I will not accept, he plans to make me a prisoner in Windsor and dismiss my entire household!'

'But what do you hope to gain by running off like this?' she says, throwing herself down onto a sofa.

'Mama, I am showing him that I stand by you.' I sit down next to her and take her hands, trying to make her understand. 'The public are on our side. They would support us if I chose to live with you.'

'Live with *me*? *Ach*, Charlotte…'

I expect her to welcome the chance to cross the Prince Regent, but my mother's expression is far from delighted.

'Why can I not?' I demand.

She fiddles with the fringe of her shawl. 'Well, that would be delightful, Charlotte, *natürlich*, but… but it so happens that your father has just offered to increase my allowance to fifty thousand pounds a year if I will go overseas…' She trails off at my expression of dismay.

'You cannot go abroad, Mama!' In spite of myself, my voice cracks. 'Have you no care for me?'

'I do not wish to abandon you, no, Charlotte, but you must know I have many demands on my purse and poor Willy is growing out of his clothes faster than I can procure them for him.'

Poor Willy! My mother has more affection for the adopted boy than she does for me. He is a thin, whey-faced child she treats the way I treat Toby or Puff, showering him with kisses and letting him sleep in her bed. Everyone thinks it very strange of her, but she will not give him up.

So she would rather take my father's money for Willy Austin than support me in my fight for some say over my own life. Tears of disappointment prick my eyes, but I blink them away as the door opens and Henry Brougham is announced. I sent him a note while I was waiting for my mother and he has come as I knew he would.

I do feel guilty when I see how exhausted he looks, though. He is a lawyer and has, he says, been up all night working on a case.

My mother perks up as always when a man is present, and doubtless she is also glad not to have to explain herself to me any further. '*Komm!* We will eat now you are here,' she says, getting to her feet and twitching her shawl into place.

'My thanks, Your Royal Highness, but I am not hungry.'

'*Quatsch!* Nonsense, of course you will dine with us. You can carve for us.'

Brougham only sighs. 'The only thing I am fit to carve is the soup!'

I tuck a hand under his arm. 'You will be better for something to eat,' I tell him briskly and he allows himself to be led down the stairs into the dining room.

Chapter Twenty-Two

We do not sit long over the meal and have barely retired to the drawing room when my mother's steward announces the arrival of an odd couple, my friend Mercer and the Great Up, the Bishop of Salisbury.

'Show Miss Elphinstone up,' I say. 'His Grace may remain in the dining room. I have no wish to see him.'

I am eager to hear from Mercer what has been happening at Warwick House since my flight was discovered and to make sure no blame has fallen on the servants.

'No, indeed,' Mercer says when I ask anxiously after Anna. 'The Prince Regent does not suspect any of the servants. I thought he would be angry, but if anything he seemed oddly pleased.'

'Pleased?' I echo in surprise.

'He said he was glad that you had run off as now everybody would see you as you were,' Mercer reports apologetically. 'He said that if your flight were known on the Continent, no one would marry you.'

Frederick would, I think to myself. My father thinks me friendless, but it is not so. Frederick will stand by me. He must.

It is the beginning of a parade of visitors and for a while my mother and I amuse ourselves by admitting only favourites and banishing bores and the pompous and disagreeable to wait downstairs or in their carriages. The Bishop I send back to my father with a message to say that I will go back to Warwick House provided that I am allowed to see Mercer as often as I wish and that Miss Knight and Mrs Louis are allowed to remain members of my household.

Cornelia arrives a little later, bridling with the excitement and intrigue of it all. She is accompanied by my dear Mrs Louis, who just looks worried.

'Oh, I am so glad to see you both!' I exclaim, hurrying over to greet them.

'We came as soon as we could, Princess.' Cornelia lowers her voice importantly. 'I bring you these,' she says, and hands me my royal seal and, more importantly, a letter.

Pushing the seal back into her hands, I tear open the letter. It is from Frederick! Thank God! Obviously, he knows nothing of what has transpired and the letter is brief and tells me nothing that I do not already know, but the important thing is that he has written. He has remembered me. He is still there for me.

I smile and my shoulders relax for the first time that

evening. 'Thank you,' I say to Cornelia and take the seal back with an apologetic smile.

'Is it from Prince Frederick?' she whispers.

'It is.' I lay my finger across my lips. I cannot afford for anyone to know about Frederick yet. But his letter has given me the strength to continue.

For a while I am exhilarated by the knowledge that Frederick loves me still, but as the night wears on, I am worn down by the constant stream of visitors, begging and pleading for me to return. The Bishop returns eventually, bearing a message from my father that he will allow me to continue to see Mercer, but that will be his only concession. I must lose Cornelia and my faithful household too. My Uncle Frederick, Duke of York, is sent to take me back to Carlton House in disgrace, but that means that all hope of freedom will be over for me. I refuse to go.

It is the early hours when Brougham comes over to me where I am sitting dully on a sofa. My mother has gone to bed. Cornelia is asleep. Downstairs, the Duke of York is waiting impatiently, aggrieved at being dragged from the card table.

'This cannot go on.' Brougham's face is grey with exhaustion. 'Come with me, Princess.'

He takes me to the window. Outside, the summer dawn is breaking over Hyde Park where the trees are a dense, intense green. As I watch, a rabbit hops into sight, freezes and then bolts at some unheard sound, leaving tiny footprints in the dew. The sky is delicately flushed and the birds are just ruffling their feathers and trying out their songs.

'In a few hours, the park there will be crowded with your future subjects,' Brougham tells me gravely. 'You are their hope for the future, and if you wish it, they will rise up on your behalf. You know they love you and hate your father. If they know that you have fled your father's keeping, they will share your anger. But if that happens, blood will be shed and people will die. Do you truly wish that?'

Appalled at the thought, I cover my face with my hands. 'No, no, I do not want anyone to suffer for me,' I say, my voice thick with tears. 'Of *course* I don't want that.'

For a moment I am tempted to stay with my face hidden in my hands. I am so tired. I am so alone. I thought I had no choice but to run, but now it has all gone wrong. My mother does not want me. My father reviles me. Even the Whigs do not want to trigger a constitutional crisis by appearing to foment a rebellion.

I do not want that either. All I wanted was not to be forced to marry a man I do not love. Was that so bad?

Now I want only to lie down and sleep and for it all to go away.

I lift my head and straighten my shoulders as I turn back to Brougham. 'Very well, I will return. But I will not go meekly back. Write a statement for me, please, Brougham. I wish to declare that I will never marry the Prince of Orange and that if an announcement is ever made to that effect, it is to be understood that it will be against my will. Write it out six times. I want everyone here to have a copy.'

When Brougham has written the statement and I have

passed them out, I call for my pelisse and bonnet and go downstairs with Mrs Louis.

The Duke of York has been sleeping with his mouth open and his head at an awkward angle, but he wakes with a start to glower at me when I go in. He hauls himself out of his chair and rubs a hand over his hair with an enormous yawn.

'There you are,' he says. 'I hope this means you are ready to submit?'

I put up my chin. I have not submitted. I will not marry Willem. 'I am ready to *return*.'

'At last!' He shouts an order for the grooms to put the carriage to, and stomps out, telling me to wait.

A few minutes later, I am summoned out to the carriage. My uncle is waiting, looking surly and rumpled. He points at Mrs Louis by my side. 'Not you,' he says.

'I will not go without her,' I say firmly.

'Oh, for God's sake, have we not wasted enough time tonight?' my uncle explodes, but I will not back down. 'Oh, very well,' he says, exasperated, at last. 'I told the Regent I'd get you home so let's get this over with.'

A strange kind of hush lies over the city as the carriage rolls through the silent streets. There are very few people about. A goose girl drives her flock towards Hyde Park. A yawning milkmaid carries her pails into Green Park to milk the cows that graze there. A befuddled dandy weaves along Piccadilly on his way home from his club perhaps, or a more sordid encounter somewhere. In the grand houses, servants are stirring. Ranges are being lit judging by the wisps of smoke curling up into the early morning sky.

None of them realise that an errant princess is being driven home in disgrace.

I am not to go home to Warwick House, my uncle informs me. I am to stay shut away at Carlton House until the rumours of my isolation have died down and then I will be taken to Windsor where my true punishment will begin.

My mother has a water closet, dark and foul-smelling. I went in there on the pretence of needing to relieve myself and tucked Frederick's letter into my stays. I could not bear to destroy it as the only sign of hope that I have, but was fearful that my uncle would demand to read it if he saw it. It crackles comfortingly against my skin as the carriage turns into the courtyard of Carlton House.

Mrs Louis is swaying with exhaustion, and I am bone-weary, but it seems my father has a final humiliation in mind for me. An equerry is sent out with a message that I am to wait in the carriage and we sit for a full half an hour before I am allowed to enter Carlton House. We are both so stiff that we have to be helped down from the carriage and it is a huge effort to straighten my back and walk in with my head held high.

I am escorted to a bedroom which is doubtless one of the lesser rooms, but which is nonetheless many times more luxurious than my room at Warwick House. Muttering at the indignity of my treatment, Mrs Louis helps me to undress and I fall into bed. By now I am too tired to sleep and I lie throbbing with the events of the day.

My hand creeps under my pillow to touch Frederick's letter for reassurance. I may be comfortable, but I am to all intents and purposes a prisoner.

Chapter Twenty-Three

Balmoral, May 1981

Diana peers down through the window as the plane hauls itself into the sky and banks over London. It never fails to amaze her how quickly the city drops away into toytown, with tiny cars running along tiny roads, street upon street of neat little houses with miniature gardens, distance lending them an enchantment that the suburbs quite lack close-up.

The last time she was in a plane she was on her way back from Australia, brimming with such excitement about her engagement that she could barely sit still. This time the flight is much shorter, only to Aberdeen, and the thrill of capturing the Prince of Wales has been tempered more than a little by reality.

During that long, long flight from Sydney, she imagined being swept up into a romantic fairy tale: Charles would adore her, the public would adore her, the papers would adore her. Her family and friends would envy her. The Queen and courtiers would see at once how she could transform the royal family's image, making them warmer and more empathetic and more popular. She would have everything she had ever dreamt of.

Only it hadn't been like that. The public do seem to adore her, true, but their adoration comes with an intensity of interest in everything she does that is overwhelming at times. Whenever she goes out in public she is met with a kind of hysteria that feels very unBritish somehow. The reporters who track her every move were waiting at airport, cameras rattling like machine guns. Even walking through the terminal with her detective shadowing her and officials clearing her path felt like going into battle while the other passengers stopped and stared or waved and called her name as if they knew her.

They don't know her.

The papers like to call her Shy Di. She isn't shy at all. She just puts her head down to get past the photographers. Once a reporter hounded her down a street and she nearly walked into a lamppost, so now she peeps out from under her fringe so that she can see where she is going.

So while it is nice to be popular, there is a definite downside to it. Diana wishes that she could even out the adoration so that there was less from the public, more from Charles.

Her other expectations have fallen flat. There is no sign that the court sees her as anything other than someone to be managed into doing things the way they have always been done. They don't want to have their image transformed. And while Charles can be fond, tender at times, often indulgent, even Diana's starry-eyed sense of romance can't persuade herself that he adores her. She has barely seen him for the past three months and even now that he has a few days free of engagements, he has chosen to go fishing at Balmoral. Diana is flying up to join him. Left to herself, she would have preferred a beach holiday, but it was Scotland or nothing, and she knows that Charles would probably be just as happy to be fishing by himself.

Well, that's not going to happen, Diana has resolved. She has found herself thinking more and more about Princess Charlotte and her determination to find happiness in spite of all the obstacles. Diana wants to do the same.

If nothing else, it is a treat to get out of Buckingham Palace, even if it does mean travelling with her private detective glued to her side. The plane climbs into the clouds and as London is blanked out, Diana sighs and pulls out the British Airways magazine from the seat back in front of her. The pilot is talking about bad weather ahead, but she ignores him. Her detective knows better than to try to make conversation. They have been given seats with no one across the aisle which at least affords some privacy. First Class is not as luxurious as it is on long-haul flights, but at least there is more legroom for her.

As they fly over the north of England, the clouds get darker. When the stewardess offers her something to drink, her detective looks up. 'I wouldn't,' he says briefly, gesturing out of the window. 'It looks as if it's going to get bumpy.'

Diana sends the stewardess a brilliant smile. 'Tea, please,' she says.

She doesn't really want it, but she hates being told what she can and can't do as if she's a child. When he suggests that she fastens her seat belt, she refuses, but no sooner has she accepted the cup than the plane hits a pocket of turbulence and it jerks in her hand, spilling tea down her front.

The detective says nothing as she dabs, tight-lipped, at the stain with a napkin.

The captain is back, advising the cabin crew to take their seats and everyone to do up their seat belts. Biting her lip, Diana does hers up just before a great flash jolts the plane and she sucks in a frightened breath. She has never been afraid of flying but all at once, her heart is hammering in her throat and she's annoyed to see that when she slides a sideways glance at the detective he is looking perfectly calm, although his eyes move constantly around the cabin as if looking for an exit.

They have a nasty few minutes, and Diana is not the only one muttering under her breath when the captain tells them that the plane has been hit by lightning. It doesn't seem to affect the flight, which eventually lands at Aberdeen in the pouring rain.

A car is sent to meet Diana. Charles doesn't come. Fishing is obviously more important than his fiancée, Diana thinks, miffed, but she has promised herself that this trip will be a fresh start. Balmoral has good memories for her, for both of them. It was at Balmoral that she and Charles really got to know each other the previous August. He was staying at the Queen Mother's house on the edge of Glen Muick, while Diana stayed with her sister Jane and Robert Fellowes in a grace and favour cottage on the Balmoral estate. In spite of the nine-mile distance, Charles rang every day, asking her for walk or to a barbecue. It had been so easy to talk then, Diana remembers wistfully, thinking of those long, chatty walks when she had really begun to think they could have something special. She had even been invited to one of the Queen Mother's picnics, complete with table napkins, silver cutlery and menu card. Diana loved it. She had thought royal life would always be like that.

Even better had been being invited back to Balmoral for the Braemar Games that September when the Queen was in residence. Diana had known then what a big deal it was, and how important it would be not to put a foot wrong. The surest way to alienate Charles would be if the Queen had disapproved. She had been shitting bricks before she went up that time. There was so much to remember at Balmoral itself: what to wear and when; where to sit or not sit; the steps of the Scottish country dances; the rules of the interminable after-dinner games.

But in the end it had been fine. Diana got points for pitching in to clean up and help with the dishes after various barbecues and picnics. She just had to be jolly and not complain about the midges or the mud or the endless rain. And the food had been great. Sausage rolls and scones for tea every day. She would have to be careful not to eat too much this time. She couldn't afford to put on weight again.

The best thing about that visit had been how much time

she got to spend with Charles. She sat for hours on the banks of the River Dee watching him fish, being quiet when he needed her to be quiet, enthusiastic when he wanted encouragement. She had made it clear that she was ready to adore him, and Charles had been ready to be adored.

There had been that one time when she caught the glint of binoculars in the bushes across the river and had told Charles that she would make herself scarce. Hiding behind a tree, she had used the mirror from her powder compact to watch the photographers as they tried to capture evidence of Charles's latest girlfriend. She had foiled their efforts, though, by swathing her head in a scarf and walking away through the trees before they could identify her. Charles had been proud of her that day. He had boasted about her quickness in outwitting the photographers to everyone that evening and Diana had glowed under his praise.

That had been a good day.

And now she is back at Balmoral, walking along gloomy corridors lined with hunting trophies, endless animals and birds, their fur and feathers going mouldy. The whole house smells like a museum. Everything is smothered in tartan. Privately, Diana thinks the decor is tacky in the extreme, but she knows better than to express an opinion about it.

Her room, she is pleased to see, is closer to Charles's than the last time, although they are still decorously separated. She barely has time to change into something suitable for afternoon tea before the gong is rung and she goes down to the sitting room where a spread of cakes and sandwiches is laid out on the table for those returning from a day on the hills or river.

Charles is there and he smiles at her. 'Ah, good, you're here,' he says.

He must have just come in because Diana can see raindrops spangling his hair, and when he kisses her cheek his skin feels cool and damp still.

'I nearly wasn't!' she tells him. 'My plane was hit by lightning!'

Charles looks vaguely surprised. 'I didn't think you'd run into bad weather. It's been fine here.'

'By fine, you mean this?' Diana looks out of the window to where the view is obscured by a veil of steadily seeping rain. There is something peculiarly Scottish about it.

At least he has the grace to grin. 'It's fine fishing weather,' he acknowledges. 'Sorry you had a traumatic journey,' he adds. 'Never mind, a few days here will calm your nerves.'

Diana isn't so sure about that. She doesn't fancy sitting in the rain to watch him fish again, and although she had put on a good show last year of being a country girl, she has no desire to tromp miles after shooting parties again. She would really rather curl up in a chair and read more of Charlotte's journal which she has brought with her.

'Did you have a good day?' she asks Charles.

'Marvellous,' he says.

'I suppose the really big one got away?'

'It did!'

'It's funny the way that happens,' she says, enjoying being with him, making him laugh, but then another member of the party comes up with some comment about the day's sport and with that they are all off, talking about fish. Diana helps herself to a sausage roll and pretends to listen, then, because it was so delicious, she has another one. There are delicious little sandwiches, too, and as no one is interested in her plane being hit by lightning, she has several of those and a couple of scones for good measure.

'I'd forgotten how much you liked the teas here,' Charles teases as they head upstairs to change once again for the evening.

Guiltily, Diana realises how much she has eaten and there is still a huge dinner to come. Even as she churns with anxiety about the additional calories, she remembers that Balmoral is so old fashioned that there are no en suite bathrooms here. When Charles asks if she wants to come into his room, she is too edgy to take advantage of the invitation. She is desperate to get to a bathroom before anyone else, to bring up everything that she has so foolishly eaten.

Afterwards, she sits on the cool bathroom tiles, rests her head on her knees and feels better.

Chapter Twenty-Four

Weymouth, September 1814

A military band is playing the national anthem as I step down from my carriage at Gloucester Lodge. Toby and Puff jump down after me and shake themselves vigorously. A crowd has gathered on the esplanade to watch my arrival and I smile and lift a hand in acknowledgement of the rapturous reception before lifting my skirts to climb the steps into the house, somewhat stiff after the last few hours in a coach and wishing I could shake the fidgets out as easily as my dogs have done.

After the last miserable few months, it is impossible not to feel warmed by the affection the public have for me. Only last night, when we broke our journey from Windsor in Salisbury, we had to press through the eager crowd to get from the carriage to the inn. General Garth, who is now in charge of my household, was bellowing at the footmen to 'get all these damned people out of the way' while Mrs

Louis clutched my jewel box to her chest. The clamour for me was so great in fact that I had to stand at my bedroom window with a candle held high so that the people could see me. I felt rather foolish, I must admit, but the crowd seemed delighted, jostling with each other to get a good view and applauding loudly whenever anyone called out my name.

I do sometimes wonder why they love me so much, given that my father rarely allows me on public view, but perhaps it is enough for them that I am not him. I will not forget their loyalty when I am Queen, I vow. I will do what I can to make their lives easier, and hope that they will cheer me for what I have done for them and not for who I am not.

At the top of the steps, I pause and turn. Over the heads of the crowd I can see the beach and beyond it the sea, heaving and swelling in the brisk wind. The air is bright and smells of salt and seaweed while above, the seagulls wheel with their raucous cries.

Oh, how good it is to be here and away from the stultifying tedium of Windsor! I feel better already. The last few months of imprisonment have worn me down. After my return to Carlton House that dreadful day, I was confined to my room for five days and kept an utter prisoner. Mrs Louis was, in the end, allowed to remain with me, but she was treated just as much as a prisoner. She had to sleep on the sofa in my room and by day she was always accompanied by two of the Regent's own servants, one watching her and one guarding the door.

As for me, I am 'attended' by my new gaolers, Lady Ilchester and Lady Rosslyn, and Lady Rosslyn's two nieces, the Misses Coates, Amelia and Wilhelmina, all of whom I heartily dislike. Lady Rosslyn is so skinny I call her Famine – though privately, of course – while her two interchangeable nieces are the Consequences.

They have been charged to guard me at all times. There is always at least one of them watching me and at night, one of them either sleeps in my room or else in the room beside it with the door open. The constant surveillance is intolerable. My letters are opened and read, an insult I find hard to forgive. They do not know, however, that I have written to Uncle Augustus, the Duke of Sussex, on stolen paper with a pencil dipped in milk or that there is, in spite of all their efforts, a secret postal service thanks to my obliging French master, Monsieur Sterkey, who passes on letters to Cornelia Knight or Mercer, on whom I rely for news of Frederick. It is an outrage that I should be forced to such underhand measures, but I will not tamely submit to being treated like a common prisoner.

In truth, Cranbourne Lodge is a good deal more comfortable than Warwick House. At least there I am able to ride in the Great Park if it is fine, although my afternoon entertainment is limited to sitting with the Queen and my dreary aunts. I miss the King, who is shut up in Windsor Castle, even more of a prisoner than I am. He was a sweet, kind grandfather who played with me as a child. I wish I could visit him but they will not allow it. The Queen says flatly that he is completely mad and would not recognise me, 'or worse'. I don't know what she means by that and none of my aunts will tell me.

At Cranbourne I spend long hours practising my music

and dreaming of Frederick, turning his turquoise ring endlessly on my finger to remind myself of him.

The question of my marriage continues to consume everyone. In spite of everything, the Regent is still holding out hopes for the Orange match. My grandmother is pushing the claims of her nephew, Prince Charles Mecklenburg-Strelitz, and my Aunts Mary and Sophia have been discussing Prince Leopold. Sophia thinks his lack of fortune is an issue. 'I hear he has but four hundred pounds a year,' she tutted, 'and when he accompanied the Tsar to London he had to be satisfied with rooms in Marylebone High Street.'

Mary is more forgiving. 'What do you think of him, Charlotte?'

Honestly, it was an effort for me to summon up an image of Prince Leopold. I remember meeting him at the Pulteney and he visited me once, I think, but mostly I think of him as 'not Frederick'.

'He is handsome,' I allowed, as that seemed safe to say, 'but he does not suit my taste.'

Nobody does. It is only Frederick I want, and his name is never mentioned.

Through the good offices of Monsieur Sterkey I managed to get a letter out to Frederick, begging him to write to the Regent and request my hand in marriage, but his reply was evasive.

'*I do not wish to run the risk of a refusal,*' he wrote cravenly. '*I am manoeuvring petit à petit, my dearest Charlotte. It would be better for me to arrange to come to England and do the deed in person.*'

'Come then!' I cried out loud in frustration when I read his letter.

But if he comes to England, I will not be able to hide my feelings for him and my aunts will straight away guess that I was not entirely truthful when I said my reasons for refusing the Prince of Orange were simply dislike of him personally.

Now I do not know what to do. I have been in turmoil for months, longing for Frederick, yearning for him, only to feel unsatisfied when I do hear from him. I fear that my feelings for him are stronger than his for me.

The pressure on me to marry is intense. My father wants me married and out of the country. The Queen and my aunts and uncles want the succession secured. Politicians want the matter settled; the people want the matter settled.

I must marry *someone*. I cannot live with this constant surveillance, the censoring of my correspondence. My father will never allow me the independence I long for until I am wed and in another man's keeping. I have not forgotten his threat – *while I live and you are unmarried, you must be subject to me* – but I do not accept that I do not have a will of my own.

The stress and anxiety have been making me ill. I have a constant pain in my side that no application of plasters seems to be able to relieve. My knee is so swollen that I have had to give up riding and walking which means that I am stiff and lethargic and my head aches the whole time, so much so that at length my grandmother has persuaded the Regent to let me have a holiday in Weymouth.

And now that I am here I am determined to get well

and enjoy myself, even if I am to all intents and purposes still a prisoner and must endure the company of Famine and the Consequences. How I miss Cornelia, my dear Chevalier! Oddly, perhaps, I do not mind General Garth. He is a bluff, sturdy character who is at least more cheerful company than the dreary Misses Coates. Rumour has it – according to Anna anyway – that General Garth was once the lover of my Aunt Sophia and that they had a child together. They are both so old and ugly, I find it hard to imagine, I confess.

I have not been to Gloucester Lodge since a holiday with my grandparents when I was six, so I remember little of the house, but I am delighted to find that my bedchamber has a view of the sea, and that an even better surprise awaits me there.

'Anna!' I am so happy to see a familiar face that I cannot refrain from embracing her, ignoring Mrs Louis's disapproving tut. 'How did you get here?' I ask excitedly. 'Do you have permission to join me again?'

'Didn't ask,' Anna says in her usual laconic way. 'I fancied seeing the seaside. Knew they'd need a chambermaid here if they were opening up the house for you and that housekeeper at Carlton House was glad enough to give me a letter of recommendation to get rid of me. Uppity, she called me.'

I laugh. Uppity is the least of it with Anna. 'Well, I am pleased she could spare you!' I glance over my shoulder at the door. The Consequences are lying down, exhausted by the journey, so for once I am not being closely watched. 'But we must take care. If Lady Rosslyn and the others know how glad I am to see you, they would certainly try to send you away.'

'Shouldn't think they would even notice me,' Anna says.

I suspect that she is right. I have often marvelled at how my family or the few ladies or gentlemen of my acquaintance do not appear to see the servants sharing our rooms. It is as if they are invisible and not real people, and yet how would we live without them? Who would lay our fires or beat our carpets or light our candles? Who would bring us water to wash and help us to dress and undress? How well would we eat if we had to prepare and serve our own food? The least we can do is to acknowledge that our servants are people like us, with their own desires and dislikes. My childhood friendship with Anna and my isolated life at Warwick House has taught me that at least.

After the bustle of arrival we are all tired and settle to a quiet evening. I am playing backgammon with General Garth when I notice that the heart-shaped turquoise has fallen out of the ring Frederick gave me.

'Oh, my ring!' I exclaim.

'Eh?' The general looks up from the board. 'What about it?'

'The stone has fallen out!' Ridiculously, tears prick my eyes. The ring is all I have from Frederick. I have had to burn his few letters, and the ring is the only tangible proof I have that he ever loved me at all.

Jumping to my feet, I hunt around on the carpet in case the stone has only just fallen out but there is no sign of it. The Consequences stir themselves to look too, although not with any enthusiasm.

The General is clearly baffled by my distress. 'What sort of stone is it?'

'A turquoise, shaped like a heart.'

'Upon my word, all this fuss for a trumpery turquoise? I had thought you had lost a fine diamond at least,' he says.

I ignore him as I tug on the bell and when the footman – his name is Robert, I think – appears I ask him to desire my dresser to come to me with all haste.

When Mrs Louis arrives, I ask her to look everywhere for the stone. 'I had it this morning when I put it on,' I told her. 'I would have noticed if the stone was gone then. Get the coachman to check the carriage, too.'

I try to settle back to the game but I cannot concentrate. The stone is just a trifle, I know, but my throat is tight with bitter tears. I make my excuses as soon as I can and retire to my bedchamber where Mrs Louis shakes her head when I ask if the stone has been found. Sick at heart, I cry myself to sleep, the empty ring on my finger seeming to symbolise all my lost hopes.

Chapter Twenty-Five

I have been so looking forward to being by the sea, but the loss of the turquoise sinks me into gloom. It is a bad omen, I am sure of it.

Mrs Louis promises me that they have scoured every inch of my rooms for the stone, and Anna has been to the mews to check the carriage. She reports back that no one has seen any sign of a turquoise and that the groom is a cheeky beggar – but she says it with a smile that tells me she likes him. I wish I could be like Anna and discard one lover for another when it suits me, but it is easier said than done.

'Why do I have such bad luck with love?' I ask Toby glumly, as I stroke her ears. I am sitting with her at the window while Mrs Louis mends a tear in a petticoat and Anna tidies the bed. I have woken to a fine drizzle and all my plans to swim or ride along the sands have had to be put on hold.

Just like my plans to marry for love.

Frederick refuses to commit to marriage. Charles Hesse's behaviour has been abominable. Mercer's father has made repeated requests for him to return my letters and gifts, but all he has said is that he destroyed the compromising letters as soon as he read them and that the gifts are locked in a trunk and left in the care of a 'friend'. He has broken his word as a gentleman and now, to make matters worse, he is travelling with my mother to Italy. It is a thought that makes me burn with mortification. Did Charles ever care for me at all? Or was it my mother he wanted? The mother I have stuck by in spite of everything and who has now abandoned me too.

'It is all very lowering,' I tell Toby with a sigh. Charles didn't love me and nor, in spite of his assurances, does Frederick, it seems. Perhaps I am too direct, too loud? Too robust? Too little able to feign being fragile and helpless? I am not good at pretending. I can only be myself. 'Perhaps I am simply unlovable?'

My parents have little love for me. My mother clearly prefers her adopted son, Willy, while the Prince Regent openly dislikes me. My grandmother is disapproving, my aunts are distant. And how many of my few friends would love me if I were not a princess?

I touch my nose to Toby's cold, wet one. 'At least you love me, don't you?' I say forlornly.

Anna pauses, her arms full of sheets. 'England loves you,' she says. 'The people love you.'

'They don't know me.'

'They know you're their hope for the future. The old King is mad,' she says bluntly. 'The Regent is booed whenever he goes out. We're longing for things to change, for a fresh start. We're all tired of watching greedy men get richer and richer while we starve. They have carved up the country for their own profits and we are left with nothing. All we've got is hope, hope that things will be better when you are Queen.'

It is not quite the same as being loved for myself, but it is something.

———————————

Life in Weymouth is very quiet, but that suits my mood. I am eager to try bathing in the sea, and as soon as it can be arranged the Consequences, who must of course always come too, and I make our way to the royal bathing machine in our green baize bathing dresses covered only by a loose wrapper and a shawl. Anna follows behind, carrying our linen and petticoats and towels.

Inside, the machine is painted white and very simply furnished, with a couple of simple benches and pegs where Anna hangs the clothes. We sit on the benches and hold tight while the machine lurches forward on the sand and into the water. I can hear the waves slapping against the floor. When it stops at last, a Mrs Myall, in a slouch hat and a dark dress, is waiting to dip me. Wearing only my shapeless bathing dress, I make my way forward to the steps and pause at the top while the gulls wheel and swoop with their harsh cries. It is a bright, breezy day and the wind is kicking up little waves that knock against the machine. As I look out, I can see nothing but the sea shifting and heaving like a hungry grey beast. In spite of myself, I hesitate.

'Walk down the steps, Your Royal Highness.' Mrs Myall beckons me on with a smile that says she has seen it all before. She is standing waist-deep in the water, holding herself steady against the shove and tug of the tide. 'You will be able to stand quite safely on the sand.'

The sea is colder than it looks. It rushes at me, pressing my dress against me, and I suck in a breath at the shock of it, but I make myself keep walking. When I am up to my breast, taking quick, shuddering gasps against the cold, Mrs Myall tells me to take a deep breath and ready myself to be dipped. Her hand is firm on my shoulder as she pushes me under. My eyes are squeezed shut. I feel the salty water close over my head and there is a moment of disorientated darkness and of panic before I burst above the surface again.

It is like being born again. When I open my eyes, the sunlight is flashing and spangling on the waves. The air is dazzling. The shock of the cold water has worn off and I feel clean and refreshed as if the months – years! – of doubt and disappointment and despair have been sluiced from me. The headache that has nagged at me for months has evaporated.

Exhilarated, I wade around breast-deep, letting the sea sway me, laughing as the waves splash against me in a shower of glittering droplets. Oh, I wish I could swim!

I climb out reluctantly at last to let the Consequences have a chance, but they don't like it. They squeal when Mrs Myall dips them and cough and splutter their way back into the bathing machine as soon as they can. I refuse to let them irritate me. My sea bath has left my skin tingling and smelling of salt and I am filled with a new resolution.

I will not yearn hopelessly for Frederick any longer. If he comes to England and asks the Regent for my hand, well and good. If not, as seems more likely now, I must look elsewhere for a husband. Without Frederick, I have no prospect of real happiness in marriage and yet marry I must, not just for the sake of the country but also to bring an end to the slavery of my life, which is utterly controlled by my father.

So I will think again about the other princes that have been suggested. Of those, Prince Leopold of Saxe-Coburg may be an acceptable second choice. I remember little about him other than the strength of his arm as he escorted me out to my carriage, but my impression was of a good-tempered, sensible man and perhaps that will be enough. It might not be the love match I dreamt of, but it would be the next best thing and would offer me a reasonable hope of being less unhappy and comfortless than I have been unwed.

My aunts have mentioned his name in letters, so there must be a chain of communication open somewhere. Sitting in the bathing machine, dabbing at my wet face with a towel, I decide to write to Mercer and enlist her help as a go-between. There would be no harm, surely, in establishing a connection and finding out Prince Leopold's feelings on the matter?

Of course, Frederick may still come...

I look down at the finger where I used to wear his turquoise ring. I have taken it off as it means nothing without the heart-shaped stone. How happy I would be to wear a new ring from him, but I cannot wait for ever.

And in the meantime, I am determined to enjoy my holiday.

Weymouth does not offer much in the way of fashionable entertainment but compared to Windsor it is a heady whirl. There are evening performances at the Theatre Royal, one of the few things that the Consequences and I enjoy equally, and once or twice we attend a ball at the Assembly Rooms, where I am the focus of all eyes. It is not that comfortable to be studied so openly for so long, but I put on a good face for everyone. It is good that they have a chance to see their Princess.

I am even allowed to give small dinner parties for the few members of the aristocracy who are still in Weymouth, staying at the hotel or in rented houses. I enjoy being able to entertain, though I am less enthusiastic about my most frequent guest, the Great Up, who has taken a house for his family and, I feel sure, has been sent by my father to keep an eye on me. He always manages to cast a damper on the proceedings, but as Bishop of Salisbury and the man who has been in charge of my education for so long, I can hardly refuse to receive him, much as I might wish to. I even have to go and hear him preach at the local church one Sunday, and truly I have never heard so weak a voice and so bad a delivery.

The Bishop comes one day, full of excitement at the news that a celebrated preacher is to preach the sermon. 'Dr Dupré is a great orator, Princess,' he tells me. 'You must not miss the opportunity to listen to him.'

Well, I file obediently into church that Sunday with General Garth, Lady Rosslyn and the Misses Coates and we take our place in the front pew where we can best admire Dr Dupré. But what a disappointment! He speaks without notes, true, but with so many blunders and repetitions that he keeps the whole pew in a titter. I confess, I have never been so in charity with the Consequences as we prim our mouths and struggle to hide our giggles behind our bonnets and even Lady Rosslyn's attempts to shush us are spoiled by the smile tugging at the corners of her own mouth.

It is not long before my health is so much improved that I can ride again on the sands – what joy to gallop along the beach in the early morning with the salt tang in the air, the sea stretching out to the horizon and the sky a huge expanse above me. The Consequences are not great riders, so General Garth organises expeditions in a carriage for us. Sometimes we go inland and lunch at an inn, but I prefer it when we explore the coast. Wherever we go, we are used now to being followed by a small crowd of curious children. We are picnicking on a beach somewhere between Portland and Bridport one day when the children watching us from the cliff above dislodge a shower of pebbles. General Garth shakes his fist at them and the Consequences shriek, but I call up instead, 'Hallo there! Princess Charlotte is made of gingerbread. If you do that, you'll break her.'

When I arrived in Weymouth, I was close to breaking anyway, but I feel better now. I am stronger and more sure of myself. I will not break.

Chapter Twenty-Six

I love sea bathing, but in Weymouth my favourite thing to do by far is to go sailing on my grandfather's yacht, the *Royal Charlotte*. She is named for the Queen, of course, but I like to think that she is partly mine, too.

She is a fine ship, with three masts, billowing sails and the royal standard flying from the mainmast. Whenever I can, I ask General Garth to send word to the captain to make the yacht ready for our party and six burly sailors row us out from the harbour to where the *Royal Charlotte* is anchored. Lady Rosslyn and the Misses Coates do not share my love of sailing. They sigh and protest and complain about feeling seasick, but that is the price they must pay for spying on me. For myself, I would be just as happy if they stayed at home and Anna and I went alone.

We take a picnic to eat on deck: bread and beef and plenty of mustard. The sea air always makes me hungry. Today we are sailing towards Portland and I am on the quarterdeck, eating sandwiches and craning my neck to look up at the mizzen sail creaking and snapping in the brisk breeze. The wind stings my cheeks and I have to keep my bonnet firmly tied to stop it blowing off. Lady Rosslyn and the Consequences are huddled together, having repulsed the offer of something to eat, while the Bishop of Salisbury is looking wan but manfully tackling a plate of beef. Behind him I can see Anna, perched on a box and watching the sailors scrambling up the shrouds and hauling in the sails.

The sea is choppy but the air is bright and the glitter on the waves is so dazzling that I have to narrow my eyes. I love it out here. There is so much space and so much light. Below it is dark and cramped, to be sure, but here on deck with the groaning of the masts and the creaking of the hull and the rush and slap of the water I can forget everything else.

Captain Scott has only been commander since June, but he moves easily around the ship as if he has known it for ever. He comes over to point out a warship anchored off Portland. 'There is HMS *Leviathan*, Your Royal Highness,' he says, offering me his spyglass.

I brush the crumbs off my fingers and lap and put the glass to my eye. 'They have sighted us,' he says. 'They will be firing a salute at any moment.'

The glass feels strange against my eye, but when my sight adjusts, the ship in the distance leaps into view just in time to hear a distant explosion and see a puff of smoke.

Delighted, I hand the glass back to Captain Scott. 'Pray,

let us hove to and signal *Leviathan* to send a boat. I should like to know more.'

He bows without a blink although I know it is no small matter to turn or slow a boat like this. There are shouted orders and flags are run up and heavy canvas sails are hauled down or tightened. In what seems no time at all, Captain Thomas Briggs of *Leviathan* is being rowed over and has climbed nimbly up onto the deck to pay his respects to me.

I beam at him as we stand together at the rail and admire *Leviathan* and he explains the flags snapping in the brisk wind. 'May I come and inspect your ship, Captain? I imagine it is very different from this one.'

'It is indeed, Your Royal Highness. And I would be honoured to welcome you aboard *HMS Leviathan*.'

Lady Rosslyn moans at the idea, while the Bishop looks pale. 'I do not think that is a wise idea, Princess,' he says, casting an alarmed glance at the waves. 'The sea is very rough.'

'Nonsense, it is just a bit of chop,' I say. 'It will be perfectly safe, will it not, Captain?

He glances at Captain Scott. 'Safe, but perhaps not very comfortable. I am afraid you would get very wet.'

'Oh, what does that signify?' I say with a touch of impatience. 'I am not a fragile flower who will dissolve in a bit of wet! Come, I am most anxious to see your ship. How will we get there?'

'Are you able to climb down into the long boat?' Captain Briggs asks and I peer over the rail to where six seamen are waiting with their oars stowed. They are secured to us with ropes tossed down by the *Royal Charlotte*'s sailors and have lowered fenders to stop their boat from bumping against the hull.

'Certainly,' I say.

Lady Rosslyn refuses point-blank to accompany me but insists that I cannot go alone. I confess, I take a malicious pleasure in seeing how dismayed the Misses Coates look, but how many times have I had to slow my stride to accommodate their dawdling? To rein in my horse when I longed to gallop and plod along at their pace instead? How often have I had to endure their company when I wished only to be alone or to talk to a true friend like Mercer? I think I can be forgiven, do not you?

The Great Up swallows. 'If the Princess insists, then I will go with you.'

'Excellent,' I say cheerfully before he has a chance to argue himself out of it. 'Let us go straight away.'

Steps are let over the side and I go briskly down to where one of the burly sailors gives me a steadying hand onto the boat. The trembling Consequences and a sickly, pale bishop are coaxed down, followed by Captain Briggs, and we are rowed across the choppy water to the warship. By the time we reach her, we are all drenched from the spray but I don't mind. I have never been this close to water this deep, and I delight in the taste of salt water on my lips, the splash and sparkle of water droplets on the oars, the way the wind plasters the ribbons of my hat across my face.

All too soon, we come alongside *Leviathan* where a rope ladder dangles over the side. Close-up, the hull of the warship rears above us, much higher than the royal yacht and I look up at her in awe. The Consequences whimper.

Captain Briggs orders a chair to be sent down and one appears over the side and is carefully lowered on ropes. 'We will pull you up,' he explains, much to the bishop's relief.

I shake my head. 'I am not such poor thing that I must be hauled up like a sack of potatoes,' I say dismissively. 'I will climb the ladder.'

'Oh no, it is too dangerous!' Amelia Coates exclaims, paling even further.

'Pooh, if the seamen can do it, so can I.'

The Great Up looks grave. 'Indeed, Captain, I think you should forbid it.'

Captain Briggs looks at me. He has a quiet, weather-beaten face but a smile glimmers in his eyes. 'It is not for me to forbid Her Royal Highness anything,' he says.

'Thank you, Captain Briggs,' I say demurely.

I wait until the chair is settled on the boat and then step past it to take hold of the ropes. Watched by grinning sailors, I begin to climb. I soon discover that it is much more difficult than I thought, but I refuse to clamber back down and tamely use the chair. By the time I reach the top and am helped over the side onto the deck, my arms are trembling with effort and my palms red and raw from the rope. But I am greeted with such a rousing cheer from the sailors that it is worth it.

I watch as in turn the Misses Coates and the bishop are hauled up in the chair and am pleased that I did not submit to anything so undignified. When they are safely on deck, Captain Briggs takes me all round *Leviathan*. The ship has a noble history, having taken part in the Battle of Trafalgar, he tells me. 'Although not under my command, I regret to say,' he adds.

It is very clearly a warship, with twenty-eight guns on the gundeck, the same number on the upper gundeck, fourteen on the quarterdeck and four on the forecastle. I ask Captain Briggs why they are anchored off Portland and he tells me that earlier in the year they escorted a convoy to Jamaica. 'As you know, we are at war with the Americans and we cannot leave our ships unprotected.'

It seems sad to me that we have only just celebrated the end of the long war with France only to be embroiled in another one, but I am learning – slowly – to keep my counsel. Instead, I ask about the quarantine the ship has been under. This is to prevent the import of tropical diseases and it seems a most sensible idea to me. *Leviathan* was thoroughly inspected only a few days ago and is awaiting orders.

I can feel the Consequences drooping behind me, but I insist on a thorough inspection of the ship. Below deck, the space is even tighter than on the *Royal Charlotte* and the smell is overpowering, though I will not let it drive me back on deck. When I ask Captain Briggs what causes the stench, he smiles. 'It is the smell of men living at close quarters, Your Royal Highness. Would you prefer to have some refreshment in my cabin?'

'No, indeed, I wish to see everything,' I say to the despair of the Bishop, who has a handkerchief pressed to his nose. 'If these brave men who are fighting for our country live in these conditions all the time, then I can manage to stay here a few minutes, surely?'

Still, I am quite glad when we do finally repair to Captain Briggs's cabin. I am quite dismayed by some of the squalid conditions below deck, but the sailors themselves seem gratified by my interest and they give me three lusty cheers as I climb back down into the boat to be rowed back to the *Royal Charlotte*. It is a moving thing to realise that one day I shall be Queen and these men will be fighting for me.

To atone for making the Misses Coates brave the longboat and the warship, I have agreed to a tamer expedition today. General Garth has arranged for us to visit a monastery of Trappist monks. Women, it seems, are not allowed, with the exception of royal ladies. So while Lady Rosslyn and the Consequences wait outside, I am shown around the monastery and gardens and given a simple meal of milk, brown bread, vegetables and rice.

It is a humbling experience. There is something inexpressibly peaceful about the simplicity and silence of the monks' lives. They grow their own food and isolate themselves from the world so they may devote themselves to God. I sit on the hard bench and lift the rough wooden cup to my lips and think it would be hard to imagine a place further removed from my father's extravagance and opulence at Carlton House.

The silence is soothing. With no need to talk, no one to explain myself to, I can sit and let my mind empty of all noise. I tear the rough bread between my fingers and taste it on my tongue. I was moved by the stoical bravery of the seamen on HMS *Leviathan*, but these monks will be my people too. How can I be a good queen to them all? I do not know the answer. I only know that I will try.

Chapter Twenty-Seven

Buckingham Palace, 13 June 1981

The sound of the crowd pressed up against the gates and around the Victoria Monument rises up to the first floor at Buckingham Palace where the extended royal family is gathered. Like most family occasions, Diana imagines, there are bursts of laughter, over-excited children, teenagers hanging awkwardly at the edges, cheeks being kissed.

Of course, her own family gatherings have always been complicated by her parents' divorce and the underlying tension that has arisen as a result. Diana has never been able to accept her father's second wife, Raine, or Raine's mother, Barbara Cartland, with her grotesque make-up and ridiculous outfits and ghastly affectations. Compared to them, the royal family seem quite normal.

Well, perhaps normal is not quite the right word... Diana glances at Charles who, like the Queen and Prince

Philip, is in regimental uniform and has a sword at his side. The scarlet coat makes him look very dashing, she thinks. He is bedecked with gleaming medals and with the blue sash, gold collar and loops of thick gold braid, he could be one of the romantic heroes her step-grandmother writes about.

Today is the Trooping of the Colour, one of the highlights in the royal calendar and one of the few occasions for which almost every member of the royal family turns out. And today, as Charles's fiancée, Diana is included. It has all been rather wonderful. Charles rode with Prince Philip behind the Queen at the head of the procession while Diana was glad to share a carriage with Andrew in his naval uniform. She has always got on well with him. He is much closer in age to her than Charles and she remembers playing with him as a child at Sandringham. Her family used to tease her about planning to marry him one day and become Duchess of York and to this day they still call her Duch. None of them ever dreamed that she would become a princess instead.

But Diana did.

She always dreamed of that.

And now it is happening.

The procession was fun. She chatted happily to Andrew and waved to the crowd, all of them caught up in the excitement of the spectacle. At one point they were aware of a kerfuffle ahead, but there was little to see when they passed apart from a larger number of policemen than usual and she forgot about it as they turned into Horse Guards Parade. She loved seeing the Household Division in their scarlet uniforms and the glossy horses. The sound of the trumpets and pipes and drums made her smile. It was impossible not to be moved by the precision of the marching, by the stamping feet and the shouted commands ringing across the parade ground. Diana's spirits lifted watching the display.

'It makes you proud to be British, doesn't it?' she said to Andrew. The soldiers were so immaculate down to the last brass button glittering in the sunlight, their movements so well trained that they seemed invincible. What other country could possibly rival that discipline, that history, these glorious traditions?

But it only takes a man with a gun to shatter that illusion of invincibility. A shadow has been cast over the day. Interspersed with the laughter and the chatter of relatives catching up with each other are more serious conversations in low voices. Someone – a lone man it seems – shot at the Queen as she rode her horse, Burmese, at the front of the procession. Diana can hardly believe that anyone would dare do such a thing. The shots were blanks, and while Burmese was startled and shied at the sound, the Queen was quickly able to get the horse back under control and carried coolly on as if nothing had happened.

Diana can only marvel at Charles's mother's calm. She can see her across the room, smiling and chatting to the Duchess of Gloucester. She herself feels oddly shaken by the mere idea that anyone would shoot at the Queen. What if they had been real bullets, not blanks? Diana can't bear to think about it.

What if someone tries to shoot at *her*? 'That's why you

have a detective following you everywhere,' Charles says patiently. 'It's his job to make sure no one gets a chance to shoot at you and, if necessary, to jump in front of a bullet to protect you. I know you don't like having someone with you wherever you go, Diana, but I'm afraid it goes with the job.'

There have been various sombre conversations about security for the wedding, but Diana hasn't paid them much attention. She has been more concerned about the threat of cameras taking pictures. She hasn't thought she might be at risk of real shots.

Now she stands next to Charles with an uncertain smile while he talks to his grandmother about Scotland and the restless sound of the crowd drifts through the windows. She fiddles with her handbag, having little to contribute to the conversation but not feeling confident enough of her role to leave his side. This is not her family yet and she is still not sure of the rules about who can and who cannot be treated with familiarity.

It is almost a relief when, at some unseen signal, two footmen open the tall windows that lead out onto the famous balcony and the noise of the crowd spills into the room.

'Here we go. Stick with me, Diana,' Charles says as the Queen and the Duke of Edinburgh lead the way outside and the cheers erupt.

Diana is glad to obey him as the whole family move out onto the balcony to watch a fly past from the Red Arrows and she blinks at the buffet of noise. The goodwill emanating from the people below is a tangible thing; Diana feels she could put her hand out and catch it in her fist. It would be hard not to respond to such excitement and affection, she thinks, smiling a little nervously.

In spite of the illusion of informality, their places are carefully choreographed. She and Charles are standing just to the right of the Queen and Prince Philip. Next to her is Princess Margaret, who always seems smartly dressed and sharp-tongued. Diana finds her rather intimidating. Today Margaret is wearing a striking orange suit and a pillbox hat and Diana is now regretting her own choice of a blue floral suit with a sheer jacket and a wide white ruffled collar and pearls. On her head she wears a tiny hat dominated by a blowsy blue flower and a blue veil. She thought it was such a pretty outfit when she first tried it on but next to Margaret's simplicity, it feels a bit much.

How much can the crowd below see? Surely they must all be just tiny, distant figures? Diana hopes they can't see the nervous twitch of her smile, the way she keeps fiddling with her bag until a look from Princess Margaret makes her put her hands behind her back.

It is the strangest feeling to stand here and look down at so many people and feel their intense interest and goodwill. For some reason Diana thinks of Princess Charlotte on the beach near Weymouth being stared at by the curious children and calling up to them: *Princess Charlotte is made of gingerbread. If you do that, you'll break her.*

What would Charlotte have made of the numbers of people here today? How would she have dealt with intrusive photographers? Diana has a feeling she would have given them short shrift. She took Charlotte's journal to

Balmoral and spent most of her time there reading it, because God knows it was more appealing than trudging through the rain or waving away the midges on the riverbank. Last year it was different. Charles sought her out and it was thrilling just to be with him, but this year they are engaged and the uncertainty has gone. The matter is settled. They are to be married and it feels as if already they have stopped bothering with each other.

Diana knows that Charles was puzzled by her change of attitude. Last year at Balmoral she had been keen to do everything, but this year she was content to curl up on a sofa with Charlotte's journal. When everyone else was out getting wet and muddy and tired, she would slip down to the kitchens for a snack to make herself feel better and chatted happily to the cooks until a sour-faced senior member of staff suggested with glacial politeness that she would be happier in guest quarters. Which she definitely wasn't.

She was glad to get back to London in the end. Plans for the wedding are gathering pace. Sometimes Diana thinks that she has jumped on a train without checking her destination. At first it seemed to chug along the track that she had imagined, but lately it has been going faster and faster and now it is unstoppable and impossible to jump off. The thought leaves her reeling between elation (she is going to be Princess of Wales!) and panic (she is going to be Princess of Wales!) That sends her to the fridge for comfort only for guilt to take her to the bathroom to bring it all back up. Diana knows it isn't right, but it is the only way she can gain any semblance of control over what's happening. Once the wedding is over, she will stop. Of course she will.

Charles touches her arm and points up The Mall. 'Here they come. Look!'

It is an extraordinary feeling to stand on the balcony at Buckingham Palace watching the Red Arrows streak towards them in perfect formation, smoke coloured red, white and blue streaming behind them.

As one, the royal family and the crowd look up as the planes sweep low overhead with a whoosh and a roar that raises a great cheer. Diana looks around the balcony and then down at the people below and marvels at the sense of unity. For just those few seconds they all shared the same sense of excitement and awe at the speed and the power and the precision of planes. Moved in a way she doesn't really understand, Diana feels tears sting her eyes. The whole ceremony has been so beautifully done. It has been so British and so impressive, a powerful tribute to the Queen who stands so close beside her.

For the first time, Diana has a sense of what her wedding will mean. Only a few weeks now and she will be part of the monarchy and share in its mystique. An odd feeling snakes down her spine at the thought. She can't decide whether it is anticipation or foreboding.

Chapter Twenty-Eight

London, June 1815

I t has been six long months since I left Weymouth, and nothing has changed. Nothing. Letters go backwards and forwards to the Continent, to Frederick, to Prince Augustus, to Leopold of Saxe-Coburg. They have all indicated an interest in marrying me, but not one has made it to the sticking point. There are problems and complications, I gather from the correspondence that Mercer and Cornelia carry out on my behalf.

Chief of which is that devil Bonaparte who escaped from Elba in April and has been on the march across France, so we are now at war all over again. The princes have military strategy more on their mind than marriage.

Even Charles Hesse came back from playing cicisbeo to my mother in Italy and re-joined his regiment. He did not call on me, which I was glad about of course, but if I *had* been able to speak to him, I might have had some sense of why he refuses to explain what he did with my letters. I want nothing from him but reassurance.

As it is, the risk of the letters being public is a constant nagging anxiety that I add to my other anxieties, although none of them, of course, compared to the greater worry of war itself. The news of Bonaparte's escape meant that London was full of uniforms again and although social life continued unimpaired, there are still low-voiced conversations in the corners of ballrooms as gentlemen and officers discuss news of the campaign.

So I understand that there are graver matters at stake than my happiness, but oh, how I wish one of the princes would screw his courage to the sticking post and take a stand. There has been more manoeuvring and negotiating and skirmishing than on the battlefield and I am so tired of it. Frustration has scratched away at the calm resolution I felt in Weymouth.

'Why can one of them not make up their mind?' I exclaim. 'Am I not a prize worth winning? I am young, I am healthy. I am not a beauty, but I am not an antidote either. And I will be Queen of the greatest nation in the world! Why do they even hesitate?'

'You are not sure of your own mind either,' Mercer points out with the good sense that is characteristic of her, but which is also irritating at times.

'That is true,' I sigh.

Cornelia Knight is more sympathetic. She shares my hopes that Frederick will keep faith with me. I cannot believe that the passionate love he declared for me meant nothing to him and I am clinging to the increasingly forlorn hope that he will be true. But though Cornelia has written to him on my behalf, he has not replied to her letters.

'Perhaps he is occupied with his military duties,' she offers.

I sometimes wonder if men do not go to war to give themselves an excuse not to deal with the demands of women, for some certainty in their lives.

Mercer, of course, is more clear-eyed. She thinks I am setting my face against the truth and that I should consider Prince Leopold of Saxe-Coburg who is, she says, a much better candidate.

She is right, too, that I dither and vacillate. I nearly persuaded myself that I *would* settle for Leopold, but then I had a letter from Frederick that threw me into confusion once more. I worried then that Leopold might propose and then I wouldn't know what to say. My love for Frederick is too strong for me to believe that I could find happiness with anyone else, but if I refused Leopold directly and then Frederick after all proves to be faithless, what would become of me then? I would be bereft of every chance of settling tolerably comfortably if I rejected Leopold, who is at least a sensible man, as Mercer is always pointing out.

'I do know my own mind,' I tell her now. 'I hope still to hear from Prince Frederick, but if he should fail me, I would accept the Prince of Saxe-Coburg in preference to any other prince I have seen. More I cannot say or tell you – and besides, knowing my own mind means nothing when I have no word from either them!' I finish with a rueful smile.

The news from the Continent is increasingly ominous. There is talk of a great battle brewing and we pore over the newspapers in the hope of gleaning more information. I thank God we have Wellington in command. He has shown himself to be a great leader and a master tactician, but Bonaparte is a formidable foe. There is much to be anxious about.

And yet we all go on as if everything is normal. Weymouth was good for my health and spirits, but it was very quiet after October and the weather kept me indoors most days. There was no more sailing or bathing. My father, it seemed, was happy to keep me out of the way and I was there until Christmas, scratching against the Consequences as the rain beat at the windows. In January, however, I was given permission to return to London at last and I am reinstalled back in Warwick House where somehow my old household have crept back into place without the Regent realising what a comfort they are to me.

The servants have their own way of organising things: it is a world just like ours where who you know counts for much and money for almost everything. Or so Anna tells me. Positions in a royal household are greatly sought after as there are so many opportunities to make money. The ends of candles are sold off, along with scraps of coal, and for those who work in the kitchens or wine cellars there are even more chances to cream off what is left at the bottom of a sack or a churn that unaccountably never makes it to the kitchens. They find each other positions, too, so all are part of a vast network where relationships mirror our own: rivalries and petty jealousies and great friendships and resentments and love affairs and corruption and cruelties.

Anna assures me that things are not so bad at Warwick

House, largely because my father keeps me on a low budget. She has been despondent of late, having fallen out with the groom she was dallying – and I suspect a great deal more – with before I was sent away. It seems he objected to her taking herself off to Weymouth to join me and when she returned to London she found that he had taken up with what she calls a 'brazen-faced trull' but who is probably just another young woman who saw her chance with a good-looking groom and took it. I think Anna is now regretting treating him quite so carelessly, but then I am hardly in a position to advise on her love life when my own is so hopeless and unsatisfactory.

Sometimes I have to remind myself that we are at war and that events of national importance are being played out in Flanders while on a day-to-day level, at Warwick House at least, we are preoccupied with little domestic disasters: Puff eats something rotten from the midden and vomits the contents of his stomach onto the carpet in the drawing room; Mrs Louis falls and twists her ankle and insists on limping around instead of putting her foot up as I suggest, as if Anna is not capable of fastening my stays; a pigeon comes down the chimney and flaps around my bedroom leaving feathers and droppings everywhere, making Anna curse; a string breaks on my harp.

At the same time, we are anxiously awaiting news from Belgium. Monday's papers suggested a great victory for Wellington, but no official news has been received and for two days now rumours and counter-rumours have been circulating feverishly while so many people have gathered at Horse Guards to await the dispatches that the crowds have spilled into St James's Park. Tensions have been steadily rising. Nobody can talk of anything but the news or lack of it. Will it be victory or defeat?

Now it is Midsummer night and the heat has been building all day, refusing to dissipate even though it is past eleven o'clock. The windows are open wide to catch what little coolness there is and the murmur of the crowd drifts across The Mall. I am sitting with the Consequences and Lady Rosslyn, all fanning ourselves and too hot and fretful to make conversation. It feels as if the whole city is holding its breath. When, oh when, will Wellington send word? This waiting is unendurable.

Puff's stertorous breathing is loud in the room when Wilhelmina Coates lifts a finger and cocks a head. Instantly, we all sit up.

'What is it? Can you hear something?'

Before she can say anything, we all hear it, a great cheering and hooting rolling through the night and we jump to our feet, clapping our hands together.

'There is news!'

'Pull the bell, Amelia,' I say. 'John can go out and find out what's happening.'

It is late before John returns, sweaty and dusty but grinning broadly. 'A great victory, ma'am,' he says. 'The battle was fought at a place called Waterloo.'

Waterloo. What a strange name, though I daresay it will become as familiar to us as Vitoria has done. 'Why was the messenger so late with the news?'

'Turns out he was becalmed at sea,' John says. He has clearly enjoyed his break from being a footman. 'Major

Percy, his name is. I heard he had to abandon ship in the end. Four sailors rowed him twenty miles to Broadstairs and then he had to get to London. He didn't get to Westminster bridge till after eleven,' he goes on, getting into his story. 'He came in a yellow post-chaise and four with two of Boney's eagle standards sticking out of windows. I saw them myself, ma'am. What a sight that was! Course, soon as people saw them, they realised that Boney had been defeated and they went wild, shouting and cheering.'

'That must have been what we heard,' Lady Rosslyn says.

It appears that having made it all the way to Downing Street, Major Percy discovered that the Cabinet were dining in Grosvenor Square, so he went on there to hand Wellington's despatch over in person, but still had to find the Prince Regent, who was at a house in St James's Square. Still followed by an enormous mob, the major's carriage drove on. The major jumped out in all his dust, pushed through crowd and ran up the stairs to the ballroom, where he went down on one knee before my father, laying the standards at his feet. 'Victory, Sir! Victory!' he cried.

What a moment that must have been! I envy my father and the pride he must have felt. One day, perhaps, standards will be laid at my feet and victory declared in my name... but then that would mean that war would have been fought and I do not wish that. Perhaps I will do without the glory, though I dare say the question of war or not will not be up to me.

We hear the story of Major Percy's race to bring the news of Wellington's victory from everyone who comes to call. I wish my father would come himself, but he has much to do, I know, planning the celebrations.

The weekend brings spectacular illuminations at all the major buildings. The streets are thronged. Jubilant bands play until two in the morning. Dustmen clang their bells. There is laughter and dancing. London is having a party, and who could begrudge the people their celebrations? They have suffered because of the war, and too many families have lost a father or a brother or a son.

I fear the losses are very great, but I am so thankful for victory. And, yes, I am relieved that the war is over and now, perhaps, some thought can be given to my marriage at last.

Chapter Twenty-Nine

Royal Pavilion, Brighton, February 1816

The domes and minarets of the Royal Pavilion are sharply etched against the winter blue sky and the crisp air is laced with the sharp, salty tang of the sea. I cannot help a shiver as I climb down from the carriage, although that may be due more to the nerves churning in my belly than to the cold.

This is my second visit to Brighton this year. In January I celebrated my twentieth birthday here after several months of living quietly at Windsor. It suited my mood, giving gave me a chance to nurse my wounded heart after finally receiving Frederick's regrets. It had not, in the end, been a great surprise but still, whenever I remember how joyously I fell in love with him that sunny June, my chest feels so tight with disappointment I can barely breathe.

It was a chance, too, to get to know the Queen and my

aunts. In the past I have chafed against the oppressive dullness of their routines and the strictness of my grandmother's views, but this winter I have come to value their support. The Queen's tongue is as sharp as ever but it is she who has promoted a rapprochement with my father.

Everyone wants to see me suitably wed. The Queen, my aunts and two of my uncles are all in favour of Prince Leopold of Saxe-Coburg and now I am, too. With all hope of Frederick gone, I am being sensible and settling for second best, just as everyone has urged me. Mercer has been corresponding with Leopold and he is willing, it seems. It is time to put aside silly, romantical notions of love, just as my grandmother says.

With that decided, all that remained was to win my father over to the idea. My birthday visit was a success. We found him in an unexpectedly jovial mood in spite of the fact that his gout was so bad he had to wheel himself around in a merlin and I wrote to him on my birthday, saying that I was anxious to be married and declaring my partiality for Prince Leopold. Fortunately, the Hereditary Prince is now married so there is no longer any question of the Orange match and although I went down to dinner that night with some trepidation, my father was – for once – inclined to be indulgent.

'Well, so Coburg takes your fancy, does he? My ministers tell me that it would be an unexceptional match. Shall I invite him to come to England?'

I remember letting out a breath. 'If you please, Papa. I should be glad of it.'

And now Leopold is here in Brighton and so am I.

I barely remember him: a strong arm beneath my hand, an impression of courtesy. That is it. What have I done, committing myself to a stranger whose face I cannot recall?

I have been a fool all my life. I have made so many mistakes. I have been defiant, disobedient, wilful, reckless, impetuous. But all I ever wanted was to be able to choose my own husband.

Well, now I have my wish. I have chosen Leopold. But after so many mistakes, what if he is another?

He will not be, I tell myself as I am escorted to my apartments past dragon columns, statues of mandarins and colourful Chinese vases. He must not be. I cannot back out of another engagement.

Mrs Louis follows, holding my jewel box and looking disapproving. My father's exotic tastes are ungodly, in her view. In that, she and my grandmother are as one.

She wants me to lie down and rest, but I have been shut up in a carriage all day and I am too nervous to sit still. 'I will go for a walk,' I decide. 'Call Anna and she can come with me.'

'I'll ask them to send a footman too.'

'I don't need a footman, Louis,' I snap, nerves making me irritable. 'Anna will be protection enough.'

'A footman would give you consequence,' she says stubbornly.

'My grandfather the King was happy to mingle with the people at Windsor without pomp and I will do the same.'

'Brighton is very different to Windsor,' she says with a dark look.

'And thank goodness for that!'

Anna has travelled in the coach with the luggage – or more likely, rugged up on the seat and flirting with the grooms. I am glad that she is here. Other maids dawdle and complain that their feet hurt, but Anna is always happy to keep pace with me.

Outside, it is very cold and I thrust my hands into a fur muff. 'Let us go to the sea,' I say to Anna, and we set off at a brisk pace. We are both wearing hooded cloaks, though mine is lined with fur, and the pattens that keep our hems out of the mud clink on the pavement as we stride through the town. Even in winter, Brighton is busy. We pass bath houses and coffee houses and libraries and shops, accompanied by the banging of hammers and the shouts of labourers constructing new houses.

The sight of the sea is as stirring as always. Today it is as restless as I feel, surging and choppy, its waves foaming white on the pebbly shore. I am invigorated by the wind and the sting of salt on my skin. I remember bathing at Weymouth and that wonderful feeling that all my doubts had been washed away.

I wish Mrs Myall were here to dip me now.

The opulence and extravagance of the Pavilion is suffocating after the chill and challenge of the sea, but at least it is warm and a welcome fire burns in my room.

Mrs Louis allows grudgingly that the sea air has brought colour to my cheeks and brightened my eyes. She dresses my hair in a becoming style and laces my stays.

'Not too tight,' I say. 'I want to be able to breathe.'

Mrs Louis has refurbished my best evening gown for the occasion, trimming the hems with bands of green silk satin to contrast with the dots of paler green silk gauze that cover the skirts. She has altered the sleeves too, puffing them up with layers of gauze so that they look like flowers.

'Very nice,' she says, turning me with a firm hand to fasten the back of the bodice.

I touch the base of my throat where my skin is blotched with nerves. 'Do you think I should cover this up?'

'What I *think*, ma'am, is that the Prince will realise he's a lucky man,' she says, handing me an embroidered shawl.

My heart is slamming against my ribs as I walk down the staircase. For the first time I notice how the banisters have been cast to resemble iron sticks of bamboo. How strange it is that I should register such insignificant details when I am on the cusp of such a momentous change: the hiss of the gas lighting, the tassels dangling from the glass lamp shades, the glare of a porcelain dragon, the intricate pattern of the carpet beneath my feet.

A liveried footman conducts me to the Saloon. As I wait for the door to be opened, I press a palm to my stomach to steady it before pinning a smile to my face. I am announced and walk into the room, remembering too late my grandmother's repeated instruction to moderate my stride.

'You walk like a man, Charlotte, and an uncouth man at that. Try for some dignity.'

Having faltered, I am now marooned in the middle of the room, my cheeks still stretched in a false smile, with everyone looking out me.

The Prince Regent has managed to get out of his gouty chair for this evening, which is a good sign. He is standing next to a young man. I am too shy to stare, but I get an impression of dark good looks.

My father beckons me over with a benevolent smile. 'Ah, here she is! Come over here, Charlotte. There is someone I think you would like to meet.'

Forcing myself to take tiny, slow steps that threaten to trip me over my skirts, I go over and make my curtsey to my father, who has grown even more obese if possible. His features have been swallowed up by fleshy jowls, his jacket, waistcoat and breeches all seem to be stretching at the seams, and the scent of eau de Nile makes my eyes water.

'You remember Prince Leopold?'

Only now do I look at the man standing next to my father and he is so close that it is something of a shock. My first impression is of steady dark-brown eyes and dark hair. The planes of his face are clean, although one cheek is slightly swollen. My gaze narrows as if I am adjusting Captain Scott's spyglass. Now I can see a scattering of little scars, perhaps from smallpox, high on his cheekbones, and the wiry hairs in his eyebrows. I see a firm, serious mouth and a tiny nick on his jaw where a shaving blade has slipped.

I see little bits of him, but I have no sense of a whole. My father clears his throat. They are waiting for me to respond.

I put my smile back in place. 'Of course. Prince.' I hold out my hand and he takes it, lifting my gloved knuckles to his lips.

'Princess. *Enchanté*,' he says.

'I daresay you young people would like to get to know

each other,' my father says with forced joviality. 'I will leave you to get acquainted.'

There is an awkward silence. As aware as I, no doubt, that we are the focus of all eyes in the Saloon, Leopold gestures to two chairs set by the window.

'Shall ve sit?' He has a strong German accent.

Consumed with shyness, I nod, but I must play my part in the conversation. The best I can manage is to say that I am glad to see him again.

'I too… I am sorry,' he says. 'My English is not good for me to say what I feel.'

'And my German is also not good… Shall we speak in French?' I suggest, switching to that language and he looks heartily relieved.

'I am anxious to improve my English,' he promises, 'but for now… thank you, *Princesse.*' He breaks off with a wince and puts a hand to his cheek. 'Toothache,' he confides.

'Oh dear,' I say sympathetically. 'Have you seen an apothecary?'

'I am afraid to,' he admits. 'He will say I must have it drawn and I would rather go back into battle against Bonaparte himself than have my tooth taken out!'

I cannot help smiling. 'It will only get worse if you do not,' I say and then realise I sound like a wife.

Leopold does not seem to notice. 'No, no, do not say that,' he says, rolling his eyes humorously. 'Let us talk of other things.'

'Very well, if you wish. Tell me how you like Brighton and my father's Pavilion.'

'It is very... very exotic.' He looks around the Saloon. 'Although this room is magnificent,' he adds politely.

It is certainly opulent. The round ceiling is painted to resemble a sky, and two great, glittering chandeliers hang from it. The windows are framed with spectacularly swagged crimson and gold curtains which are reflected in the huge gilt mirrors while underfoot is an exquisite carpet most beautifully patterned.

'What is your taste in decor?' I ask.

'Ah, generally I prefer things a little more simple,' Leopold says carefully. 'Simple is not always plain, of course. Simple can be elegant and beautiful.'

'I agree,' I say. 'That is a taste that we share.'

His eyes drop to my bust where my breasts swell over the low neckline. 'I hope it will not be the only taste we have in common.' He leaves enough of a pause for me to colour and then adds that we both like walking. 'I saw you walking out this afternoon,' he tells me. 'I recognised you at once. No one else walks with your vigour.'

'The Queen is always telling me to keep my eyes demurely downcast and to walk in a more regal way,' I confess.

'Walking demurely is for young ladies,' Leopold says. 'You are a princess and a future queen. I admire the confident way you walk with your head up as if you are ready to meet every challenge.'

I am not quite sure what to make of this. I am not quite sure what to make of *him*.

'What's he like then?' Anna asks as she unlaces my stays that night.

I sat next to Leopold at dinner and we talked about all manner of things. I do not feel the thrilling passion I felt for Frederick, but he seems steady and sensible. He seems like someone I could marry.

'I don't know,' I admit. But I go to bed happier than I have for a very long time.

Chapter Thirty

A nd so it is done. Leopold asks permission to see me alone and proposes. He is very formal. It is not the romantic proposal I once dreamt of Frederick making, but I am glad to be asked at last.

Before I accept, I have to tell Leopold about my indiscretion with Charles Hesse. My father has insisted it is necessary that I confess that the letters and gifts I sent him are still unaccounted for. I know it is right, but I dread disclosing my foolishness in case it will give Leopold a disgust for me, but he listens gravely.

'You were very young,' is all that he says. 'He took advantage of you.'

I am so relieved that tears prick my eyes. 'So, you... you still wish to marry me?'

'Ah, Charlotte, how could I not wish that?'

'Well, I am not always very wise, it seems,' I sigh.

'You have had bad luck, that is all,' Leopold says firmly. 'You deserve better. I wish only to be worthy of you.'

'I don't suppose that you have ever done anything foolish,' I say without thinking and he laughs.

'Of course I have!'

I am almost startled by how the humour changes his face, and for a moment I can only stare.

'What did you do?' I ask, intrigued.

Well, perhaps it is a vulgar question – I am sure my grandmother would say so – and Leopold raises an eyebrow.

'I have confessed my own folly,' I remind him. 'I would like to feel that I am not alone in my youthful foolishness.'

He relents and smiles. 'That is fair.' He pretends to think. 'Well, when I was fifteen, I hid in an attic when the French invaded Coburg. I felt very foolish crouched behind an old rocking horse!'

'Hiding when your home is invaded is not foolish,' I point out. 'It is surely the only sensible thing to do. I meant foolish affairs of the heart.'

'Ah, that is a different story…'

'Go on,' I say, folding my skirts beneath me to sit on one of my father's exquisite sofas and making it clear that I am getting ready to listen. 'I have told you of my first love. Who was yours?'

'Her name was Polyxène,' Leopold admits. 'I was eighteen and she was seventeen and I wrote her very many passionate love letters. Alas, she was the daughter of a French émigré, so marriage was out of the question and we had to part. My heart was broken for at least a week!'

'Come, I am most encouraged to know that such a

romantic heart beats beneath that sensible exterior,' I say. 'Was this Polyxène the last of your follies?'

'No, indeed. When I came to London as a very junior member of the Tsar's entourage, I was not given rooms at the Pulteney or at Carlton House. Instead I lodged in Marylebone High Street where the landlord had a very pretty housemaid. I made of myself... what is the expression in English... something to do with a *gâteau*?'

'You made a cake of yourself?'

'Yes, that.' I see him filing the phrase away for future use. 'Oh, I made myself a very big cake! I must have been a great nuisance to this maid, always loitering on the stairs and getting in her way. I am ashamed to admit it now. I took her to the gardens at Vauxhall and spent many pennies I could not afford on her, at which point she threw me over and took up with her employer so I lost not only my heart but also my accommodation.'

I cannot help laughing at his rueful expression. 'Is it wrong of me to be encouraged that you are capable of folly too?'

'We all have it in us to be foolish and to be wise; we must forgive ourselves for the first and try for the second, do you not think?'

'Yes, yes, I do.'

He comes over and kneels in front of me and takes my hands in his. 'So let me try again. My dear Princess Charlotte, will you do me the very great honour of becoming my wife, so that we may forgive each other our foolishness and learn to be wise together?'

'I will,' I say.

Leopold lifts my hands to kiss my knuckles. I am not wearing gloves and am very aware of his lips on my skin. When he straightens, he bows formally but his eyes hold a gleam of humour that makes my own mouth curve in response.

'You have made me very happy, Charlotte,' he tells me. 'I will do my very best to make you happy too.'

'I am happy,' I say, and it is true. I do not feel the infatuation I once felt for Charles Hesse or the violent desire I had for Frederick. It is more the comforting sense that I have reached safe harbour at last after a storm-tossed journey and the hope that in Leopold I have found a friend as well as a husband.

We have only a few days to get to know each other in Brighton. Leopold does not mind my stride and we take brisk walks by the sea, regardless of the squally rain showers that send our companions scurrying back to the Pavilion. Walking at his side, raindrops clinging to my lashes and the wind snatching at my bonnet, I am filled with hope about the future. We agree on almost everything. Leopold has a horror of debt and is determined to live within his means and I am more than happy to surrender management of our household to him as I have never been able to manage my money in spite of long hours being made to labour over my accounts. Our only disagreement is about riding. Leopold says that it is too violent an exercise for ladies, while I have always been a neck or nothing rider. I love the freedom of galloping, love the beauty and power of the horse beneath me, but I will be a married woman and it will be worth sacrificing some of my pleasures for domestic harmony.

The more I see of Leo, as I call him now, the more I like him, but I do not feel desire for him, certainly not the way I felt it for Frederick. I am not in love with him. I am perhaps a little disappointed that my marriage will not be the romantic and passionate one I once yearned for, but I think that I will be content with Leo, and that contentment will be enough.

The wedding date is set for 2 May. I say goodbye to Leo at the Pavilion knowing that I will not see him again until the wedding. The carriage journey back to Windsor is a slow one on the winter roads, but I feel so much more certain than I did on the way there.

The Queen and my aunts are delighted at the engagement and it is a novel feeling to know that, for once, I am approved of. My grandmother insists that the ceremony should be a quiet one and the Regent is so unpopular in the country at the moment that it seems to make sense for the ceremony to be hidden away in case there are protests. I do not wish to be married with stones being thrown at the windows.

But the announcement of my engagement to Leo provokes such an outburst of excitement that we are all taken aback. It seems that hundreds of engaged couples are postponing their weddings so that they can be married on the same day as Leo and me, and the public interest in every aspect of the wedding is so great that all the plans have to be rethought.

I had known that I was popular with the public before,

but now the people seem obsessed in a way that is quite disturbing. Every time I go out in my carriage I am mobbed by cheering crowds. There is something almost feral about the eyes fixed on my every move. It is heartening, of course, that so many people are pleased for me and wish me the best, but at the same time there is something oppressive about the goodwill. All those avid faces become a blur, trapping me in my carriage, their gazes battening on me. Sometimes it feels as if I can't breathe.

My wedding is not just for me, I remind myself. It will join me intimately with Leopold as a person, but it matters for the state too. It is a marriage which has implications for Britain. These will be my people and I represent their future. I should be glad of their love for me. How much better this than to be jeered at and have stones thrown at your carriage, which my father endures.

Still, the obsessive interest in the wedding makes me uneasy and I have moments, too, when I realise how little I know of Leo. We write to each other often, but it is not the same as being with him. There are times when I cannot remember exactly what he looks like.

'I remember 'im all right,' Anna says when I confess that. 'He's bang up, he is.'

Mrs Louis clucks as she always does when Anna uses cant. 'The Prince is very handsome,' she reassures me.

For once, Mrs Louis and Anna are in accord. They approve of Leo, which is very reassuring to me. Anna never liked Frederick, I remember. If I cannot always rely on my own judgement, I trust theirs and if they both believe that Leopold is the right choice, then he must be.

I have been concentrating my energies on marriage as a way to find independence from the Prince Regent that I haven't really thought until now about what that will mean, sharing my life and my home with a man.

Now that I *am* thinking about it, I am getting nervous. As Leo's wife, I will be under his control. I will be exchanging my father's mastery for that of a man I barely know. Leo may say that he will not play the tyrant, but what if he does?

I will also be sharing a bed with him. The truth is that I am not entirely clear what that will mean. Frederick kissed me: I remember that tingling, tugging feeling low in my belly, the fever in my blood, the yearning for *more* without really knowing more what. But as to what actually happens once *more* is permitted and I am alone in bed with a husband, I am vague.

I do try to raise the subject with my grandmother who has, after all, had fifteen children, but she simply barks at me to do whatever my husband wishes me to do, which is not very helpful. My Aunt Sophia was there and she took me aside afterwards. She is unmarried, but if the rumours are true, she bore a child to General Garth – although I still find it hard to believe. 'It does not have to be unpleasant, Charlotte,' she told me awkwardly. 'Indeed, it can be very pleasurable if you and your… your husband are in accord.'

But what does being in accord mean? Mrs Louis's title is a courtesy. She has never been married. Nor has Anna, but she is the one who tells me what I really want to know. By the time she has finished, my cheeks are scarlet.

'But that will be so embarrassing!'

Anna grins. 'You can be embarrassed or you can enjoy it. That'll be up to the Prince, I reckon, but 'e looks to me like he knows what 'e's about.'

Chapter Thirty-One

Wimbledon, 3 July 1981

Thwak... thwak... thwak... Diana watches the ball being smashed backwards and forwards across the net. There are fourteen thousand people crammed into the seats, but the Centre Court is utterly quiet except for the sound of the ball hitting the racquet strings and the grunting of the players. It is the Women's Singles Final between Chris Evert Lloyd and Hana Mandlikova, and like everyone else's, Diana's head goes from side to side like a metronome. The moment a shot is won, a great *ooooh* goes up from the crowd, followed by a smattering of applause.

Diana has a good view, of course. It is a definite perk of her new position, she thought as she took her seat in the royal box with the kindly Duke and Duchess of Kent. Her sister Sarah is with her. It feels good to be able to take her eldest sister for a treat. It is not long since Sarah allowed Diana to tag along with *her*. This time last year, Diana had a job cleaning Sarah's flat. All that has changed now. She doesn't have to clean anything. In a funny way, she misses it. She's always liked to tidy up. She was a good cleaner. It might not be much to boast about, but at least she was good at *something*.

She was a good nanny too, now she comes to think of it. She still misses the children at the nursery and especially dear little Patrick. She misses his mother, too. Mary Robertson became a kind of mother figure for her, someone she could talk to without feeling that her every word was being judged for how appropriate, how *princess-like* it is.

Diana's own mother is in Scotland. Oh, she is at the end of the phone, but it is not the same and it is so hard to articulate her anxieties when it seems to the outside world that she has everything. Even courtside tickets to Centre Court at Wimbledon.

Chris Evert – Diana can never remember to refer to her by her married name – is well in control of the game. Diana envies her athleticism, confidence and control. She wins the first set easily, by six games to two, and while they rest Diana slides down in her seat to avoid attention. She feels as if she is in a kind of match of her own with Camilla, she muses. It means that she can never relax. Like Mandlikova, she has to be always on her toes. No sooner has Mandlikova hit the ball successfully to Evert, back it comes, twice as hard. That is what it is like for her, looking for attention from Charles who all too often now seems to be with Camilla. Diana knows that it is partly her fault. The more jealous and demanding she is, the more he retreats, but she can't help herself.

'You were so jolly and relaxed last year at Balmoral,' he said to her only the night before, baffled. 'What's changed?'

Diana can only marvel at his obtuseness. *'What's changed?'* she echoed incredulously. 'What *hasn't* changed? I've left my old life behind and now I'm shut up in Buckingham Palace with a whole lot of people droning on about duty and telling me I have to be someone quite different from the person I am! I'm the focus of attention wherever I go. My every move and mood are assessed by the public, everything I wear studied and copied. This time last year I was a nursery school assistant and part-time cleaner and nanny; now I'm going to be Princess of Wales. How can you possibly ask me *what's changed*?'

Charles hates being criticised. Dull colour stained his cheekbones. 'I appreciate that it's a difficult adjustment for you,' he said. 'This is precisely why I asked you to think carefully before you agreed to marry me.'

'You sound like you wish I hadn't!' she said tearfully and he sighed.

'Of course I don't wish that,' he said, clearly picking his words carefully.

'Then why do you spend so much time with Camilla?'

'Camilla is an old and dear friend, and I'm not going to pretend that she's not,' he said. 'But you're the one I asked to marry me, Diana. I've promised myself to *you*. We're going to get married and you will be my wife. What more can I do?'

He doesn't understand, Diana thinks in despair. As far as he's concerned, there is no more to be said. But if that is so, why isn't she enough for him?

She constantly feels inadequate now. It has never bothered her before that she isn't clever. She would cheerfully admit to anyone who asked that she is thick as two short planks.

Charles, on the other hand, is serious and thoughtful. It is one of the things she admires most about him. He thinks about philosophy and architecture and horticulture, things that Diana has not the slightest interest in. She would so much rather play with children or chat to people. When she is Princess of Wales, that is where she is sure she will be able to make a difference, but for now she is hidden away at Buckingham Palace. On odd occasions, like today, she is on display but generally she is supposed to sit quietly until she is married and can take on a proper role. She is interested in people, not politics or ideas, but the only people she meets at the moment are the palace staff and she is not supposed to natter with them, although she does. They are so much more fun than the courtiers she thinks of as the 'grown-ups'.

Evert and Mandlikova take to the court again. Diana sits up to watch. She is wearing a pink-striped, slightly quilted jacket over a cream blouse with a ruffled collar. The ruffles have become part of her signature look. Whatever she wears is seized on and copied. Diana was amazed to see how after she was photographed at Balmoral in her old cords and a Fair Isle sweater and wellies, the shops were suddenly full of copies and green wellies are now a fashion statement. Clothes aren't as deep as philosophy, but she's enjoying seeing how what she wears has an impact.

Fashion is a way for her to relate to people, and she

intends to take it seriously. It is one thing she can do better than Camilla, anyway! She is enjoying her new slim figure, too, and is determined to create a new and stylish image for the monarchy. Diana has no intention of wearing fusty dress coats. Yes, she will have to wear a hat and gloves for certain occasions, but even the stuffy courtiers aren't expecting her to dress like the Queen. She has been given a free hand with her wedding dress and for other events she has started working with young British designers. Her sister Jane introduced her to Anna Harvey of *Vogue*. Anna contacts designers and gets them to send round sample outfits to Vogue House. One of Diana's favourite activities now is to sit down with Anna and the former model Grace Coddington and choose designs with their advice.

So it is not *all* bad, Diana reminds herself. She fiddles absently with the engagement ring on her finger as she watches Evert serve, admires the controlled way the ball is tossed in the air, the fluid curve of the tennis player's body as she arches back and brings the racquet down in a clean, powerful movement.

For once, all eyes are on Chris Evert and not on Diana. It is something of a relief. She has just been reading more of Charlotte's journal and remembers her sense of being suffocated by the obsessive interest in her marriage. Diana knows how she felt.

She is beginning to feel a real sense of kinship with Charlotte, especially now that the earlier princess has accepted her marriage won't be the fairy-tale romance she had hoped for. It is funny how many parallels she can find with Charlotte's life. It was Diana's twentieth birthday two days earlier. She will be the same age as Charlotte when she married. Like Charlotte's eighteenth birthday, she celebrated with a small party in her rooms. Not with her fiancé or her family, but with a few members of palace staff who have been particularly kind to her. Diana was so touched that one of the palace chefs made her a chocolate cake. She invited her dresser, Evelyn; Cyril Dickman, the fatherly palace steward; her detective and Julie, the housemaid; as well as the chef who made the cake. They sat in her sitting room and drank too much Pimm's and ate too much chocolate cake, and Diana felt more at home than with any members of the royal family. Afterwards, she wandered down to the steward's office and gave everyone there a slice of the cake that was left over.

Then she went back to her empty apartment. Julie had cleared up and there was nothing left for her to do but feel guilty about all the cake she had eaten, so she brought it all back up. Diana knows it isn't the healthiest way to lose weight, but it is definitely working. Elizabeth Emanuel made a face at the last fitting for the wedding dress.

'We'll have to take in the waist again,' she said. 'I really don't want to cut the fabric and sew if your measurements are going to keep changing.' She twitched the sample skirts into place and didn't meet Diana's eyes. 'You really don't need to lose any more weight. You look marvellous.'

The trouble is that Diana doesn't *feel* marvellous. She is pleased with her new, slimmer figure but it is about more than losing weight now. Binge eating followed by vomiting is the only thing that helps her feel that her life is under control.

The second set is soon over. Evert has taken only an hour to win her third Wimbledon singles title. Diana stands to applaud her achievement. She is going to be more like Chris Evert, she decides. If she is in a contest for Charles's attention and good opinion, then she is determined to win.

Chapter Thirty-Two

Carlton House, 2 May 1816

I am too nervous to sleep the night before my wedding. At least, I suppose I do sleep a little because I definitely wake when Anna pulls the curtains on a dull grey morning. I suppose I should be glad that it is not actually raining. I do not know what has happened to the weather. It has been unrelentingly dreary and cold since winter was supposed to have ended. It is as if the sun has forgotten how to shine.

I should be feeling cheerier. This is my wedding day. I have been longing for this day for years now. After today I will be free of my father at last.

But I will be tied to Leopold for ever.

I *like* Leo, I remind myself. I am glad to be marrying him. It is my decision. Still, my treacherous mind keeps sliding to Frederick and how deliriously happy I would be if I were to be marrying him today.

But Frederick does not want me.

Perhaps Leo is not as passionate as Frederick, perhaps his eyes do not glint in quite such a delicious way. He may not make my heart beat faster the way Frederick did, but he is handsome. He has a nice smile. He is steady and sensible.

And he is here.

He is staying in Clarence House and has promised to come and visit me this afternoon before our wedding this evening. I will feel better when I have seen him and remembered what he looks like, I am sure.

I hope.

Anna turns from fixing the curtains to study my face. 'Losing your nerve?' She knows me too well.

'No,' I say, though even I can tell that I don't sound very certain. I pull myself up against the pillows. 'I'm just thinking that everything will change after today.'

'In a good way,' she says firmly. 'We're all going with you, remember?'

I came up to Carlton House from Windsor with the Queen and my aunts yesterday. It is strange staying here, instead of in poky Warwick House. I almost miss it. But I have gathered most of my household together again. Last night I gave them all gifts to mark my marriage and tried to tell them how much their loyalty has meant to me. Mrs Louis will come with me on the honeymoon, but the rest will wait for our return to Camelford House, the London residence the government has provided for us.

'The only difference will be that we'll be in a better house and we'll have your husband underfoot,' Anna goes on and I cannot help laughing.

'I am sure he will soon learn his place!'

'And think of all the new gowns you have to wear.'

I brighten. Last night two trunks were delivered, one from Madame Triaud in Bond Street and the other from Mrs Bean. Madame Triaud has made my wedding dress, my going away dress and eight other dresses. Mrs Bean's trunk contained twenty-six dresses and eighteen lace-trimmed caps. I unpacked them with Mrs Louis, Anna and my ladies-in-waiting, who still include Amelia and Wilhelmina Coates. We were all united in exclaiming at the exquisite workmanship, the gorgeous fabrics, the sheen and glitter of them as the gowns were lifted out of the trunks one by one, provoking *oohs* and *aahs* every time.

In addition, I have night chemises made of the finest muslin and gauze, so fine they are almost transparent, and decorated with absurd satin bows and swansdown. I have never worn anything so frivolous. Or so revealing. I blush just imagining what it would be like to wear them.

My wedding wardrobe has cost ten thousand pounds. It is an enormous sum of money and having been kept on a strict budget up to now, the lavish spending makes me almost uncomfortable. I know how badly the people are suffering. The aftermath of the war has left families struggling. The streets are full of terribly injured soldiers begging for a crust of bread, and the terrible weather has only compounded the misery of farmers. The ceaseless cold and rain feels like a punishment from God and yet how can we be punished for beating Bonaparte?

The Prince Regent's extravagance has made him deeply unpopular. I do not want to be associated with his excesses and was hesitant at first about lavish spending on my wedding, but there has been so much interest from the public that no one seems to begrudge it. It is as if they want a spectacle to cheer right now – or that is what I tell myself. The people need to see a princess looking like a princess. What is the point of us otherwise?

But perhaps I am just making excuses. The truth is that I am delighted with the wedding dress that Mrs Louis drew out of the trunk yesterday. It made us all gasp: a rustle of white satin and silver lamé and net, glittering in the candlelight, trimmed with a froth of Brussels lace and exquisitely embroidered with shells and flowers. I have never worn anything so beautiful. I am not a dainty person. I am too loud, too strong, too voluptuous. I know this, but in that dress I will feel like a fairy queen.

By the time Leo comes to visit me in the early afternoon, I am more myself. The moment he is announced and walks into the room I recognise him straight away. Of *course* I have not forgotten him! I know him at once and the relief as I get up to greet him is so great that I actually feel weak at the knees.

As we are still not married, my ladies are in attendance, but they withdraw to the other side of the Rose Satin Drawing Room to give us some privacy. Leo leads me over to one of my father's ornate French sofas and we sit together. After that first rush of recognition, I find myself tongue-tied. The ease of our conversation in Brighton has been lost. I am abruptly aware of him as a stranger, a man, tall and dark and serious and somehow out of place in this ornate room. Perhaps he is feeling as awkward as I as we both speak at once.

'How—'

'Did—'

We break off at the same time.

'You first,' I say quickly.

I have written loving letters to this man sitting beside me. We have exchanged thoughts about everything from art to domestic economy to the diplomatic ramifications of Russia's new power to remedies for toothache, but now I cannot think of a thing to say. I am overwhelmed by his physicality – which I never noticed before.

It is Anna's fault. I should be thinking about the sanctity of the vows we will exchange this evening, but in fact I am thinking about what she told me. I am trying to imagine him without his neckcloth and his coat and his waistcoat and his breeches. What will it be like when he climbs into bed with me? When he puts his hands on me? When he does *that* to me?

'I was only going to ask how you are feeling,' he says.

'Nervous,' I confess.

'I am too.'

'Really? You do not look nervous,' I say almost accusingly.

'I have learnt to hide my feelings,' Leo says. 'Is that a good thing or a bad thing, I wonder?'

'It is a good thing, I think.' I sigh a little. 'I have never been able to do the same.'

'That is because you are a woman of honesty and open

emotion. Of passion. I will try to be the same, but I fear I am too used to restraint,' he says.

I wish he had not mentioned passion. It is making me think about what will happen tonight when I am wearing one of those absurd chemises and practically naked.

I moisten my lips. 'Perhaps we will complement each other?'

'I hope so indeed.'

A silence falls, stretches uncomfortably. One of his hands rests on a strong thigh. My eyes dart around, trying not to fix on his fingers or the material of his breeches or the hint of stubble on his chin. I stare at a pair of gilt griffins holding up a side table, at their golden paws, their carved beaks and beards, but my eyes keep being dragged back to the long legs so close to mine.

Belatedly, I realise that Leo has made another attempt at opening a conversation and is waiting for me to say something. I blush. 'I beg your pardon, what were you saying?'

A rueful smile tugs intriguingly at the corner of his mouth. Does he think I am bored? 'I am sorry,' I say. 'I am a little... distracted... today.'

'That is understandable. It is a great day, and not just for you and me. I was saying only that the crowds are already massing to watch the procession later. They are standing in the damp and cold for hours in the hope of seeing you. I have never seen anything like it. When I left Clarence House to come here just now, the footman who opened the door of the carriage for me was nearly pushed under the wheels by the crush of people.'

'Was he hurt?' I ask.

'No, he is a brawny fellow and he regained his feet quickly, but he could have been.'

'It is as if the people have lost their senses,' I say, shaking my head. 'Do they not know that we are just people like them? We bleed like them and bruise like them.'

Leo thinks about that for a moment. 'But we are not like them,' he says. 'We are royal, and royalty confers on us a glow, a distinction that sometimes we may not deserve, but which sets us apart. For you and I, our marriage is between a man and a woman. For the people of this country, it is between their future Queen and an unknown German Prince. We cannot blame them for being curious. Certainly, their only interest in me is in being the man fortunate enough to win the hand of their beloved Princess Charlotte – and I wonder at my good fortune myself!'

Our marriage is between a man and a woman. When I am stripped of my titles and my beautiful wedding gown, a woman is all that I am. And Leo is just a man.

My eyes slide away from his again. 'Our wedding has caught the imagination of the public, it seems,' I agree. 'I wonder how all those couples who postponed their weddings so they could be married with us today are feeling now?'

'They are probably as nervous as we are.' Amusement threads Leo's voice and I peep a sideways glance at him.

'Are you *really* nervous?'

This time he laughs, just as he laughed when I asked if he had ever been foolish and just as then, the way the laughter transforms his face makes my heart give a little kick of… something. It is not quite surprise, not quite desire. It definitely makes me look twice anyway. The laugh creases his cheeks and crinkles the edges of his eyes. It warms his serious expression and makes him look younger and more approachable.

He leans forward and takes my hand in an intimate gesture that catches the breath at the back of my throat.

'Charlotte,' he says, 'I am about to wed the most eligible princess in Europe and a future queen in front of the British royal family and the cream of the aristocracy while outside thousands of people are waiting to see us. I think I may be allowed to feel a little nervous, don't you?'

His fingers are warm and firm around mine. I am excruciatingly aware of his touch. Until now he has only kissed my knuckles. This, this feels more intimate even than Frederick's passionate kisses. Our palms are pressed together. I can't decide whether I want to pull my hand away or cling to his. Across the room, my ladies exchange indulgent glances.

'It is different for you,' he says. 'Surely you are not truly nervous?'

I cannot tell him that it is the thought of the night to come that is making me so edgy and unsettled.

'There have been so many negotiations and so much waiting that I can hardly believe that I will actually be married at last,' I say instead. 'I have been disappointed before,' I remind him. 'I keep thinking: what if he has changed his mind? What if he is not there when I get to the altar?'

Leopold lifts our clasped hands and presses his lips to the back of mine. It is not a polite gesture. It is a real kiss and the touch of his mouth on my flesh makes something clench inside me. 'I will be there, Charlotte, I promise you,' he says. 'I will be there.'

Chapter Thirty-Three

The back of my hand is still tingling from the touch of Leo's mouth as I set out for Buckingham House where I am to dress. My ladies travel in the carriage with me while Mrs Louis and Anna are to follow with the dress, my jewellery and everything else I will need to prepare for the wedding ceremony.

The Regent's coachman himself, gorgeous in his full livery, is in charge of the carriage, much to the disappointment of William, my own coachman, who scowled when he was told that he would not be driving me in the procession himself. He is to take us to Oatlands for the honeymoon later so I hope that will console him for what he considers a great blow to his pride. Anna tells me that he has contented himself with pointing out where the brass on the carriage could do with an extra polish, with examining the horses from top to tail and generally making himself extremely unpopular in the Carlton House stables.

I can see him watching critically as I climb into the carriage and I smile at him and give him a wave. All he does is bow and nod back, but I can tell that he is pleased.

The cheers when my carriage appears are deafening. The plan is to drive down The Mall to the Queen's House, but the press of people is so great that we have to take the long way round through St James's Park instead.

'Bless me, *look* at all those people!' says Wilhelmina Coates.

There is no need to look. We can hear the crowd, a good-natured roar that rolls before us. I did not know there were this many people in London! How can they all be here, squeezed into The Mall, waiting for *me*?

They are gathered outside the railings at Buckingham House too, and the guards have to push them back so that the carriage can drive through the gates and up to the entrance. The King bought the unpretentious house after his marriage to my grandmother. It was to be a comfortable family retreat from the formality of St James's Palace, and the Queen still uses it when she is in London.

Our footsteps echo on the stone steps as we are conducted up the grand staircase. The King always considered carpets unhealthy, although what he thinks now no one knows. I feel a pang for his kindly presence. It is hard to think of him shut away at Windsor with guards at his door. I wish he could be at my wedding. They say he is mad and that I cannot see him, but to me he will always be the grandfather who got down on his hands and knees to play with me.

The Queen and my aunts are waiting to greet me in the Crimson Drawing Room, which looks out over the gardens at the back of the house. Unlike my grandfather's rooms which are painted a plain grey-green and furnished with restraint, the drawing room is carpeted and the walls hung with red damask and covered with paintings. It is a comfortable room, miles from the ornate formality of my father's houses, and normally I would be glad to sit here, but today I can barely keep still. My aunts are all of a twitter about the wedding and although my grandmother is more restrained, even from here we can hear the crowds at the front like the murmur of the sea. So much for her determination to keep it a small, private wedding!

I am outwardly calm, but there is a restless fluttering in my stomach and along my veins. It is happening, it is really happening… I am to be married… tonight! Rational conversation is beyond us all and I am glad when I can withdraw to prepare for the ceremony. Mrs Louis and Anna are waiting for me in the chamber that has been set aside for my use.

Anna pours warm water into a bowl while Mrs Louis helps me undress. It is unseasonably cold and I am glad of the fire that has been lit when I stand in my shift and sponge myself clean. My mother has a reputation for a lack of personal cleanliness and I have a horror of anyone thinking the same of me. I do not want Leo to take a disgust of me on my wedding night as my father did for his bride, so Anna brings me some lemon juice to dab under my armpits.

When I am clean and dried, and my stays are laced up, I step into the petticoat and Mrs Louis fusses about, making sure it sits properly before she dresses my hair. We have decided on a simple, elegant style, as my hair is thick enough not to need curling.

Next comes the net dress and the train, which is six feet long, made of the same material as the petticoat and fastened with a diamond clasp. I keep twisting to see the pretty embroidered shells and flowers until Mrs Louis clicks her tongue at me to keep still. The final bow at the back is tied and then my aunts and attendants come in, cooing and exclaiming at the dress.

There is a brief discussion about whether I should wear some rouge or not, but I decide against in the end. That, too, is associated with my mother, who wears it to excess. No one, surely, could blame me for being pale on my wedding day?

At last, the jewels. Leo has given me a beautiful diamond bracelet which Mrs Louis clasps on my left arm. Pearls circle my neck; diamonds dangle at my ears. Finally, the watching ladies gasp as Mrs Louis lifts up a superb wreath of diamonds fashioned in the shape of rosebuds and leaves and settles it very carefully on my hair before fastening it into place with a diamond pin.

'There now,' she says briskly, stepping back so that I can see myself in the long mirror.

'Oh...' It is all I can say. I scarcely recognise myself. I am golden-haired, all silver and white, a-glitter with diamonds.

In the mirror I can see Anna waiting unnoticed at the

back of the room. Our eyes meet and she winks at me, and I smile back a little shakily. Mrs Louis is twitching the train into place, disguising her emotion by being brisk. When she looks up, I can see that she has tears in her eyes all the same.

'You must not cry,' I tell her, 'or I shall cry too, and then where shall we be?'

'It is just that you look so beautiful, Princess,' she says, her lips pressed firmly together to stop them wobbling, and then this woman who has cared for me so intimately for so long, curtseys to me.

'Thanks to you.' I raise her up and kiss her cheek, ignoring the audible sniff of disapproval from my aunts and ladies. I meet their censorious gazes steadily. I will not be ashamed of showing affection to my servants. They are my family and they know me better than anyone. 'Thank you for everything, dear Louis. And thank you too, Anna,' I add deliberately, beckoning her forward. 'I have one last task for you today. Would you go up to Miss Elphinstone in Harley Street and tell her how I look?'

It is my only sadness that Mercer cannot be at the ceremony when she has done so much to bring about the marriage. She has sent a message to say that she is unwell. It feels wrong to hope that this is true, but it would be worse if she were staying away because she and Leo do not agree, as I fear is the case.

The clock on the mantelpiece chimes to mark the half hour. 'It is half past seven, Charlotte,' says my aunt, Princess Mary. 'It is time to go.'

The carriage is open so that everybody can see me in my finery. The crowds are pressing so close that it takes the combined efforts of the Life Guards who are escorting us, and the constables and Bow Street Runners, who are supposed to be providing security, to clear a path for us.

Never have I seen so many people or felt so much goodwill! Fearful of dislodging my wreath, I sit very straight and still, but I smile and lift a hand in response to the cheers while beside me the Queen, in a magnificent gold and silver dress, relaxes her severe expression to concede a gracious nod every now and then.

At Carlton House a band is playing 'God Save the King', though it can barely be heard above the cheers. I descend very cautiously from the carriage, to be met by my bridesmaids who gather up my train to spare it dragging on the ground, and with a final wave for the crowd, I take a deep breath and head up the steps to the entrance. I am making myself walk more slowly than usual. I cannot bounce around as I usually do with a head topped with diamonds and a great train behind me.

Uncle William, the Duke of Clarence, is waiting for me in the entrance hall, resplendent in military uniform. 'What a crowd!' he greets me in his bluff naval way, as if I might not have noticed. 'Never seen anything like it!' He tells me that when Leopold returned after visiting me earlier, there was such a surge of people anxious to see him that the women and children at the front were shoved right through the doors of Clarence House.

'They'd no sooner got rid of them than the poor fellow

was mobbed again by women and girls when he set out to come here!' My uncle's protuberant Hanoverian eyes roll. 'Then while the coachmen were distracted by them, a gang of men took the horses off their traces and announced they were going to draw Leopold's carriage themselves.'

'Oh, my goodness!'

'Your Leopold took it in good part, but the Guards were afraid of an accident so they drove the men off and put the horses back. So we got him here for you, all right and tight,' he adds.

The noise and the crowds and the churn of nerves have left me feeling quite overwhelmed. I feel as if I am being borne forward on an unstoppable tide and am helpless now to do anything but go along with it, but it is all happening so fast that I am struggling to get my bearings.

Somehow I arrive at the entrance to the Crimson Room where a temporary altar has been brought from the Chapel Royal. The room is so crowded that at first I am dazzled and can only blink at the scene, a blur of silk and jewels and colour and faces all turned towards me. The great chandeliers are ablaze, the candlelight glinting off the gilding on the ceiling and making the crimson velvet furnishings gleam.

My father is waiting for us, looking every inch the Regent in the uniform of Field Marshal, his vast chest smothered in the star of the Order of the Garter and countless other honours and orders that have been bestowed on him by other sovereigns as well as those he has kindly given himself.

And there is Leopold, as he promised he would be, waiting at the altar with the Lord Chamberlain. My eyes fix on his lean figure with relief. Next to my father he looks a model of restraint in his white waistcoat and breeches and general's uniform coat.

'Ready?' Uncle William whispers.

I swallow and nod.

Part of me longs to rush forward to Leo, but I force myself to take slow steps as I tread carefully towards him. The train tugs at my shoulders, almost as if it is urging me away from the altar where the Archbishop of Canterbury waits, wreathed in unctuous smiles.

I peep a glance at Leopold as I reach him, and he smiles at me as our eyes meet. He has a nice mouth, I find myself thinking irrelevantly as my own smile feels more of a grimace.

The Archbishop clears his throat.

We turn to him and the service begins. It is such a strange feeling. I can hardly believe that I am here, getting married at last. My attention keeps drifting to tiny details: the line of Leo's jaw, the embroidered edging on the Archbishop's stole, the weight of the diamond wreath on my head, but I pull myself together when it comes to saying my responses in a clear voice.

There is a rustle of surprise around the room when I promise to obey Leopold. When I am Queen I will be answerable to no one but God, but I wanted Leo to feel that he will be truly my husband and not a subordinate. Still, I cannot forbear a giggle when Leo promises to endow me with all his worldly goods, which are not very many. He is not bringing wealth to this marriage or any great diplomatic advantage, but I hope – oh, how I hope! – that he will bring me happiness and comfort.

At last it is over and we are enveloped in a babble of congratulations. I kiss my grandmother and my aunts and shake hands with my uncles while across London bells are pealed, bonfires are lit, cannons boom at the Tower and in St James's Park guns fire a salute.

I stay only long enough for the guests to drink our health before leaving to change. Mrs Louis has a travelling dress laid out ready for me. The white silk is trimmed with satin and lace, and the pelisse, also white with an ermine collar, is worn over my shoulder in the latest fashion.

It is a relief to remove the diamond wreath and put on a white satin bonnet decorated with a plume of ostrich feathers. I study my reflection in the mirror when Mrs Louis has finished fussing. It is not as beautiful as the wedding gown, but I look smart.

I look like a married woman.

Now I need to feel like one.

I do not re-join the guests in the Crimson Drawing Room. Instead, I go down the private staircase from the state apartments to the courtyard where Leopold is waiting beside our new green carriage. *Our* carriage. It feels strange to think it.

My ladies are there, my servants behind them, smiling broadly. Also there in high good humour are my father and uncles and aunts and even the Queen, who is barking at

Mrs Campbell, who is to be my new lady-in-waiting, to stop standing there and get into the carriage.

'Grandmama, I do not need a chaperone,' I point out. 'I am married now.'

And as Leo hands me into the carriage and climbs in beside me, it feels true at last.

Chapter Thirty-Four

Buckingham Palace, July 1981

Diana closes the journal, drops it on the sofa beside her and stretches her arms above her head with a yawn. She can't help thinking that Charlotte had it easy, no matter how daunting the crowds.

Charlotte's guest list was limited to the numbers that could squeeze into the Crimson Drawing Room at Carlton House. Diana has no idea how big it would have been, but even if it was comparable to the White Drawing Room here at Buckingham Palace, there could not have been more than a couple of hundred, surely.

Three and a half thousand guests will be at *her* wedding to Charles at St Paul's Cathedral. Some two *million* people are expected to line the streets to watch the procession from Clarence House to the cathedral and back to Buckingham Palace after the service.

Two million people watching her.

As if that weren't enough, the procession and service will be televised in more than seventy countries around the world, they've been told. If she giggles at the wrong moment, as Charlotte did, there will be an awful lot of people listening to her mistake.

'Will people really watch it overseas?' Diana asked Charles doubtfully the evening after the complicated televising arrangements had been explained.

'Only about seven hundred and fifty million, I'm told,' he said with one of his wry smiles.

'*Seven hundred and fifty million*?' She remembers goggling at him. 'I can't even *imagine* that many people!'

'Then don't try.' Charles took her hand and drew her down onto the sofa beside him. 'This wedding is for us, Diana. You and me. You only need to imagine the two of us. Forget about everyone else.'

Diana glows, remembering. When Charles is like that, she is reassured that he loves her. It had been a nice evening for once. Too often lately, Charles has been preoccupied by events that are out of his control, as far as Diana can see. He wants her to fret with him about the riots in Toxteth, about unemployment, about the lack of opportunities for young people. It is as if he saves his compassion for issues rather than for people. It is good that he is such a serious person, Diana knows, but sometimes she can't help wishing that he worried more about her than about the environment, say.

But last night there was no disturbing footage of burning buildings or Molotov cocktails or police moving crab-like behind riot shields on the television news. For once, Charles was relaxed and they enjoyed a quiet supper alone together

– apart from the footman serving, Charles's valet in the background, his private secretary popping in and out with queries and various other interruptions. But as far as life in the Palace went, it had felt reassuringly normal.

She found his naval commander's cap and larked around with it tipped over one eye, twirling and giggling, while Charles watched her indulgently. It reminded her of the first heady days of their romance when she had been giddy with the thrill of his attention and she had let herself think that everything will be all right after all.

He likes it when she's fun. Too often lately, she's been sulky and demanding, Diana can admit that. She knows that Charles hates it, but she can't help it. He doesn't understand how hard it is for her to stay cheerful when she spends so much time on her own, when the doubts about how much he really loves her crowd in, when she thinks about how close he is to Camilla Parker Bowles…

But she's not going to think about that now. Diana jumps up, suddenly restless. She'll go down to Charles's office on the ground floor and see if there is anyone to talk to there. The office has been the hub of the wedding planning, with a whole team charged with dealing with the invitations, security, the service, gifts and every other aspect of the biggest royal celebration since the Coronation.

Diana's role has been largely to write thank-you letters, but she has been allowed some say on the guest list, at least. All sorts of foreign dignitaries apparently need to be invited, and she has accepted them, but there are some names she drew a line through. One of those was Barbara Cartland. Her stepmother's mother wears ridiculously flamboyant outfits and is always grotesquely made up; no one can help staring. Diana has no intention of being upstaged by her. She has come under a lot of pressure from her father and from others who claim that it will look bad if such a famous and close connection is banned from the wedding, but Diana doesn't care. It is *her* wedding.

She drew a line through two other names as well. Charles was still close – too close – to ex-girlfriends Camilla Parker Bowles and Dale Tryon. Diana didn't see why she should have them at her wedding, but Charles had put his foot down.

'You're inviting your old friends, Diana. I'm inviting mine.'

They had a filthy row about it and in the end he agreed that neither Camilla nor his precious 'Kanga' would be invited to the more private wedding breakfast at Buckingham Palace after the ceremony. That was for family and friends and Diana did not want either of them there. She had her way about that, at least.

'Very well,' Charles said wearily at last. 'Not the wedding breakfast.'

'Not anywhere,' Diana said angrily. 'Can't you see how it makes me feel when you spend so much time with your old girlfriends? It's like you can't bear to let them go.'

'They're *friends*.'

'You don't need friends,' she spat. 'You've got a fiancée, although you'd never think it, the amount of time you spend with me!'

Charles rubbed a hand over his face. 'I'm busy.'

'Not too busy to spend hours on the phone to Camilla!'

There was a long, charged silence. 'We're going round in circles,' Charles said, sounding tired. 'It sounds like you want me to give up all my friendships.'

'I just want to feel that I matter more to you than they do.'

'You do, Diana,' he said. 'Of course you do. I wouldn't be marrying you if you didn't.'

'Then prove it,' she said tearfully.

So Charles promised that he would distance himself from his closest friends, by which Diana sincerely hopes that he means Camilla. She suspects that he is doing it for a quiet life rather than because he really wants to, but she has made her point.

She hopes.

There is a buzz of activity in the Prince of Wales's office that pauses briefly when Diana breezes in.

'Michael in?'

Michael Colborne is Charles's personal secretary. Diana likes him, and often chats to him when she's in the office.

A secretary is at a desk just outside Michael's office. She is on the phone but pauses her conversation to put her hand over the mouthpiece. 'He's just popped out to see Edward.'

Edward Adeane is Charles's private secretary rather than his personal secretary, so the two men work closely together.

'I'll wait for him in his office,' Diana tells her and wanders in.

Michael's desk is piled high with parcels. More wedding gifts, she assumes. All will have to be noted, acknowledged, and an appropriate thank-you letter sent. Diana doesn't envy Michael his job.

She sits in the chair behind the disk and spins it idly for a couple of minutes, watching the bustle in the outer office. Phones ring constantly, people walk purposefully. Only she, it seems, has time to sit and wait.

Bored already, Diana picks up one of a number of smallish packages on the top of the pile. Poor Michael having to deal with all of this. She can at least open a few of them.

She draws out a jewellery box and regards it, a little puzzled. It's not that she wants grand gifts, but the Crown Prince of Saudi Arabia sent a stunning sapphire and diamond set of a watch, a bracelet, a pendant and ring *and* earrings. This looks a much more modest gift. It might actually be something she could wear, she thinks as she opens the box. That would be nice.

Inside lies a bracelet, quite plain, but with two letters engraved on it. Those letters are not the D and C Diana expected.

G and F.

It is as if a bucket of cold water has been thrown in her face. Diana knows only too well what those two letters stand for: Girl Friday. Charles's nickname for Camilla.

This bracelet isn't for her. It is for Charles to give Camilla, the 'friend' he has promised to give up.

Rage, hurt and disappointment rise in Diana, a thick, choking tide. She throws the bracelet onto the desk in disgust. Disgust with Charles, disgust with herself for being stupid enough to believe that he would change.

Her fists are clenched and she is taking short, jerky breaths.

'I'm so sorry to keep you waiting, Lady Diana...' Michael Colborne appears in the doorway, smiling his urbane smile, but when he sees the bracelet glittering on the desk, his face changes.

'Lady Dia—'

'Don't say anything!' Diana says, shoving back the chair and jumping to her feet. 'I know what this is!'

'Lady D—' He tries again, but Diana can't stand any more.

'Oh, what's the point? Just forget it!' Unable to stop the bitter tears, she pushes past him, rushes out of the suddenly silent office and runs weeping along the empty corridors to her apartment.

When she finds and confronts Charles, he doesn't even deny it. 'Yes, I bought the bracelet for Camilla. It's a farewell gift.'

'Am I supposed to believe that?'

'Believe what you want,' he says coldly. 'You want me to say goodbye to her. I'm doing that.'

'With a very expensive bracelet!'

'It wasn't expensive. It's a token of affection. I've bought similar gifts for other old friends that I'm saying goodbye to because that's what *you* want. I'm not going to cut any of them off without acknowledgement.' Charles won't even give Diana the satisfaction of raising his voice. 'That's not the kind of friend I am. So make up your mind, Diana. I can say goodbye with affection or not at all.'

By this point Diana is too angry and tearful to think straight. 'I don't want you to see that woman again!'

'I'm afraid you're just going to have to accept that I *will* see Camilla again.' His jaw is tight. 'We're having a farewell lunch on the twenty-seventh. I will be giving her the bracelet then and I'll be saying goodbye.'

He's waiting until two days before the wedding to say his goodbyes! Diana is beside herself. It's all too much: the disappointment, the pressure, the intense press interest, the terrible sense that she has got on the wrong train and it is bearing her remorselessly away from where she needs to be.

While Charles is giving Camilla the bracelet, Diana is having lunch with her sisters. 'I can't bear it,' she says tearfully. 'I've got this awful sense of foreboding. It feels all wrong. How can I marry Charles feeling like this? Knowing how *he* feels?'

'This is just pre-wedding jitters,' Jane says soothingly. 'All brides get them.'

Diana looks at her sister in frustration. 'This is more than jitters, Jane! I'm seriously thinking of calling the whole wedding off.'

'Sure,' says Sarah with a snort. 'Your face is on all the tea towels now. Bad luck, Duch, but it's too late to chicken out now.'

Chapter Thirty-Five

Oatlands, Surrey, May 1816

S o this is what it is like being married.

I am so tired by the time we reach Oatlands, where we are to spend our honeymoon, that I am beyond even being shy. Mrs Louis clucks around me and brushes out my hair and puts me into the bed before retiring with a wordless pat of... what? Sympathy? Reassurance? I am not sure.

Leo comes in wearing a splendid dressing gown and sits on the edge of the bed. 'You look very tired, Charlotte.'

'It has been a long day and it is all very strange,' I say, plucking at the sheet and keeping my eyes down.

There is a pause. 'Would you like to just sleep tonight, *liebling*?' Leo asks after a moment. 'We are on our honeymoon, after all. There will be time to consummate the marriage.'

I am perverse, I know. I should be grateful that my new

husband is so considerate, but it feels almost like a rejection. Clearly Leopold is not consumed by desire for me! Frederick would have been eager to seduce me. Or so I tell myself.

Part of me longs to accept his offer, but the day has been so long and overwhelming and my thoughts are so jumbled and I am so nervous about the intimate side of marriage that I don't know *what* I want.

'I think I would like to get it over with,' I blurt out in the end and Leo smiles wryly.

'It will not be as bad as all that, I hope!'

'I don't *know* what it will be like. That is the problem,' I say almost sulkily.

'The first time may be painful for you, but it will get better,' he promises.

'Very well,' I say with false bravado, 'let us do it then!'

And so we do. Leo is gentle with me and it doesn't hurt exactly, but it is not very comfortable either and it is certainly not at all dignified. Afterwards, he falls asleep while I lie awake in spite of my tiredness.

Is that it? I wonder. Anna made it sound more enjoyable. Would it have been different with Frederick? The thought of him brings tears to my eyes, even though I cannot in all honesty picture him clearly anymore. I just have a memory of flooding happiness when I was with him. I hoped that being married would bring me happiness at last, but I don't feel happy. I don't feel anything.

Still, I am glad to have the first time over. It is very strange having someone else in the bed. I am afraid of rolling into Leo and disturbing him, and I lie so stiffly that I hardly sleep at all.

Breakfast is a constrained affair. We regard each other from opposite ends of a long table, which has been cursorily laid by the Yorks's famously ill-managed servants. Still, there are rolls and butter on the table and Leo carves himself some ham while I nurse a cup of lukewarm coffee and try not to think about the intimate thing we did together.

Was Leopold satisfied with me? Did I do it right? I need to know, but I can't ask him, not when he is immaculately dressed as usual in a jacket and snowy neckcloth and we are being so polite to each other. Doubtless it is normal for newlywed couples to feel shy with each other, but it is all very awkward.

'Well, we have a day of leisure at last,' Leo says eventually. 'What shall we do?'

I look at the rain streaking the windows. The weather continues so dismally that we were lucky it did not rain for the wedding yesterday. I wonder what he would say if I confessed that I would really like to go back to bed. I am desperately tired from the strain of preparing for the wedding, and then a sleepless night.

But I do not want to be a languishing bride. I make myself sit up straighter and fix a brighter expression on my face. 'I could show you the menagerie,' I suggest.

'Menagerie?' His brows rise. 'Are there not enough animals in this house?'

Nobody warned Leo about the Duchess of York's love of animals. As many as thirty or forty dogs are often in residence, along with a number of birds, and when you first walk into Oatlands, the smell can be eye-watering.

Leo was aghast last night to be welcomed by a whole pack of dogs. They were perfectly friendly, though there was a scuffle as Puff took foolish exception to a mastiff ten times his size and I had to snatch him up, while Toby cowered behind my skirts. Anna took them both last night as I was afraid they might take exception to Leo's presence, but I missed their comforting warmth curled up against my legs.

'I must have counted at least twenty dogs on my way to the breakfast room this morning,' Leo goes on. 'And yet more in here!' He eyes the three mastiffs panting happily in front of the fire. Misinterpreting his interest, one hauls itself to its feet and pads over to shove its massive head onto Leo's lap.

'You have made a friend,' I say.

'I like dogs,' he says, pulling the mastiff's ears gently. 'They are fine creatures. But one or two in the house is plenty. I don't understand why the Duchess of York needs have quite so many.'

'People know that she loves dogs, so they keep giving them to her,' I explain, 'and she is so soft-hearted, she cannot bring herself to refuse them. She has taken her tiny Pomeranian and her elderly pug with her so that we can have Oatlands to ourselves, but she could not take them all.'

A spaniel noses through the door and bustles in, bringing a strong odour of wet dog with it. It quarters the room in search of scraps, before settling with the others in front of the fire with a heavy sigh. It may be May, but the weather is so inclement that the servants have lit a fire in the breakfast room, and the dogs are certainly enjoying the warmth even if little enough reaches us at the table.

My eyes meet Leo's involuntarily, and we both smile which eases the atmosphere somewhat.

'I love dogs too,' I say, 'but I agree, two is enough.'

'I am glad to hear it,' Leo says drily.

'You get used to the smell after a while,' I offer. I have been to Oatlands several times before, as Frederica has always been kind to me.

'I thought it was a great honour to be offered the Duke of York's residence?'

'It is. Freddie and my uncle lead largely separate lives, but when they do entertain together here the guests always enjoy themselves because everything is very relaxed.'

'Relaxed is one way to describe the service here,' he says. The footman who opened the door for me and who would in any other house be standing expressionless by the sideboard to attend to our needs has disappeared and we have the room to ourselves.

'Oatlands is famous as the "worst managed establishment in England",' I tell him, relaxing a little. 'There are a great many servants but never anybody to wait on you, it is said.'

'As we are discovering for ourselves,' Leo says. 'I would call for the footman, but it would be easier for me to serve you myself, I think.' He gets to his feet and carries the coffee pot down to fill up my cup.

'Thank you,' I say shyly.

'I had heard the Duchess of York was eccentric,' Leo says

as he sits back down. 'I did not realise quite how eccentric she was though.'

'She is,' I agree, 'but she is also very kind. Freddie has been a good friend to me. She does not like court and goes as little as possible. She is much loved by the people hereabouts,' I go on. 'Many of the poorest children in the neighbourhood are clothed and educated at her expense. She has established charity schools and supports infirm pensioners.' I pause. 'I would like to follow her example in that, if not in other things.'

'What in her conduct would you not want to follow?' Leo asks me. 'Apart from having quite so many dogs,' he adds with a glance at the hounds sprawled in front of the fire.

'She does not sleep like other people. She might go to bed for an hour or two, but more usually sleeps fully dressed upon a couch. She insists on open windows when she sleeps too, against all the doctors' advice. She will often go out for a walk with her dogs late at night or very early in the morning, or at other times she does not dress or breakfast until three o'clock and she seldom appears before dinner time.'

'Stop!' Leo holds up his hand, smiling. 'I am grateful not to have her as a hostess!'

'I like the way she does not pretend to be anything other than what she is,' I say, and to my surprise Leo nods.

'That is one of the things I like most about you too, Charlotte.'

Is that what I do? I feel as if I spend my whole time pretending to be someone I am not: a demure lady, a dutiful princess, a future queen. I do not have Freddie's confidence to just be myself.

Unsure of how to answer him, I push back my chair. 'Shall we leave all this for the servants to find when they care to come back? We should go out and explore.'

'It would be good to get away from this smell,' Leo agrees, rising with me. 'But it is very wet.'

'If we wait for a fine day we will spend our entire honeymoon indoors with nothing to do but sit and look at each other and smell the dogs,' I point out.

Mrs Louis makes me put on a voluminous cloak with a hood and sturdy walking boots before I go downstairs to meet Leo in the hall. Neither she nor Anna are impressed with Oatlands. Anna complains that the house 'stinks worse than a gypsy's midden' while Mrs Louis finds the servants lazy and slovenly.

Toby, Puff and some of Freddie's dogs accompany us to Oatlands' famous grotto where at least we have some shelter. Leo's eyes widen as he looks around the grotto, which is lined with crystal spar and seashells that Freddie herself collected.

'What an extraordinary place,' he says, peering at the statue of Venus that presides over the pool of cold, clear water.

'It is one of the principal curiosities of the kingdom,' I tell him, trailing my fingers over the shell walls. 'They say it cost fifty thousand pounds to construct. There's a cascade, too – see, over there – and a fish pond lined with gold and silver.'

'I think if I had that kind of money to squander, I would

rather spend it on a well-organised house,' Leo says in a dry voice. 'For the cost of a golden fish pond I could surely afford a servant or two to clean up the muddy pawprints of the dogs and fetch fresh coffee.'

He could not be more different from my father, who if he wanted a fish pond would undoubtedly line it with gold and decorate it with diamonds. That is a good thing, I remind myself. My own taste is for a more restrained elegance and yet for a moment I find myself wishing that he were the kind of man who would commission a golden bath for me to soak in, or shower me with jewels. But he is not going to be a husband who will make extravagant gestures, I think with an inner sigh. I should be glad of it.

On the way back from the grotto we inspect the graveyard Freddie has made for her dogs, and pick our way through the puddles as we visit her menagerie. She has an ostrich, peacocks, eagles and all sorts of other fowl who sit with feathers hunched against the rain, while wallabies, exotic goats and a colony of monkeys hide sullenly.

The rain drives us back into the house in the end, and means a long afternoon and evening where we are still constrained with each other, followed by a night which is even more awkward than the last one.

All in all, I am beginning to wonder where the pleasure is in married life, and my mood is not improved when the Prince Regent honours us with a surprise visit. He stays two hours or more and bores us very much by discoursing on the subject of uniforms, which is one of his pet interests. He explains the merits and demerits of such and such a uniform, the cut of one's coat compared to the cape of another, and generally offers a learned dissertation of every regiment under the sun. Leo bears it well. We both wear fixed smiles for the whole of my father's visit, our jaws clenched to stop the yawns.

The relief when the Regent leaves is indescribable. I collapse into a chair with a groan the moment we are alone.

Leo warms his backside at the fire. 'Have I ever told you about the epaulettes we wear in Saxe-Coburg?' he asks with a mock pompous air.

'Oh, stop!' I cry, throwing up my hands. 'If I never hear about another uniform, I will be a happy woman indeed!'

'But the buttons are most interesting…'

I cannot help a giggle. He has caught my father's manner exactly. 'No more please!'

'And the braiding on our jackets is particularly noteworthy.'

'Stop it,' I say, laughing, until Leo gives in and laughs too. For the first time since we have been married, I feel truly in harmony with him. I am wiping my eyes when I meet his gaze without thinking. There is an odd moment of stillness while our smiles fade simultaneously and the silence lengthens until Leo clears his throat and makes a performance of taking out his pocket watch.

'It is nearly time to change for dinner.'

'Oh… yes… yes.' Unaccountably flustered, I get to my feet. 'I will go and change now.'

Chapter Thirty-Six

Camelford House, June 1816

The weather continued to be miserable for the whole of our honeymoon. Leo and I both caught chills while Mrs Louis and Anna spent much of the time altering my expensive new clothes, hardly any of which actually fit me. It is just as well there were only the dogs to see me until my wardrobe was ready.

Now we are back in London to take our place in society. There are still times when I have to pinch myself to realise that I am married and cannot be sent back to Warwick House or to Windsor on a whim of my father's. I begin to see more advantages to the married state. My old household has expanded, and we now have six footmen who wear our simple green state livery. Mrs Louis and Anna stay on, of course, as do most of the Warwick House servants who served me so loyally for so long. I no longer have to endure the company of Lady Rosslyn and the

Consequences. Instead, Mrs Charlotte Campbell is my lady-in-waiting, and Mercer and Cornelia Knight are frequent visitors.

The government has given us Camelford House as a London residence. A meagre brick building on the corner of Park Lane and Oxford Street, it is hardly ideal but I am told that is all that was available. It has dark, pokey rooms, a narrow hall and only one staircase which we share with the servants. It will do for this season, but really for the next we must look out for another house. Fortunately, we have also been given Claremont as a country residence and that is an elegant and well-appointed house near Esher with every advantage. As soon as the season is over, I look forward to removing there.

In the meantime, we must adapt ourselves to the cramped quarters of Camelford House. Leo has his own rooms. I had thought that he might retire there after the marital act, but he continues to sleep with me and I am becoming accustomed to the weight and the warmth of him in the bed beside me. I am learning the sound of his breathing when he sleeps: the long sigh as he turns over, the snore that I can stop by poking him in the side, the little snort he gives before he wakes.

As for the act itself, I am used to that too. I don't mind it, but I am always expecting something more. It leaves me feeling flat, that is all. But Leo is a good husband. He is attentive, and if my heart does not soar when I look at him, I like how clean he always looks, how clean he smells. I don't often make him laugh, but when I do it feels as if I have single-handedly beaten Bonaparte himself.

We both enjoy the theatre and between attending the Queen's Drawing Rooms and assemblies and receptions and formal visits and dinner parties, we have been to see Mr Kean in *Bertram* at Drury Lane, and to the opera. I no longer have to sit out of sight at the back of the box as my father insisted. Now the audience hiss until we move our seats forward so that we can be seen, and the band plays 'God Save the King' when we go in.

Tonight we are going to Covent Garden to see the great Mrs Siddons in *Henry VIII*. I am in my dressing room and about to draw on my new kid gloves, when Leo comes in. As always, he is quietly but immaculately dressed in a black coat, white waistcoat and white neckcloth.

Mrs Louis bobs a curtsey and withdraws.

'I have a gift for you, *Fledermaus*,' he says.

'A gift?' Surprised, I turn to look at him properly.

'To say how happy I am that you are my wife.'

'Oh…' My heart warms and a smile trembles on my lips as I take the box from him. 'What is it?'

'Open it and see.'

It is an oval brooch, made of diamonds, the large central stone surrounded by a starburst of smaller ones. It is simple and exquisite. I raise my eyes to his. 'Leo… it is beautiful! Thank you.'

He clears his throat. 'I am glad that you like it.'

Our eyes meet, and for some reason my breath catches. I look quickly away.

'I… I will wear it now. It will go perfectly with this dress.'

I am wearing a green silk dress with short puffed sleeves

that are gathered with a pearl drop at either side. The neckline is cut low, but a ruffle of fine lace adds modesty. My fingers fumble as I try to open the brooch.

'Let me.' Leo takes it from me and undoes the catch. 'Where would you like it?'

I point at the centre of the neckline, suddenly, ridiculously, shy, and my colour mounts as he fixes the brooch into place with deft fingers. His head is bent as he concentrates on what he is doing. I can smell his cologne. His hands are close to my breasts and it feels unbearably intimate. It is stupid: he is my husband. He has touched my flesh, but I am aware of him in a way I never have been before.

Leo steps back. 'There,' he says. Is it my imagination or his voice not quite even? 'It looks perfect,' he says. 'Just like you.'

Perfect? I have never been that. 'Ha!' I manage a shaky laugh. I am not sure what has changed, but *something* has. Moistening my lips, I turn away to pick up my gloves once more and fight for composure. 'What did you call me just now?' I say, trying to sound lightly amused rather than disconcerted.

'Perfect?'

'No, when you came in?'

'*Fledermaus*?'

'It was that! I thought I must have misheard.'

'It is an affectionate name,' he says defensively.

'It is a *bat*!' I laugh at him, on surer ground now and feeling more myself. 'You cannot call me a nasty nocturnal animal! If you call me a bat, I shall call you a… a toad!'

'Well, what would you prefer? Would you like me to call you a wallaby?'

'Only if I can call you a camel!'

'An ostrich then?'

'A giraffe? Dear donkey?'

'Darling crocodile?'

It is silliness, but we are both laughing, and we are laughing still as we climb into the carriage.

'Enough,' Leo says with mock sternness. 'We cannot arrive at the theatre tittering together. We must be serious. Surely we can agree on a name that does not make you burst out laughing every time I use it?'

'What is wrong with Charlotte?'

'Other people call you Charlotte,' he says. 'I want a name that is only mine.' He purses his lips as he looks out of the window and thinks, while I am very aware of his shoulder bumping lightly against mine in the close confines of the carriage as we rattle over the cobbles.

'I have it!' he says at last. '*Mäuschen*.'

'Little mouse… it sounds too small and sweet for me,' I say. 'I have never been a dainty thing.'

Leo takes my gloved hand and raises it to his lips. 'In Saxe-Coburg we also use it to mean sweetheart.'

I swallow. 'Well, it is better than *little bat*, anyway,' I say gruffly.

When we enter the Prince Regent's box at the theatre, we have to acknowledge the cheers of the crowd and a rousing rendition of the national anthem before we can sit and enjoy the play. Usually I cannot take my eyes off the stage, but tonight I am distracted by Leo. My mind keeps wandering to the memory of his hands at my breasts, to the laughter in his voice and the warmth in his eyes. It is as if I have never noticed him before and now I cannot *stop* noticing him. My eyes slide to his jaw, to the edge of his mouth, to his hand resting on his thigh. On stage, Mrs Siddons is declaiming, and I should be riveted by the greatest actress of the age. Instead, I am thinking about going back to Camelford House and lying in bed with my husband. I'm thinking about how he will turn to me, how it will feel when he puts his hands on me and draws me towards him. A thrill of anticipation shivers through me.

Leo leans towards me. 'Are you cold, *Mäuschen*?' he whispers.

I am the opposite of cold. I am burning. 'No,' I whisper back and put my hand on his arm. I remember the feel of his arm beneath mine when we met at the Pulteney. How could I have not realised then what I would feel for him? 'No, I am not cold.'

Never has a play lasted so long. Never has the carriage ride back to Camelford House seemed so slow. We do not speak, do not touch, but the air is charged between us, and when I climb the stairs to my bedchamber, Leo follows in silence.

Mrs Louis is waiting as usual to help me undress. Leo's eyes flicker towards her and then rest on me.

'Send your maid to bed,' he says, his voice very deep.

I glance at Mrs Louis, who dips a curtsey, her face expressionless, and leaves softly.

'Now who will help me undress?' I say, pulling off my gloves, one finger at a time.

'It would be my pleasure,' says Leo.

He unfastens the brooch at my breast. He undoes my bracelet and my earrings, his warm fingers grazing my neck. He takes the coronet of roses from my head and draws out the pins, one by one, until my hair tumbles over my shoulders.

I stand stock-still as, very slowly, he loosens the fastenings of my dress until it can fall in a puddle at my feet. He draws out the lacings of my stays while my blood pumps wildly, turns me between his hands until I am facing him.

I feel myself unravelling with each brush of his fingers, with each hammering beat of my heart, and when he lays me on the bed, I understand at last what Anna meant.

———————

This is the year without a summer. The incessant rain floods the fields and the crops fail in the cold. There is unrest in the country as the poorest go hungry. The streets are full of beggars. I distribute money wherever I can, knowing that it will make little difference to the misery the people are enduring.

And I feel guilty. Guilty for not being able to do more. Guilty for being so happy when people are suffering.

I have fallen in love with my own husband. Everything has changed. Oh, I thought I loved Frederick. I remember how my heart soared with tremulous excitement at the very idea of him.

That was nothing like the way I feel for Leo. My love for him is quieter, less fevered, but more intense, *real*.

I look at him over the breakfast table and my mouth dries with desire. I watch the faint pucker of concentration between his brows as he reads or listens to music and I want to go over and coil myself around him, to press kisses along his jaw and down his neck, to ruffle his immaculate appearance. I glance at him across a crowded ballroom just as he glances at me and we smile and I am filled with a wordless, heart-swelling joy. I feel so safe with him, so sure of myself. He is the steady centre around which I can whirl, and bounce and talk too loudly.

I only have to think of his mouth on my skin, of the warmth and solidity of his flesh beneath my hands, and desire thumps and thuds inside me. Strange now to remember how awkward we were together at first! Now we fit perfectly together, two pieces of a lock. Leo is the missing part of me. When we lie together, it is as if life has clicked into place. I used to long for a home, but I realise now that home is not a place. It is Leo.

I am so consumed by desire for him that I lose track of the days and the weeks. It is Mrs Louis, who has been carefully watching for when my monthly rags might be needed, who alerts me. Until she mentions it, it has never occurred to me, but I call in Dr Baillie, the King's physician, who confirms what Mrs Louis has known all along.

I am to have a child.

Chapter Thirty-Seven

Buckingham Palace, 27 July 1981

S he is trapped. *Your face is on the tea towels.* Sarah is
right, Diana knows. She has left it far too late to back
out now.

She paces around her apartment, too jittery to sit still.
It's not just a matter of tea towels and souvenir mugs.
Literally millions of pounds have been spent on
preparations for the wedding. Foreign heads of state are
jetting in tomorrow. The security budget alone is immense.
For the past two weeks, every single room in every building
along the processional route to St Paul's Cathedral has been
checked by the security services, and armed police
disguised as footmen are to travel with the Queen's coach
and with Charles's in case of a terrorist attack.

The carriages in the Royal Mews have been spruced up
and polished. The Royal Navy have made two identical and
gigantic wedding cakes. The florists have their displays

ready. The palace chefs are busy in the kitchens preparing for the wedding breakfast and the housekeeping staff whisk around making sure that everything is immaculate for the royal guests arriving from around the world. There is an undercurrent of excitement amongst the staff with all the preparations. Only Diana feels marooned with nothing to do but feel sick with nerves.

What would happen if she called it off now? If she went to Charles and said that she couldn't marry him? If she refused to get into the Glass Coach and didn't turn up at St Paul's Cathedral?

The thought leaves Diana teetering on the edge of an abyss. For a moment, just a moment, she is tempted to simply step off and give everything up, but a feeling like vertigo makes her head spin and she puts out a hand to steady herself.

Of course she can't call it off. She can't do that to the hundreds – thousands – of people who have been beavering away behind the scenes to organise the celebrations. She can't do it to the Emanuels, whose future is riding on the wedding dress. She can't do it to the people who are already lining the streets with folding chairs and sleeping bags, determined to stake a place at the front of the crowd.

She can't do it to Charles.

And she can't do it to herself, Diana realises heavily. Where would she go? What would she do? She would be vilified for backing out so close to the wedding. Who would give her a job after that? It's not as if she has any skills. She's not qualified to do anything.

Like Charlotte, Diana has always assumed that she will

marry and have children. She hasn't been brought up to be a career girl with a life of her own, and she doesn't want that. If she doesn't marry Charles, what will she be left with? A Hooray Henry with an estate in the country? Or a merchant banker? Is that *really* what she wants?

Diana sighs, wriggling her shoulders restlessly. She has always, always had a sense of destiny. She's always believed that she can make a difference, somehow. And she can't do that married to anyone in the huntin', shootin', fishin' set, and certainly not to a man who works in the City, however well connected he might be. Those men were her friends. They were great company at dances or dinner parties. She could lark around with them. But she couldn't imagine marrying any of them.

Always supposing anyone would marry her if she jilted the Prince of Wales at the altar.

Just imagining the fallout makes Diana shudder.

No, she is being silly. She has always dreamt of marrying Charles, hasn't she? As Princess of Wales, there is so much she could do. She can change things. Diana can *feel* it.

And she loves him, she reminds herself. Perhaps their engagement hasn't turned out to be as romantic as she had imagined – an understatement! – but he might change once they are married. Diana has enjoyed reading Charlotte's journal, and sympathised with her determination to find some happiness for herself even when she is resigned to doing her duty, a word Diana now loathes, it has been flung at her so often over the course of her engagement.

Charlotte hadn't loved Leopold to begin with. He had

been second best, chosen only when it became clear that she would have no future with Frederick. Everything had changed once they were married and she had fallen in love with her husband. What if the same happened to Charles? Diana wonders. What if marriage would change things for them too, and Charles learnt to fall in love with his wife?

Perhaps she is clutching at straws, but why not be hopeful? Diana tells herself. It is not as if she has any choice now. She's not going to chicken out. She won't think about what Charles said to Camilla today at lunch or whether he meant it when he said it would be a farewell. She will think only about going forward to her destiny, whatever that may be, and making the best of it.

There is a soft knock at the door and Diana's dresser, Evelyn, comes in, carrying a ballgown in her arms. 'I've just been pressing out the creases,' she says. 'I'll hang it up for you.'

'Oh… yes, thank you.' Diana has almost forgotten the ball tonight. Some eight hundred guests have been invited to Buckingham Palace for the traditional pre-wedding ball, and she will need to be on sparkling form. She glances at her watch. 'I should be thinking about having a bath.'

'Would you like me to come back a bit later to help you get ready?'

'Would you? Thank you, I want to look my best tonight.'

Evelyn is a wonder. Diana is amazed at what a difference it makes to have a dresser, someone who sets out your outfits for you, who sews on any loose buttons and checks no hems are drooping. Who makes sure what you wear fits properly. Who makes sure that your clothes are ironed, your shoes cleaned and that the whole outfit works. Evelyn is not as close to her as Mrs Louis was to Charlotte, but she has a good eye for accessories and Diana values her opinion.

Tonight, she purses her lips while they consider what necklace Diana is to wear with the fuchsia-pink taffeta ballgown designed for the occasion by the Emanuels. Diana has long ago learnt to put her feelings into compartments and she makes a conscious decision to put away her doubts while she thinks about what to wear. On Evelyn's advice, she selects a diamond and pearl necklace and she studies her reflection in the long mirror while her dresser fastens the necklace and settles it on her neck.

She looks happy, Diana thinks, surprised. That awful diet has worked and she has lost the puppy fat that so dented her confidence when she was first engaged. Now she is slim and radiant, and there is not a trace of the turmoil in her heart as she turns to thank Evelyn.

'You look beautiful,' the dresser says.

'Thank you, Evelyn. Are you coming to the party tomorrow night?' She and Charles are hosting a party for all their staff at Mark's Club in Mayfair.

'I wouldn't miss it for anything. Enjoy tonight, ma'am.'

With so much anxiety churning in her stomach, Diana doesn't really expect to enjoy the evening, but the moment she steps through the discreet entrance into the White Drawing Room and sees the state rooms crowded with everyone in their finery, she puts her worries into a drawer and closes it firmly. For tonight, she will just enjoy herself.

It would be hard not to. Some eight hundred guests

have been invited to the pre-wedding ball, including most of crowned heads in Europe – apart from the Spanish King and Queen, to Diana's regret. She has met Juan Carlos and he is charming. Very attractive too, with his smile and downturned 'bedroom eyes'. Sadly, she and Charles are spending part of their honeymoon on *Britannia* and the decision to meet the ship in Gibraltar has offended the Spanish. The Prime Minister, Mrs Thatcher, is here tonight, as is Nancy Reagan, the US President's wife, tiny and beautifully dressed. The rooms are full of famous faces, in fact, the men formally dressed in dinner jackets and making the perfect foil for the women's glamorous ball gowns. Buckingham Palace, which has seemed so empty for much of Diana's engagement has come into its own, the magnificent rooms alive with laughter, with beautiful colours and fabrics and jewels glittering in the light from the chandeliers.

Diana is delighted to find friends here, too, from her light-hearted Coleherne Court days. Charles's friends are here as well, of course, but among eight hundred it is easy enough for Diana to avoid them.

She comes face-to-face with her sister Jane and her husband, Robert Fellowes, and kisses their cheeks. 'You look absolutely gorgeous, Duch!' Jane lowers her voice, obviously remembering Diana's distress at lunchtime. 'All right now?'

Diana hopes that Jane hasn't confided her doubts to her husband, who works in the Queen's office and is a consummate courtier. 'Yes, fine,' she says. 'It was just... bride's jitters.'

'That's what I thought,' says Jane, reassured.

It was more than jitters, but what is the point of talking about it? There is nothing that can be done other than make the most of the party.

In spite of Diana's doubts, it is a riotous night. The footmen, many of whom Diana recognises with a smile, are serving cocktails called A Long Slow Comfortable Screw up against the Throne with deliberately impassive faces. Diana wouldn't have wanted to be the courtier getting the Queen's OK to *that* idea!

Everyone seems to be in a euphoric mood. Princess Margaret, normally so conscious of her dignity, ties a balloon to her tiara. Prince Andrew has one attached to the tails of his dinner jacket. Diana dances once with Charles and the rest of the night with old friends. Sometimes she catches herself thinking: what if I'd married *you* instead? But then she wouldn't be here in this glittering palace, dancing in a beautiful dress and getting ready to marry the Prince of Wales. For tonight at least, it feels as if the fairy tale is coming true after all.

Chapter Thirty-Eight

Camelford House, July 1816

I keep pressing my hand to my stomach. The thought of a baby growing inside me makes me dizzy at times. It never occurred to me that I wouldn't have a child, but I never thought about what it would be like to have one either. It is almost a surprise. Do other women think like me: oh, so I am just like everyone else? I may be a princess, but I am not unique in this, not at all.

I am elated, but I am terrified too. It is no small matter to give birth, but my grandmother did it fifteen times so there is no reason to fear, I reason. And I feel well, extraordinarily so, in fact.

Leo is delighted, of course, but he fusses around me, reminding me that I promised to obey him when we wed. I am not to walk too far or too fast. I must not tire myself. I must sit quietly, which he knows quite well is not something I have ever been able to do. He would forbid me the theatre if he could!

I am glad in the end to have our first important party to distract him. We have invited the Duke of Wellington and his staff to dinner. I received a most obliging acceptance from the Duke and have planned a special menu. To my sorrow, Mrs Brough and Mr Thomas decided that they would not move to Camelford House with me after my marriage.

'You'll be wanting fancy dishes like that Monsewer Carême when you're married,' Mrs Brough told me. 'I'm just a plain cook. Me and Mr Thomas, we're going to get married and run an inn back in Banbury.'

'I'll miss you,' I said, and I do. Mrs Brough was part of my childhood, more constant than my own mother. I miss being able to go down to the kitchen and sit in the steamy warmth, eating tarts warm from the oven and listening to Mrs Brough's steady chiding of the kitchen maids.

We now have a chef, a Frenchman called Boutillard, who thinks very highly of himself. He complains bitterly about the inconveniences of the kitchen here at Camelford House, but nonetheless produces excellent meals. I have not dared trespass into his domain! Instead, he comes to me to discuss the menu for the day. Today, I have asked him to prepare a special menu for the nation's hero and we have agreed upon a haunch of venison for the first course with veal and a sorrel sauce, vol-au-vents with pigeons, neck of lamb with a braised cucumber sauce and red mullet. For the second course we will be served, amongst other things, roast fowls, stewed peas, artichokes in a sauce and the sweet dishes on which Boutillard particularly prides himself: raspberry creams, almond pastries, fruit comfits. I am hungry just thinking about it.

All day the house has been in a bustle of preparation. Anna tells me that 'the Frenchie' has reduced the kitchen maids to tears and almost come to blows with Turner, our new steward, but otherwise seems to have the dinner in hand.

I don't like the idea of the kitchen maids crying. 'I wouldn't,' she says when I wonder aloud if I should intervene. 'You'll just encourage him. Leave them all to get on with it.'

And indeed, when it is time to welcome our guests, the house is miraculously calm. The dining table has been polished to a gleam before the tablecloths have been snapped open, floated into place and laid with our new silverware. The napkins are crisply folded, the candles lit and appetising smells are drifting up from the kitchen.

This is the first time I have entertained a guest as important as Wellington. He is the hero of Waterloo, the man who delivered us at last from the threat of Bonaparte. It feels like an honour for him to come, but when I said as much to Leo, he pointed out that I will be Queen one day, and that it is time for me to meet the country's political and military leaders. That the Duke might feel it an honour to dine with *me*.

When my father heard that Wellington would dine with me, he was jealous, like a child seeing a playmate with a toy he could have at any time. There is no other explanation for it. He told Lord Castlereagh to give a dinner for the Cabinet tonight as well and invite Wellington to attend! Leo could scarcely believe it when he heard. Naturally, the Duke sent his regrets as he was already engaged to dine with me but I do think it was the outside of enough for my father to try and ruin my party out of petty jealousy!

But when our guests arrive, Wellington is not amongst them. His aide-de-camp bows low to me and explains that the Prince Regent sent a messenger to Wellington ordering him to join him at Lord Castlereagh's dinner.

I see Leo's mouth tighten at the insult.

'His Grace had no choice but to obey a royal command,' the aide-de-camp says, clearly embarrassed. 'He has asked me to apologise most sincerely, and to say that, if he may, he will join us as soon as possible.'

So Boutillard's grand meal is served to Wellington's staff, who are all very pleasant, easy gentlemen. Leo has much in common with them, having fought in the same campaigns and he has been working hard to improve his English. Mrs Campbell and I leave them to their port but they do not leave us alone for long and barely have they joined me in the drawing room than the Duke of Wellington himself arrives, having come straight from Castlereagh's house in St James's Square, and sits beside me.

The Duke has a brusque, blunt manner that I like. I have a tendency to be blunt myself, so I am not likely to hold that against him. He says what he thinks and speaks to me as if I am one of his officers, which offends me not in the least. I am delighted to hear his views on our diplomatic and military alliances, and we discuss as well the terrible situation in the country where the bad weather and poor harvests are causing the people much suffering. He looks around the drawing room and tells me that he approves of the simple style of decoration that both Leo and I prefer. I cannot imagine his upright figure in the ornate surroundings of Carlton House. We did not discuss my father, of course, but I cannot imagine that the Duke would relish being forced into the discourtesy of not attending my dinner party after he had accepted the invitation.

I am flattered, I must confess, by his plain speaking and interest. Wellington is a great hero and to him I must appear but a young woman with little to recommend me other than my parentage. That he should make the effort to come in honour of his first acceptance speaks well of him.

My father's stratagem to embarrass me speaks less flatteringly of *him*. Leo was furious, but he does not know the Regent as I do. Since my marriage my father has been in good humour, but it is clear that he could not bear the thought of me playing hostess to Wellington.

It has been a lesson to me. I am determined that when I am Queen, I will not treat my ministers – or anyone – like that. I will not force them to break engagements or refuse to listen to their advice. Dinners like these are important. I need to be well informed and able to converse on serious subjects.

I am learning to be a queen.

Nobody ever taught me to be a princess. The Queen is burdened with the King's madness. My father ignored me, my mother abandoned me. My tutors and governesses did their best, but what did they know of kingship? So I grew rough and ready, too loud and too impulsive, too reckless and too open.

They are not all bad qualities, Leo says, but he is helping smooth down my edges, encouraging me to be quieter and more thoughtful. *Doucement, chérie*, he says when my voice rises in excitement. Gently, darling. *Doucement, chérie, doucement.*

He says it so often that I have taken to calling him *Doucement*, while I am still *Mäuschen*, his little mouse. I pretend that I think it is a silly name, but secretly I like it. It makes me feel daintier than I am.

Leo and I are agreed that we will teach this child that I carry from the start. It will not grow up isolated and alone, that it will learn how to be a prince or princess, that it will understand how to treat people with kindness and courtesy, no matter their rank. We will not pass on the ugly Hanover pattern of the eldest son continually running counter to the father.

The year without a summer: that is how 1816 has been dubbed. We are now in July and I cannot remember the last time I saw the sun shine. The cold and the endless rain mean that we are all constantly recovering from a chill or catching a new one. I am tired after the dinner and for a couple of days afterwards. It feels as if I am going down with a new chill. Leo wants me to stay at home but I am wild to see the new opera at Covent Garden.

'It will do me good to go out,' I tell him.

Leo looks dubious, but in the end he agrees. Having insisted on going out tonight, I am ignoring the heavy feeling in my belly. It is just the effect of the chill, I tell myself.

'You look pale,' Mrs Louis says, frowning, as she hands me my gloves.

'I'm fine, Louis,' I say, but I know I sound shorter than usual. 'Don't fuss.'

The audience stand and sing the national anthem when we enter the royal box. I smile and acknowledge them, but I am glad to sit down. The walk from the carriage and up the stairs to the box seemed to take a very long time and I was aware of Leo glancing at me in concern.

At last, everybody sits down with a rustle and the curtain rises on the opera. For so many years I was not allowed to attend, or had to sit hidden at the back of the box lest anyone should see me, so now I take every opportunity I can to come to Covent Garden. But tonight I have made a mistake. I should have done as Leo bid me and stayed at home.

I fix a smile to my face and try to concentrate on the music, but I cannot shake the sense of something being terribly wrong. That dull ache in my belly is spreading, sharpening, and I shift in my chair, ignoring Leo's worried look. I just have to get through the evening and then I will go to bed and stay there until I am better, I promise myself, and I am still telling myself that when a stab of pain makes me gasp and lean forward involuntarily.

'Charlotte!' Leo is out of his chair and Mrs Campbell is on my other side. They are helping me up, drawing the chair back to the rear of the box so that I can sit.

'Get the carriage,' Leo snaps at the footman. 'Quickly!

And send a message to Dr Baillie that he attend us at Camelford House immediately. '

But I am afraid that it is too late for Dr Baillie. I can feel the blood loosening in my womb, feel the tiny life inside me giving up.

I fold my arms around my belly and bend forward. 'I'm sorry,' I whisper, unsure whether I am talking to Leo or to the child we had such hopes for and who will now not live. It will not be a prince or princess. It will not be born into a loving family. It will not break the Hanover curse. It will not live at all. 'I'm so very sorry.'

Chapter Thirty-Nine

Claremont, September 1816

The nation has gifted us Claremont as our country residence. Leo takes me there to recover. After the dank, damp summer with the dirty London fog coating everything, it is like stumbling into paradise. The grounds are extensive and the house is a fine square one set atop a rise. True, both house and gardens have been sadly neglected, but the air here is sweet and I feel as if I can breathe.

Warwick House and Camelford House are both narrow, gloomy houses facing the street. At Claremont, at long last, I have a home of my own that fills me with joy. The rooms may be shabby, but we can clean and refurbish them. And as for the grounds and gardens, Leo and I have great plans to restore them to their former glory.

I mourn the child that I lost, but privately. Leo tells me that I am not to blame myself, but of course I do. I know that I would have lost the baby whether I insisted on going to the opera or not, but however much I tell myself that it was God's will, there is a little worm of guilt that wriggles inside me.

It is easier to bear at Claremont, though. What a gift the nation has given us! All our furniture and servants came down in a procession of coaches and military wagons at the end of August, while Leo and I followed the next day. As we drove through Esher towards the gates, the church bells pealed a greeting. We feel so welcome here and are glad to be able to support the local shops and provide employment to the villagers.

Already local men are putting up new paling around the park and building me a narrow gravel road so that I can take out a little pony cart. My doctors and Leo are in agreement that it would be unwise for me to ride, and after losing the baby I am doing as I am told. I miss riding, but I look forward to my daily drives out with Jenny, a sweet-tempered pony who trots along happily while I sit holding the reins behind her in the cart.

Between the paling and the road, we are employing a good number of local men who would otherwise be idle. We have found less-demanding jobs for the poor, elderly men of the village who are happy to tidy up the walks through the gardens and weed the grass plots as we slowly bring order to the grounds. Young lads have found work assisting the gardeners or in the stables while any number of girls from the village are now employed as maids for the rooms, for the kitchen, the scullery and the stillroom. Leo is organising the repair of the dairy, so we will need dairy maids too before long.

Mrs Louis keeps aloof from them all, but Anna is in her element. As my personal maid, she has considerable status in the servants' hall, and soon knows which maid is in love with which groom or struggling farmer. She knows which footman supports a struggling family in the village, who is greedy and who is kind. I miss not knowing all the servants personally, but Claremont is a royal establishment now. It is not just Leo and me: Mrs Campbell, my old sub-governess, has become a friend as well as my lady-in-waiting while my equerry, Colonel Addenbrooke, is a straightforward military man. Leo has two equerries, both capable and courteous, Baron Hardenbroek and Sir Robert Gardiner, and now we have been joined by Dr Stockmar as Leo's personal physician, who is a great addition to our household. Stocky, as I call him, is a young man of many abilities; I see why Leo values him and his advice. Before long, we are all at ease with each other and living in harmony. I give thanks every day for the love I have found with Leo and for the peace and tranquillity of Claremont.

In the country I find new pleasures in the changing seasons. There may not have been a summer this year, but the autumn offers its own delights. On my drives I note each day the changing colours of trees, from every shade of green to gold and bronze, red and brown. I have taken pleasure in nature before in the Great Park at Windsor or in Hyde Park or even Carlton House Gardens, but there is a new enjoyment here at Claremont. Perhaps because I am home at last, perhaps because I am happy, but there is a kind of piercing pleasure in the way the wind tumbles fallen leaves along the paths, in the sharpening of the air which carries a faint smell of apples and woodsmoke. Claremont has its fogs too, but they are not the dense, dirty, smothering fogs we get in London but a pale, pearly greyness that hangs over the lake and drifts through the trees.

Leopold's favourite thing is to shoot in the park, which is teeming with snipe. He goes out with his equerries or Stocky and they all come home damp and brimming with self-satisfaction after tramping around ponds and ploughing through the bogs with which the park abounds. I am happy for them to enjoy themselves, although I do not see the pleasure in shooting myself. I have made one stipulation only, which is to forbid Leopold, or anyone, to shoot blackbirds or hares. I have not forgotten those dark days when I watched the bright-eyed blackbirds from my window, and hares are such beautiful, golden creatures. I cannot bear to think of them killed.

The winter is almost as cheerless as the summer. I feel desperately sorry for the poor after the bad harvests left so many in distress. I do what I can to distribute food and money to the poor in Esher and I pray to God that more can be done to help them. I am so grateful for my good fortune in having Leo and Claremont, where the rooms are warm and cheerful and the candles alight on the dark winter afternoons.

We lead a quiet life, but a very, very happy one. Leo and I would happily remain engrossed in each other, but we entertain, as we must. Some guests are more welcome than others: my father visits, as does the Queen, but we also have Freddie, Duchess of York, who brings three of her dogs with her, the Duke of Orléans and the Tsar's brother, Grand Duke Nicholas, a handsome young man who is natural, unaffected and good-natured.

I am reluctant to leave, but it would be rude to refuse an invitation to join the Prince Regent at the Royal Pavilion in early December for a family reunion of sorts. It is good to see my grandmother, uncles and aunts again. The Queen finds me 'much improved' and puts my quieter behaviour down to marriage. She does not know that Leo's gentle murmur of *doucement, chérie, doucement* whenever I forget to speak quietly is having its effect.

Leo and I soon tire of the stuffy, over-decorated rooms at the Pavilion and are glad to return to Claremont in time to celebrate Leo's birthday on 16 December. We have planned a grand entertainment and have invited guests from London who brave the muddy roads to come and celebrate with us. For my twenty-first birthday on 7 January, though, I have chosen to make the celebrations local ones. The Regent is holding a ball in my honour at the Royal Pavilion in Brighton, but I will not be there. I will be here, at Claremont, at home. I give a hundred pounds to the poor while a band plays in the streets of Esher and we throw open the house to play host to the locals. The celebrated soprano Joséphine Fodor-Mainvielle sings Zerlina from *Don Giovanni*, creditably accompanied by Leo who has a fine tenor voice. Listening to their voices soar, joy shivers through me. I want to hold on to this moment, listening to my husband sing, my friends around me, with the music filling my drawing room, my house filled with light and with the people who have come to mean so much to me. It is as if after so many sad and lonely years, life has decided to fill my cup of happiness to the brim.

In February it overflows: I discover that I am with child once more. This time I will take no risks. This time I will stay quietly at Claremont and let the world carry on without me for a while.

This time, I am sure, the baby will be born.

———————

As the weather slowly improves, Cornelia Knight comes to visit. I am glad to see her again. She proved herself a loyal attendant, but when I think about how she aided my obsession with Prince Frederick, I can only marvel at both of us. What were we thinking? And what if Frederick had been true? I would never have married Leo. Sometimes I lie in bed with my arm over his body, my face pressed against the warm flesh of his shoulder and I feel cold at the thought at how my life might have been without him.

I know Cornelia thinks the same. Today she put her head around the door to find Leo and me seated at a desk covered with receipts and other papers.

'Oh, I beg your pardon,' she said instantly. 'I did not know you were in here. I mustn't disturb you.'

She made to withdraw, but I called her back gaily. 'Come in, come in,' I cried. 'It is just Mr and Mrs Coburg doing their accounts! We will be glad of the interruption, will we not, Mr Coburg?'

'I think you mean you will be glad not to have to explain this receipt for a very expensive bonnet!' Leo said, but he was smiling and he pinched my cheek tenderly as he said it. 'Come in, Miss Knight,' he went on, having risen to his feet as Cornelia came tentatively in. 'I know my wife is eager to have a comfortable cose with you, so I will leave you.'

'Yes, go away, Leo,' I said, laughing and waving my hand at him. 'I have so much to tell Cornelia and you will be very much in the way. We will return to these horrid accounts another time.'

As Leo bowed, shaking his head at me, and took his leave, I moved over to the sofa and patted the seat beside me. 'Do come and sit down, Cornelia,' I said. 'I am so glad to be able to talk to you alone. One can never converse properly about the things that really matter over dinner or with gentlemen present. Now, you must tell me—' I broke off as I saw her eyes fill with tears. 'Whatever have I said?'

'Nothing, nothing, it is just that I am so happy to see *you* so happy, Princess! Prince Leopold is the perfect husband for you.'

'I truly think he is,' I said, smiling reminiscently.

'I do not think I advised you well when I was your companion in London,' Cornelia confessed, dabbing at her eyes.

'Dear Cornelia, what could you have done? I was too headstrong to take advice then,' I said. 'I thought then that I loved Prince Frederick and it is only now that I know what love is that I realise what I felt for him was mere infatuation. Or worse than that, if I am honest, he was a reason to break my engagement to the Dutch Prince. I can never be sorry that I withstood my father's demands then. I wanted to be in love and so I was. I held on to the idea of Frederick longer than I should have done,' I went on reflectively. 'I did not see what was right in front of me, and even when I married Leo, I was a fool. I thought that I was settling for second best instead of realising that I had the best possible. That is on me, not you.'

Cornelia looked unconvinced. 'I just feel that I encouraged you when I should have been wiser,' she said.

'You were a loyal friend,' I told her, patting her hand. 'That was what I needed then. I missed you very much when I was sent away to Windsor without you. I hope you will come to Claremont often,' I went on. 'You will always be welcome here, Cornelia.'

Chapter Forty

Claremont, June 1817

S pring is glorious this year, but perhaps that, too, is because I am so happy. It is as if the trees have never been so freshly green, the grass so lush, the blossom so heavy. My belly swells with the warmth and the sunlight.

Family duties take us to London at times, and we have a box at Drury Lane, but we are always eager to return to Claremont, where we can forget about the rest of the world. Leo has been shocked by the way the papers lampoon those in positions of power or responsibility. He is mortified by criticisms of him as a parasite, a foreigner tied to his wife's apron strings and dependent on her for money. Radicals jeer at him for being paid a dowry as if he were a woman and, unused to ridicule, he takes it very ill.

In Saxe-Coburg they do not treat their leaders this way. He writes to his sister, Sophie, appalled at the savage treatment of the royal family here. He does not understand why the newspapers in this great country of ours both fawn over and revile its royalty. The Prince Regent comes in for the greatest criticism of course. His extravagance and swelling girth make him an easy target, but even I have suffered at the hands of the cartoonists and the radicals constantly complain that the country bears the cost of supporting us to live quietly at Claremont instead of… what? What do they suppose I can do? I cannot set myself up in opposition to my father, and for now I have little influence. When I am Queen, of course I will take my responsibilities seriously and be more visible, but for now I hope most of my people will not begrudge me this tranquil time to bear and raise their future King.

It is true that we received a handsome settlement of £200,000 on our marriage, but the expense of running an estate like Claremont is very great. We give as much as we can to charity; thirty pounds here to the lacemakers in Honiton, fifty pounds there to poor Irish labourers. We ordered two thousand yards of silk to help the Spitalfields silk weavers and four hundred pounds recently to the poor most in distress, but it is never enough for the radicals! Leo dare not give his opinions or do anything that might bring the wrath of the press down on him. Marriage to me has placed him in the public eye, which he accepts, of course, but he does not relish being the butt of such savage criticism and so we go to London as rarely as possible.

It means that we miss the theatre which we both loved, but there is much to do at Claremont to keep us busy and we have new enthusiasms. We have appointed a botanist, a Mr Fairbairn, to oversee work on the gardens. He is restoring the views and vistas, pruning trees and suggesting planting and we have many long conversations about what will grow best where. I have learnt a new passion for botany. We have built a camellia house, all glass windows and graceful cast-iron arches, and we like to take our coffee there. The Prince Regent's taste is for the ornate, for gilt and elaborate, exotic decoration but to me no extravagant decor can match the beauty of camellias with their glossy leaves and flamboyant blossoms and the rich, pungent fragrance of growing plants.

Leo and I are learning a new appreciation for nature in the wild at the same time. A daisy is no less a marvel than the exotic camellia. As the evenings lengthen, and when it is fine, we often stroll out into the park after dinner, to where the lush grass is tangled with wildflowers. Here is nature at its simplest and most beautiful. The most talented artist could never arrange flowers in a display as artless and astounding as nature has done in the meadows here.

It is a warm June evening and the golden light throws long shadows as we walk out to our favourite spot beside a hedge where dog roses scramble with honeysuckle. Blackbirds twitter with thrushes and swifts swoop and dart after insects and somewhere nearby a wood pigeon burbles. The grass is long here and we sit carefully to avoid crushing the flowers. I have been teaching Leo their English names and he practises, repeating the name as he points: stitchwort and herb Robert, daisies and red campion, celandine and cowslips and cow parsley.

I lie back in the grass until all I see is the blue sky fading slowly to violet, framed by the feathery tips of grasses above me. Leo leans over me and holds a buttercup under my chin.

'So, *Mäuschen*, it seems you have a weakness for butter,' he says, mock stern as he inspects the yellow reflected onto my skin.

'I have a weakness for *you*,' I say, smiling up at him, and he tosses the buttercup aside so that he can lower his head and kiss me. I wind my arms around his neck and kiss him back, careless that we are outside. No one can see us, hidden as we are. It is just my husband and me, alone in the sweet grass, loving each other.

Afterwards, Leo rolls onto his back and laughs softly. 'If all those people who adore their dutiful Princess Charlotte could see their future Queen now!'

I giggle as I straighten my clothes. 'If your friends could see sober, sensible Prince Leopold now!'

'It is true. They would not recognise me, driven to distraction by my reckless wife!'

With a contented sigh, I settle back next to him and we link hands as we lie together looking up at the sky. I yearn, as I have done so often lately, to stop time, to stay poised for ever in this shimmering moment of intense happiness. It is not possible, I know. Sooner or later, we will get up and brush each other down, and we will walk back to the house through the lengthening shadows. There will be other joyful moments. There is the child to look forward to, perhaps more, and one day a coronation. We will move forward as we must.

But until then I lie next to my dozing husband, his fingers slack with sleep around mine. I am listening to the birds, feeling the babe shift inside me, and my heart is so full I am close to tears.

When Leo wakes with a little splutter, he rubs a hand over his face, embarrassed. 'I did not mean to fall asleep on you.'

'It doesn't matter.' I turn on my side to face him. 'There's something I want to tell you.'

'That sounds serious.' He frowns. 'Is something wrong?' His voice sharpens. 'The baby?'

'No, there's nothing wrong. It's just something I need to say.' I swallow, searching for the right words. 'When I married you, Leo, I didn't love you. I thought I would prefer to marry someone else. I thought... I thought that with you, I would settle for second best. It seems hard to believe now,' I go on with a half-laugh. 'Because now I cannot imagine being married to, being happy with, anyone but you.

'I don't think I've ever told you how much I love you,' I say haltingly. 'I'm sure you must know, but I wanted to say it, and I wanted to thank you for making me so happy.'

Tenderly, Leo puts his palm to my cheek. 'You don't need to say anything, *chérie*.'

'I do need to,' I insist. 'I don't want to take anything for granted. I don't want to look back when it's too late and realise that I never told you what you mean to me or how very, very grateful I am to have you in my life.'

'Ah, *Mäuschen*... it is I who thank you for making me the happiest man on earth. And since we are being honest with each other, I did not love you either when we were married. How could we love each other when we did not know each other?' he asks. 'But I liked you. When we met in 1814, we were both just pawns in a game. I had to make a dynastic marriage; you were the most eligible princess in the world. But I could see then that you had no interest in me, and for me you were just a young woman with someone else on her mind.

But I remember watching you from my bedroom window at the Pavilion, when the matter had been largely agreed by letter and without either of us knowing any more about the other. You had just arrived, and you were walking out with your maid. It was a cold, blustery day and most ladies would be huddled by the fire, but not you. You were striding out to the sea and you looked so vigorous, so alive. I thought, here is someone who does not shrink from the world but who goes out to meet it on her own terms. I liked the way you walked into a room, the way you looked me in the eye and shook hands like an equal.'

'All the things I was constantly being told not to do,' I say a little ruefully.

'I admired that about you. So yes, I liked you, but I didn't love you. I thought then that love was just desire, an itch that was easily scratched, but you have taught me that it is so much more than that. It is the way my heart warms when you walk into a room, how everything feels lighter and easier when you are near. It's knowing that I can catch your eye and that you will smile, that I can turn in the night and that you will be there and that everything will feel... *right*.'

I let out a sigh. 'Oh, Leo, that is just how I feel!'

'How lucky we are then to have found each other,' he

says. 'It does not matter that we did not truly love each other when we married. What matters is what we feel now. I have come to love so much about you, my *Mäuschen*. Your warmth and your merry laugh. Your frankness. Your kindness and your bravery. Your honesty, and the way you are not afraid to admit your mistakes.'

'Of which there are many!' I interpose, more moved than I want to admit.

'But most of all,' Leo says, 'I like the way you look at me as if you really see me. You look at everyone properly. It doesn't matter if they are a tsar or a footman, your eyes don't slide off their faces. You *see* individuals, no matter their rank. It is a gift,' Leo says seriously. 'You will make a great queen, Charlotte.'

'I hope I will,' I say, and it is my turn to touch his face. 'But for now it is enough for me to be your wife.'

Leo puts his hand on my swollen stomach. 'And the mother of my child.'

'It is a boy,' I tell him. 'I can feel it. He will be King.'

'Our son, the King.' Leo nods, smiling. 'But first and foremost, our son.'

Chapter Forty-One

Clarence House, 28 July 1981

Diana wanders over to window. She is back in Clarence House, in the same room with the four-poster bed and the view out over the gardens towards The Mall. Could this be the room where Leo stayed before his wedding to Charlotte? Diana likes the idea of a connection between them. She has grown fond of both Charlotte and Leo while she's been reading the journal and knowing that they deal with so many of the same issues, particularly the intrusive British press which can still seem positively feral at times in its relentless pursuit of royalty.

Yesterday was an exhausting roller coaster of emotions: despair knowing Charles was lunching with Camilla; her anguished confession to her sisters that she couldn't go through with the marriage met with a bracing dose of reality; the daunting rehearsal at St Paul's and realising how much there was to remember; the unexpected fun of the ball.

Today there was just a last-minute fitting for the wedding dress – Elizabeth Emanuel had to take in the bodice yet again, by another quarter of an inch each side – and the television interview to get through before she and Charles hosted a party for the staff who weren't invited to the wedding ball. Diana didn't watch the interview, which was broadcast on the BBC and ITV. She isn't sure about her choice of a demure grey dress with a Peter Pan collar and is afraid that she came across as awkward and shy. Better not to see it and obsess over it, Diana decided.

Now all the preparations are done, the run-up is over. Decisions have been made and cannot now be changed. The whole wedding enterprise has been like a massive steam-roller rumbling unstoppably towards this moment and there is nothing to do but get through tomorrow.

She is spending the last night before the wedding at Clarence House, apparently to preserve the notion that she has been living apart from Charles throughout the engagement. The truth is that they *have* been effectively living apart, but apparently nobody trusts the public to understand that you can live under one (huge) roof without what the papers would doubtless call 'hanky-panky' going on.

Waiting for the fitting earlier, and trying not to feel anxious about the interview, Diana had picked up Charlotte's journal once more. She was glad to know that Charlotte and Leo were so happy in the end. It's reassuring that they grew to love each other after their marriage, to know that it's possible. She hopes it will be the same for her and Charles. As Leo said, how can they love each other if they don't really know each other?

She and Charles are so rarely alone that they have never had the chance to get to know each other properly, Diana realises now. She remembers a moment in Australia, after she had accepted Charles, but before the engagement was announced. Her mother was afraid that marriage to Charles would have too many echoes of her own disastrous marriage to Diana's father. She tried to dissuade Diana from going ahead: she was too young, the age gap with Charles was too great, they had too little in common. Diana wouldn't listen.

'Mummy, you don't understand,' she said. 'I love him.'

She remembers the heat that day, the smell of dust and dry gum leaves, and how beyond the shade of the veranda the fierce Australian light hammered the red earth.

'Love *him* or love what he is?' her mother asked.

'What's the difference?' she asked.

She hadn't understood. The love she has always felt for Charles has been infatuation, she can see that now. And for Charles, perhaps she seemed to offer everything he thought he wanted. She adored him so openly last year, Diana remembers. For a while he really did seem besotted with her. But just as she did, Diana is afraid that he fell in love with the idea of her and not the reality of her.

One of the interviewers earlier asked her what interests she and Charles shared and her mind went momentarily blank. 'Music,' she remembered at last, and at least that was something they do both love, but then she rambled on about the sports that Charles likes to do and that she hates. She even suggested that she shared his passion for polo, for God's sake! Diana laughs wryly to herself. If she never had to sit through another wretched polo match, she would be more than happy!

But perhaps all is not lost, though, she comforts herself. Perhaps like Charlotte and Leo, once they are married, they can find a way through, they can share more interests and come to love each other after all.

Charles has gone to Hyde Park to light the first in a great chain of bonfires across the country before a celebratory firework display. When Diana opens the window she can hear the screams of the rockets, the bangs and whistles and pops as they explode across the London sky, but she can't see anything. Beyond the garden of Clarence House, people are settling down for a night in the open to ensure they have a good view of the procession next day. They can see: they are oohing and aahing at the firework display, their excited chatter and laughter and occasional bursts of song blurring into a swell of sound.

'The crowds are absolutely amazing,' Jane says when she arrives to spend the evening with Diana. 'There are people *everywhere*. On the streets, on balconies, on rooftops. Hyde Park is packed – they're saying half a million people are there watching the fireworks. Traffic is at a standstill. It feels as if the whole of London is at a party!'

'Everyone except me,' Diana says dolefully. 'And now you. Why is it the bride isn't allowed to have any fun before a wedding?'

'Tomorrow's your day,' Jane assures her. 'You need to be

resting, not having fun. Tomorrow is going to be a long day. Now, have you had anything to eat?'

'I'm not sure I could eat anything. I'm too nervous.'

'You must have something or you'll be faint.'

Jane takes charge. She is used to royal households, and before Diana can marshal any arguments, she has arranged for a meal to be served. As soon as Diana sits down, she realises that she is starving. She eats everything and then asks for more, and even when they have retired up to her room, she sends a request down to the kitchen for more ice cream.

'Are you sure?' Jane asks dubiously. 'I thought you couldn't eat?'

'Now I can.' Diana has been starving herself for months. She recognises the signs of a bingeing session, but she is too jittery with nerves to try and control the craving for food. The wedding is tomorrow. Elizabeth Emanuel told her that her waist measurement has gone down from twenty-nine inches to twenty-three and a half. The wedding dress has had to be altered repeatedly. So tonight, surely, she can eat what she wants?

They make the mistake of putting on the television to watch the news, which is all about preparations for the royal wedding. Diana eats bowl after bowl of ice cream or custard or cereal, which an impassive footman brings to the room and listens to a reporter talking to the cheerful people waiting out in The Mall, all of whom tell him how thrilled they are to be there and how much they are looking forward to the next day. Another report speculates wildly about what Diana's dress will look like. The guest list is excitedly analysed, the processional route outlined, the security arrangements hinted at, the timetable for the day described in detail.

Diana feels dizzy. God, all those people! All that planning! What if she comes out in spots tonight? What if the dress doesn't fit? What if she trips over her dress? What if her father can't make it up that long, long aisle? What if she falls over when she curtseys to the Queen? What if Charles runs off with Camilla tonight and isn't there when she gets to the cathedral? What if—?

'Gosh, this is going to be *huge*,' Jane interrupts her frenzied thoughts. 'And it's all about you, Duch. Can you believe it's actually happening?'

Diana stares at the screen without speaking, the enormity of what she has set in motion with her casual acceptance of Charles's proposal – 'all right then' – bearing down on her.

'Excuse me,' she says abruptly, and leaping to her feet she runs to the bathroom where she is violently, blessedly sick.

Afterwards she feels better, purged, clean and calm.

Jane fusses worriedly around, making Diana splash cold water on her face and do her teeth. 'I *knew* you shouldn't have had all those puddings.'

'I'm fine, Jane. It was just nerves.'

'You mustn't worry about tomorrow,' Jane says. 'I know you'll be marvellous—' She breaks off at a soft knock on the door. 'Don't tell me you ordered *more* ice cream?'

'Not me,' Diana says. 'I'm done.'

When Jane opens the door, she finds a footman who

proffers a small package on a tray. 'For Lady Diana,' he says.

'What is it?' Diana asks as Jane closes the door and passes her the package.

'You'd better open it and see.'

Diana sits on the edge of the bed, turning the package over in her hands curiously before ripping it open and upending it.

A signet ring tumbles into her lap. When she picks it up, she sees that it is engraved with Prince of Wales feathers.

'It's from Charles,' she tells Jane.

There is a note with it. Unfolding it, she reads it to herself, and then out loud to Jane. *'I'm so proud of you and when you come up the aisle, I'll be there at the altar for you tomorrow. Just look 'em in the eye and knock 'em dead.'*

'Ah!' Jane looks gratified. 'There now, he's thinking of you. What more do you want?'

A word of love, perhaps? But Diana slips the ring on her finger and smooths out the note so that she can read it again. It is just the reassurance she needs. *I'm so proud of you.* Perhaps, perhaps, this will work after all.

Jane smiles. 'Do you think you can sleep now?'

'I hope so.'

'I should go and let you get some rest.' Jane gives her a hug. 'We're *all* proud of you, Diana. Really we are.'

When her sister has gone, Diana stands at the window once more, turning the ring on her finger and listening to the crowds outside. They are still in a jolly mood, with outbreaks of singing – and dancing, too, judging by the roars of 'Whoah, the hokey cokey! Whoah, the hokey cokey!' She envies their uncomplicated enjoyment and anticipation of the day to come.

She knows that she should go to bed, but she can't imagine sleeping. Charles's note has steadied her. She can do this, she vows. She will put all thoughts of how many people will be watching tomorrow out of her head and just think about Charles and how it will feel to marry him. She will do as he says and knock 'em dead, she thinks, smiling.

In the meantime, it is far too noisy to sleep yet. The crowd is still at full volume, putting their left legs in, their left legs out. Diana looks at the television, but that will just be about the wedding. What she needs is a distraction, and she turns, remembering Charlotte's journal that she has brought with her as there are only a few pages left to read.

Chapter Forty-Two

Claremont, November 1817

The baby is late. Dr Baillie thought it would be delivered towards the end of October, but October has come and gone and still there is no sign of my son wanting to join the world. I confess I am weary of waddling around. My belly is huge. The Queen's eyes widened when she visited. She thinks me immense, but the doctors say there is no cause for concern. That is all very well for them, but they are not the ones who cannot get comfortable, whose back is sore and whose feet ache.

I must not complain. I try hard not to, for does not every woman go through what I am going through? Why should it be any easier for me?

Sir Richard Croft has been engaged as my accoucheur. I am told he is vastly experienced. He seems a cheerful, good-humoured man who believes in letting nature take its course, and when I think of the alternative – forceps and other metal tools – I cannot help but agree with him. The wet nurse has been chosen. She has just given birth to a hearty boy and I envy her being on the other side of the ordeal. Mrs Griffiths, who has attended many aristocratic childbirths, is to be my nurse. The Archbishop of Canterbury, the Bishop of London and the Privy Counsellors who are required to witness the birth of a future sovereign are all waiting, their horses harnessed and their carriages readied.

I am past caring. I just want it to be over and to hold my son in my arms. His layette, lovingly embroidered by Mrs Louis, lies in a drawer. We just await the baby's pleasure. Already he is more than two weeks overdue. I tell Leo that I hope he will not be so discourteous in life.

In the meantime, Sir Thomas Lawrence has been here for nine days painting my portrait. It is to be my birthday present for Leo on the sixteenth, although I am hoping that he will be more pleased with his son – oh, how I wish this birth were over! I cannot deny that while I am looking forward to having the baby, I am also feeling some trepidation. I do not wish to alarm Leo as he is so anxious on my behalf so I pretend that I am perfectly well, which I am, just a little fearful of the discomfort and unknowability of it all. The truth is that I am a great coward, but I bluster it out like the best of them until the danger is over.

So I send Leo off to shoot with Baron Hardenbroek to distract him, while I drive around the park in my little chaise. We are both better for some air, but this evening it starts without warning, and after waiting for so long, it comes as a shock when my waters break and I am seized by the most awful pains. Then there is much rushing around and hurried footsteps and messages sent to Mrs Griffiths and the doctors while Anna helps me walk around and bears my fingers digging into her arm when the contractions strike.

'I have changed my mind,' I whisper to Anna. 'I don't want to have the baby after all.'

She grins at me. 'It's a bit late for that now, ma'am.'

'I didn't know it would hurt this much.'

'Hush now, here's Mrs Griffiths. She'll know what to do for you.'

And in fact I do feel better with Mrs Griffiths there. She seems to know what she is about, which is good because I certainly do not.

'No need to rush, Sir,' she says to Leo in a motherly way when he comes in haste. 'It'll be a while yet. You go and enjoy your dinner.'

I am glad when he refuses to leave. He holds my hand and lets me squeeze his fingers when the pain comes in savage waves. I am awed by the immensity of it, this sense of being in the grip of a force greater than I have ever known. It is stronger than the wind, stronger than the tide, stronger than time itself. What use is my royal status in the face of nature and the need for this child to be born?

I lose track of time. Leo is there, I hold on to that, but otherwise there is just a blur of faces, cheerful at first and then fading gradually to grave.

'Is everything proceeding as planned?' I ask Dr Croft when he has examined me.

'I fear there may be some irregularity in the uterus,' he tells me, not quite meeting my eyes. 'Either that or the child is unusually large. But there is nothing to worry about,' he adds quickly, putting on a more cheerful expression. 'We will let the labour proceed naturally and consider at a later stage if it might be wise to give some artificial assistance with forceps.'

I don't like the sound of that, but I must trust in him. I am almost glad when the contractions resume and I am helped to the bedroom next to the Grand Library which has been prepared for the birth. It must happen soon, I think.

But it does not. Hours, days, nights pass: I no longer know. I drift between exhaustion and pain. Sometimes I have moments of piercing clarity: the warmth of Leo's fingers tight around me, the drawn look in his eyes. Mrs Louis, her mouth pinched with worry. The stale smell of sweat and vomit.

'Is something wrong?' I ask weakly as Dr Croft straightens from peering between my legs. 'It shouldn't take this long, should it?'

'Everything is as it should be, Your Royal Highness,' he reassures me. 'The child is just taking its time.'

At other times, I am caught up in a great tide, jostling me backwards and forwards in time, sweeping me back to the past before surging forward once more.

I am playing in the stables at Carlton House with Anna, the air rich with the comforting smell of horses and leather and hay.

I'm lying in the meadow with Leo, watching a ladybird climb up a blade of long grass.

I am in the sea at Weymouth, digging my toes into the sand, feeling it rush away beneath my feet while the sun glitters fiercely on the water.

I'm driving through the crowds to my wedding, feeling blessed by their love and goodwill.

I am at the Frost Fair, laughing. That must be why I am so cold.

I am in my mother's bedroom with Charles Hesse and I am bleeding, I am bleeding, I am bleeding...

'I am bleeding,' I mutter.

'Hush, all is well.' Leo takes a damp cloth from Anna and wipes my face. 'The baby is coming now.'

'How long has it been?'

Leo looks grim. 'Fifty hours... my poor Mäuschen, it has been a hard labour for you.'

'That explains why I am rather tired,' I say, summoning a smile.

'Dr Croft says it will not be long now,' he promises.

It *feels* long. It feels as if I am trapped in a dark tunnel of pain, only vaguely aware of exhortations to push or to breathe or worried glances being exchanged.

At last, at last, when I have no more strength to do anything, I feel the child being drawn out of me, but there is no thin cry, no murmuring of relief, just an ominous silence.

With difficulty I raise my head. 'What...?' I whisper hoarsely, but when I see Leo's set face, I know.

'A boy... Charlotte, they are trying to save him.'

'He is dead?'

Leo glances over at the doctors. I cannot see them shake their heads, I can only see Leo's shoulders slump in grief.

I lie back. I look up at the canopy. My vision is grey at the edges. I am so tired, so very tired. I cannot be strong any more. I cannot even grieve. 'It is God's will,' I say.

'You are alive, that is all that matters now.' Leo is kissing my hand, again and again. 'You must rest and get well.'

I lift my free hand to touch his hair. 'You must rest too, my love. You are exhausted.'

'I do not want to leave you.'

'It's over now,' I tell him. 'Go and sleep, *Doucement*.'

His smile is twisted as he bends down to kiss my forehead. 'Only because I know you must sleep too. Dr Croft and Dr Baillie will care for you and Anna is here too.'

I nod, beyond talking any more, but the moment he goes, I want to call him back. My anchor has gone; who will hold me now? I am being selfish, I tell myself. He will only be a few rooms away. I will see him tomorrow when all this will be a terrible memory. The pain in my stomach will have gone, the ice around my heart will have melted.

They have taken the child away. I did not see him. 'A noble infant,' said Dr Croft.

Noble, but dead.

'They tried everything,' Anna tells me a little later when I ask. I have had a cup of tea and am feeling a little better. 'They put brandy in his mouth, blew in his little lungs. They gave him a warm bath and rubbed him with salt and mustard, but they couldn't bring him back.' Anna's face is set, her lips pressed hard together way she does when she is upset. 'I'm sorry.'

'Where's Mrs Louis?'

'We sent her to bed. She's been here for three days and she's exhausted, same as the Prince.'

'You're still here,' I point out. 'You must be tired, too.'

She shrugs that off. 'You know me, I always like to be where I can interfere.'

I smile faintly. 'What about Toby and Puff?'

'I've taken them,' she says. 'They don't like all these people around.'

A memory swims into my head. 'Do you remember I wrote my will when I was just a child? I left you my dogs then.'

'I'll look after them, but just until you're better, mind,' she adds, scowling ferociously.

'Good.' I stretch out my hand to hers. 'Thank you, Anna. Thank you for everything. I think I can sleep now.'

I dream of blood and wake feeling sick with a terrible ringing in my ears. Dr Croft prescribes a camphor mixture which I promptly sick up. Anna holds the chamber pot for me and wipes my face afterwards. How many times has she dealt with the vile content of my chamber pot over the years?

'I am sorry,' I whisper.

'Don't be sorry, just get better.'

'I'm trying,' I say but I feel so weak, so cold. The greyness that has been pressing against my eyeballs and my eardrums is brightening and I am floating, untethered.

'Leo!' I call out, needing to hold on to him.

Anna's face swims in and out of focus. 'Dr Stockmar's gone to get him.'

Someone is raising me up, pouring liquid down my throat. Brandy? An opiate? It burns as I choke and cough.

'Gently!' Anna's voice is sharp. 'Let me do it.' I sense her pushing someone out of the way and then she is holding me up and coaxing me to sip some more, but my lips won't work properly. I am cold, I am cold and my head is spinning.

'Here's an old friend of yours,' Dr Croft says.

I manage to focus on Stocky's worried face. 'Stocky!' I try to grasp his hand. 'Stocky, they've made me tipsy.' That explains the rushing sound in my ears again and the way I am fading in and out. 'Where's Leo?'

Stocky clears his throat. 'He is sleeping, Your Royal Highness.'

Sleeping... I need to sleep too... I need darkness, but instead the light is getting brighter and harsher, making me narrow my eyes against the sunlight on the sea. I am there in the waves, rocking in the water.

'I will go and rouse him,' Stocky says from somewhere. 'I will bring him to you.'

But he's here, I want to say. I am in the sea and Leo is on the beach. Geggy is with him, and Anna and Mrs Louis and Toby and Puff and my grandfather, the King, smiling and well, and behind them the people of Britain are gathered in a great crowd stretching as far as the eye can see. *Don't go,* they are all saying. *Don't go.*

Why are they saying that? I'm not going anywhere. I am just bathing. I am waiting to be dipped.

'Stocky!' I manage to call, needing to tell him not to go, that Leo is here after all. 'Stocky!

But the light is blinding now and the tide is insistent. It is taking me away. No, I think. *No.* I must get to the beach where the people who love me are waiting for me. But it is too late. The sand is rushing, rushing away beneath my feet and the water is lifting me and carrying me away into the dazzle.

Chapter Forty-Three

Clarence House, 28 July 1981

Diana's throat is tight as she realises that Charlotte died just when she had found happiness. Turning the page, she finds an editor's note drafted by Amelia Bell.

Charlotte died on Thursday 6 November. A post mortem revealed a concealed haemorrhage, red fluid in the pericardium and a 'Cyst the size of a Hen's Egg' on Charlotte's right ovary. Post-partum haemorrhage is sometimes given as the cause of her death, but pulmonary embolism may be a more likely explanation.

Whatever the reason, her death, and that of her stillborn child, provoked an outpouring of national grief on a scale never seen before in Britain. For many, Charlotte had represented a bright hope for the future. The public was tired of years of war, disappointed in a sick, old king, and exasperated by the extravagance and dissolute lifestyles of the Prince Regent and his brothers. People were looking forward to a new reign with a queen whose domestic happiness and dislike of ostentatious extravagance already marked her as very different from her father.

Having been reassured that the Princess was enjoying good health throughout her pregnancy, the news of her death, announced by the mournful tolling of church bells, came as a dreadful shock to the country. It was 'as if every family had lost a child', the *Morning Post* reported. Even the poorest of the poor wore a token of mourning while the better-off dressed in black and many of the nobility ordered mourning clothes as if they were at court. Shop windows were half-closed as a mark of respect and black ribbons fluttered at every door. Theatres were closed, dinners, balls and assemblies cancelled. Across the country, people paused their lives in grief.

Charlotte's funeral was held at St George's Chapel, Windsor on 19 November 1817. The previous evening, crowds began to mass, lining the road from Egham to Windsor, to watch the funeral procession bringing her body from Claremont. Inns along the route charged extortionate rates so that those who could pay could watch the hearse pass in the moonlight. Some private homes offered window space for a fee, but many chose to stand quietly in the cold to bear witness to Charlotte's last journey.

The sombre procession reached Windsor half an hour after midnight. It was headed by a coach and six containing Charlotte's heart, which had been placed in an urn, and the tiny coffin of her stillborn son. The hearse that followed carried her coffin, where her body lay on white silk, her head resting on a bolster and pillow covered in white satin. Behind, came a line of mourning carriages that took an hour to pass the crowds watching in a silence broken only by the slow clop of the horses' hooves on the gravel and the creak and rumble of the carriage wheels.

By tradition, the Prince Regent did not attend the funeral, and he was in any case distraught. Prince Leopold was the chief mourner, his carriage followed by the royal dukes and other male relatives. The Queen and Princesses, also barred by etiquette from attending the funeral, could only sit and listen as a detachment of Horse Guards escorted the child's coffin and the urn to the porch of St George's Chapel to be deposited in the royal vault.

Charlotte's body was taken to rest in a black-lined room at Lower Lodge where Leopold, still dazed with grief, sat up all night with it.

The funeral took place the following evening and was a chaotic affair. So many people wanted to attend that tickets had to be issued, but the number of guards placed around chapel meant that many were unable to see, while others were refused admission. The service itself was brief. Charlotte's remains were lowered into the royal vault. Leopold spent ten minutes alone with the coffin for a final farewell and then returned to Claremont.

Leopold was inconsolable. He had taken an opiate to help him sleep after it was clear that the baby could not be revived and when it seemed that Charlotte would recover. The drug meant that Dr Stockmar was unable to rouse him until it was too late. Charlotte's hands were already cold when he fell to his knees by her body and covered them with kisses. For many months after her death he could only drift around Claremont, desolate with grief. He was still a young man and he did eventually marry again, but he never forgot Charlotte. It was, he said, his most 'ardent desire' to be buried with her in St George's Chapel. However, by the time he died he was King of the Belgians, and the Belgian state would not allow their monarch to be buried in a foreign country, next to a foreign princess who had died decades earlier.

Charlotte's death and that of her child wiped out two generations of the royal family and cast the Hanover dynasty into doubt. King George III was still alive but old, ill and incapable. The Prince Regent was not only grossly overweight and in poor health, but also still tied to a wife he loathed. None of his already middle-aged brothers had legitimate children; barred by the Royal Marriages Act from marrying without the King's permission, they had satisfied themselves with mistresses.

The loss of Charlotte as heir presumptive changed all that and prompted an unseemly rush by the unmarried royal dukes to produce a new heir for the dynasty. Long-term mistresses were discarded and the search was on for suitable Protestant princesses. Bluff William, Duke of Clarence, and later King William IV, had ten children by his mistress, Mrs Jordan, but his marriage to Adelaide of Saxe-Meiningen was childless. The next brother in line was Edward, Duke of Kent, who married Prince Leopold's widowed sister, Victoire, in July 1818. They had a daughter, known as Victoria, born on 24 May 1819. The Duke of Kent died a year later, leaving Victoria heir to the throne. On William IV's death in 1837, she became Queen, aged just eighteen.

The Queen who never was, that was what Charles called her. Diana remembers standing in front of Charlotte's portrait with him all those months ago as she closes the file and clips the pages into place. If Charlotte had lived, or if her child had lived, there would have been no Queen Victoria. And if there had been no Queen Victoria, there would have been no House of Windsor, Charles would not be Prince of Wales, she would not be marrying him tomorrow… It makes Diana dizzy to think of the myriad different paths life could have taken had it not been for Charlotte's tragic death. How much would have been different if Charlotte had become Queen? Diana wonders. If there had been a Charlottian Age rather than a Victorian one?

'I think Charlotte would have been a good queen.' Amelia Bell had said that, and Diana agrees with her. Charlotte, she is sure, would have been a queen who looked at individuals and liked them or not regardless of their rank, who thought about the British people, and who cared more for them and their concerns than for the exquisite works of art that filled her father's palaces. One of the few bits of history that Diana has had to learn is the transformation of Buckingham House into a palace by

Charlotte's father when he became George IV. It was he who was responsible for the undoubtedly magnificent state apartments. If Charlotte had ever lived there, perhaps she could have made it into a warmer, friendlier place.

And perhaps she can do the same when she becomes Queen, Diana thinks. She remembers the promise Charlotte and Leo made to each other, that they would bring up their child as their son first, as part of their family, instead of treating him as just a future king. She and Charles would do the same, Diana vows. She will give her children a proper childhood, and make sure they understand the importance of love and of thinking of others.

She will be able to change things when she is married. Hasn't she always felt that she has a destiny? It will start tomorrow, she thinks.

Outside, the crowd are still singing, but less raucously now. Perhaps someone has suggested she might need to sleep tonight. Diana doesn't mind the noise. There is something comforting about the fact that so many strangers are there, wishing her well.

Smiling, she puts Charlotte's journal aside, climbs into bed and turns out the light.

Chapter Forty-Four

Clarence House, 29 July 1981

The room is full of people. Her hairdresser, Kevin Shanley, is there, with his wife as assistant. Barbara Daly is there to do her make-up. The Emanuels are there, with *their* assistants. Her two older bridesmaids, Sarah Armstrong-Jones and India Hicks, are there, as is her dresser, while all sorts of other people are popping in and out. Outside, the crowd is getting louder and more excited, loudly cheering road sweepers and police cars, the noise a continuous roar of goodwill that spills over the walls of the Clarence House garden and in through the open windows, competing with the buzz of helicopters hovering overhead

Strangely, after all her doubts and uncertainties, Diana woke feeling calm and composed. She has expected to feel nervous, but instead is suffused with a sense of simmering anticipation and even... could that be happiness bubbling through her? Empty after the excesses of last night, she had a huge breakfast to stop her tummy rumbling during the service and then put on jeans and a T-shirt as it will clearly be a while before the dress goes on. In the meantime, she has been practising wearing the spectacular Spencer tiara.

'That's an interesting look with jeans,' Elizabeth Emanuel jokes when she comes in and Diana giggles as she adjusts the tiara on her head.

'Perhaps I shouldn't have bothered with a dress?'

'Don't say that!' Elizabeth laughs and they both look to where the dress is hanging, shrouded in covers so no one could get so much as a glimpse before it was carried in to Clarence House. Interest in the design has been intense. The Emanuels have had reporters going through their bins in search of sketches, and the big fashion lines have designers waiting with their own sketchbooks to copy the dress the moment Diana steps out of the coach. Bets are being taken on how soon a version of the dress will be available to buy off the peg.

She has had a little television on in the background all morning, sharing in the building excitement and the cheerfulness of the crowd spills into the bedroom, leaving them slightly giddy. When the commercials come on, Diana hears the famous advertisement for Wall's Cornetto ice cream cones and she spins round.

'Oh, wait, I love this!' Still in jeans and tiara, she joins in with the song. '*Just one Corrrnetttoooo*!' she warbles with suitably extravagant gestures, and then they are all singing along and laughing together. '*Please geeeve to meee…*' It is a perfect, happy moment and when her hair is done and her make-up is done and the wedding dress is carefully lowered over her head at last, Diana feels her heart swell. It is happening, it is really happening. This is the moment she has dreamt of for so many years. It was a fantasy and then a hope and now it is real.

The bridesmaids have gone to change and wait for her downstairs. Diana stands in front of the mirror while the Emanuels twitch and tug and smooth the dress into place. She looks like a princess in a fairy tale, she thinks.

'Oh, it's beautiful...' one of the assistants breathes, and Diana smiles and nods. The Emanuels have given her exactly what she wanted, a full-skirted romantic confection of ivory silk and embroidered lace decorated with pearls and sequins and the bows and ruffles and flounces she adores. The train flows out behind her, carefully folded as the room is too small to stretch it to its full length. She stands still as the tiara she wore so casually earlier is lowered onto her head to keep the billowing tulle veil in place and she thinks of the times she practised walking with an old sheet dragging behind her in place of the train. There will be no more rehearsals, no more practising. This is it.

Her dresser is keeping an eye on the time. The guests will already be in place at St Paul's. They can tell by the waves of cheering that the carriages bearing the royal family from Buckingham Palace have driven down The Mall and are on their way. Downstairs, the Glass Coach is waiting, pulled by Kestrel and Lady Penelope, two bays from the Royal Mews.

'It's time to go...'

Diana takes a deep breath. 'I'm coming.'

Slowly, carefully, she walks to the staircase, the

Emanuels' assistants gathering up the train and veil behind her. Her father, the bridesmaids and the Clarence House staff are waiting in the hall. As one, they turn to look as she appears at the top of the stairs and there is utter silence for a moment, followed by a rustle of *oohs* and *aahs*.

Just the effect she wanted.

Terrified of tripping at this stage, Diana begins her slow descent. Her father steps forward as she reaches the bottom step, his smile shaky with emotion. 'Darling,' he says, 'I'm so proud of you.'

'Thank you, Daddy.' Diana is worried about how he is going to manage the long walk up the aisle at St Paul's. Since his stroke, he has been unsteady on his feet but he is determined to give her away and thrilled with the prospect of a carriage ride.

The Glass Coach is drawn up under the portico of Clarence House. The brass lamps are gleaming, the lacquer glossy, the scarlet wheel spokes freshly painted. A magnificently dressed coachman with a wig and tricorne hat sits impassively atop the box which is covered in scarlet cloth and decorated with gold braid and tassels. The two Windsor bays stand patiently in their polished harness while behind, six mounted police officers are waiting to accompany the coach. Two footmen in full gold livery have let down the steps and stand ready to help her father in.

Diana is next, ducking her head to climb through the door. Inside, the coach is comfortably upholstered in squashy black leather, but it is so much smaller than she or the Emanuels had realised. Her beautiful dress is crushed just getting in. There is an almost comical scene as the veil and train are practically stuffed in after her and piled on the seat opposite. The door is closed, the footmen swing up onto the back and as the coachman gives the horses the signal to move, the coach lurches a little.

Squeezed together, Diana and her father exchange a smile that is part terror, part anticipation. 'Off we go!' he says.

As the coach comes out of the gates of St James's Palace and turns into The Mall, a huge roar of welcome erupts. The police horses toss their heads and cavort while the crowd whistles and cheers and waves flags. Bells are ringing; helicopters hover overhead. It is so unbelievably exciting that Diana cannot help but smile and wave, while beside her Earl Spencer beams with pride. He is having a lovely time, waving back at the thousands of smiling faces lining the route. The noise and fervour are so loud when they come up to St Martin-in-the-Fields that he reaches for the door, assuming that they must have arrived at St Paul's.

'Here we go!'

'Daddy, no!' Diana puts out a hand to stop him. 'We're not there yet!'

'Good Lord,' he says, sinking back against the cushions. 'I've never seen anything like it!'

'It's amazing, isn't it?'

It feels as if they are being carried along the Strand and Fleet Street by a wave of warmth. Outside the coach, there is noise and laughter, the sound of horses' hooves, a blur of Union Jacks, the streets lined with uniforms standing to attention. Inside, there is the smell of leather and new fabric, the comforting bulk of her father, and the sense of being encased in a beautiful soft blur of silk and tulle, while the sequins on her veil wink and glitter in the light.

Up Ludgate Hill, and the coach is slowing at last to draw up at precisely the right spot at the bottom of the steps of St Paul's Cathedral. The footmen are there, letting down the steps, opening the door.

'*This* is it,' Diana tells her father.

He gets out first, and she's glad that there is someone there to help him up the carpeted steps. Now it is her turn. She bends again to get through the door, lifts her skirts to step down and if she has thought the cheers were loud before, they are nothing compared to the one that goes up when the crowd first catches sight of her. Moving forward a little to greet the welcoming party, she waits while the long train and veil are pulled out of the coach after her. She doesn't dare look at how crushed they must be.

Sarah and India are there to take the ends and lift them, while Diana concentrates on climbing the red-carpeted steps without tripping. It was so much easier at the rehearsal! At the top of the steps she turns, just as she practised, to face the crowd but no amount of rehearsing could prepare her for the sheer numbers cheering and waving her and her throat tightens as she lifts a hand in acknowledgement, wondering if any of the people calling her name have any idea of what their joy means to her.

The cathedral is a vast space, all stone and light and almost unrecognisable, crammed as it is with guests on either side of the long aisle. Fleetingly, Diana thinks of Charlotte and her wedding in the Crimson Drawing Room.

What would she have made of three and a half thousand guests?

Her vision is blurred by the veil and everything seems faintly surreal. Above her head, trumpets are blaring. Someone gives her the bouquet and she is momentarily swamped by the fragrance of gardenias and freesias, lily of the valley and roses named after Earl Mountbatten.

Taking her father's arm, Diana concentrates on keeping him in a straight, slow march up the long, long aisle. He is unsteady but dogged as they waver to and fro along the red carpet as the long train and veil drags behind her. She smiles, but most of the faces are a blur until one or two snap oddly into focus. That's how she sees Camilla Parker Bowles, unmistakable in a pale-grey veiled pillbox hat.

Camilla is in the congregation. Diana is the bride. Charles is waiting for *her* at the altar, not Camilla.

Diana lets go of the last of her doubts and her heart brims. She truly is the luckiest girl in the world. It is as if her whole life has been leading to this moment when Charles, Prince of Wales, steps forward to meet her, *her*, Diana Spencer, to make her his Princess.

He smiles at her. 'You look beautiful,' he says in a low voice, just for her to hear.

'Beautiful for you,' she whispers back.

The cathedral itself seems to vibrate with the sound of the first hymn. Diana is achingly aware of Charles beside her, looking marvellous in his uniform and when the Dean begins the service with the traditional reminder that the congregation are gathered here 'to join together this man and this woman', she forgets about the thousands of guests watching. She forgets about the hundreds of thousands of people listening to the service outside, about the millions watching on television around the world. That is all she and Charles are, after all, a man and a woman, and this is about them.

Everything seems to be in slow motion and yet happening too fast, pausing only for brief, vivid impressions: the roar from the listening crowd outside that rolls through the cathedral when she says 'I will'; Charles's reassuring grin as she muddles up his names; blinking at the clarity as she puts her veil back at last; Barbara Daly touching up her lipstick and powder while the registers are being signed; the rustle of her dress as she curtseys to the Queen.

And now she is holding tight to Charles's arm as they make their way back down the aisle and out into the sunlight to be greeted by a wall of jubilant sound. They are driven back to Buckingham Palace in an open carriage through a red, white and blue blur of flags being frenziedly waved by the euphoric crowds. The noise is deafening: pealing bells, the clatter of hooves, the sound of the carriage wheels, the thunk-thunk-thunk of helicopters overhead, and most of all the clapping, the shouts, the cheers, the whistles, the hoots, the calls of 'We love you!' She and Charles have to shout to make themselves heard and they soon give up trying to talk, but they are both bowled over by the joyful affection of the people sharing the happiness of their wedding day.

When the carriage drives into the courtyard at Buckingham Palace the noise is muffled abruptly, but

Diana's ears are still ringing as she climbs down from the carriage. She smiles as she recognises the staff lined up to welcome her. They bow and curtsey. Your Royal Highness, they call her. It should feel strange but it doesn't, it feels right. She is where she is meant to be.

The crowds have swarmed down The Mall after the last cars and carriages have left the cathedral, and they are surging at the gates like a sea, demanding to see the bridal couple. Inside the palace there is the usual hubbub and kissing as the guests invited to the wedding breakfast arrive. Charles finds Diana in a quiet corner, comforting little Catherine Cameron who, having had the thrill of a carriage ride back to the palace, turns out to have had an allergic reaction to the horses. Diana is sitting down on the floor with her, careless of her dress which is in any case is irredeemably crushed, and mopping her small bridesmaid's streaming eyes.

'Can I borrow Diana, Catherine?' Charles asks.

When Catherine nods solemnly, he reaches down his hand to pull Diana to her feet. 'You must be exhausted, darling. I know I am!'

'Well, it's been *quite* a big day,' she says and he smiles at the understatement.

'We can sit down at the wedding breakfast soon but first, I'm afraid, we're needed out on the balcony...'

The crowds are getting restless. Their chants of *We want Charles and Di!* or *We want the bride and groom!* beat at the palace walls and windows.

Diana smooths down her dress as best she can as the balcony doors are opened by two footmen, a sign that provokes a roar of approval from the crowd. Charles smiles and offers his arm.

'Ready?'

Out of nowhere, Diana remembers peering out of the window when she first moved into Buckingham Palace and wondering if anyone could see her. It feels as if the whole world is waiting to see her now, watching as she steps out of her old life and into her new role as Princess of Wales. She thinks of that magical carriage ride back from the cathedral, of the love and warmth of the people calling for her now. After all the doubts and uncertainties of the past few months, she is happy and eager to take on the destiny that she has always known awaits her.

She smiles back at Charles. 'I'm ready,' she says and together they step out onto the balcony and into an eruption of joy from the people waiting below.

Acknowledgments

On 29 July 1981, I was in The Mall with thousands of others to watch Lady Diana Spencer leave Clarence House for her wedding to the Prince of Wales. Most of us could see little more than the tops of the Life Guards' helmets bobbing past but we cheered along anyway, caught up in the excitement and the party atmosphere. I remember the fireworks the night before and the pubs being open all day but to my shame I don't recall wondering what it was like for Diana herself that day or, indeed, what it had been like for her since the engagement was announced.

The People's Princess is, obviously, a work of fiction, but it is based on fact. The hard thing, of course, is to decide what is fact and what is perspective, what is a real memory and what is wishful thinking. This is particularly true of Diana. She remains one of the most famous people in the world, and so much has been written about her, but the truth remains elusive. We rarely remember our own lives with total accuracy, and Diana's own account of her engagement to the Prince of Wales, as told to Andrew Morton in *Diana: Her True Story – In Her Own Words* (1992, 2017), is inevitably coloured by later events.

In spite of living though that time myself, I had to research 1981 as if it were any other historical period. I drew on Morton's book, of course, but I also found Tina Brown's *The Diana Chronicles* (2007, 2017) and Sarah Bradford's *Diana* (2006, 2017) in particular very helpful in offering different perspectives on Diana's story, and where there have been different interpretations of what was said or done or felt, I have, as a novelist, felt free to make up my own mind.

I have done the same with Princess Charlotte's story. Although most of the scenes are based on fact, I have invented or elaborated others. I am indebted to Anne Stott's timely book *The Lost Queen: The Life & Tragedy of the Prince Regent's Daughter* (2020), but James Chambers's *Charlotte & Leopold: The True Story of the Original People's Princess* (2007), Alison Plowden's *Caroline & Charlotte: The Regent's Wife and Daughter 1795-1821* (1989) and Thea Holme's *Prinny's Daughter: A Biography of Princess Charlotte of Wales* (1976) were also useful and interesting. It's impossible not to wonder what Britain would have been like if we had had a Charlottian age instead of a Victorian one. Perhaps one individual wouldn't have made much difference. Still, I cannot help feeling, like my fictional historian Amelia Bell, that Charlotte would have been a good queen in spite – or perhaps because – of her reckless, passionate spirit, her frankness and her longing for love.

Getting to the end of a book means having to wrench yourself out of a different time and place. It is always an unsettling time, but at least it gives me a chance to pass on some sincere thanks: to Charlotte Ledger, Bethan Morgan and the rest of the team at One More Chapter for all their support; to my agent, Caroline Sheldon; and to friends who have patiently listened to me talk about Princess Diana and Princess Charlotte over the past few months and who will probably be gladder than I am that the book is finished at last.

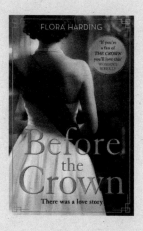

Don't miss *Before the Crown*, another page-turning and romantic historical novel from Flora Harding...

Windsor Castle, 1943: As war rages across the world, Princess Elizabeth comes face to face with the dashing naval officer she first met in London nine years before.

One of the youngest first lieutenants in the Royal Navy, Philip represents everything she has always been taught to avoid. Instability. Audacity. Adventure. But when the king learns of their relationship, the suitability of the foreign prince is questioned by all at court.

He is the risk she has never been allowed to take. The risk not even the shadow of the crown will stop her from taking...

Step through the palace gates and discover a captivating historical novel of royal secrets and forbidden love...

YOUR NUMBER ONE STOP

ONE MORE CHAPTER

FOR PAGETURNING BOOKS

One More Chapter is an
award-winning global
division of HarperCollins.

Sign up to our newsletter to get our
latest eBook deals and stay up to date
with our weekly Book Club!
<u>Subscribe here.</u>

Meet the team at
<u>www.onemorechapter.com</u>

Follow us!

𝕏 <u>@OneMoreChapter_</u>
f   <u>@OneMoreChapter</u>
⧉ <u>@onemorechapterhc</u>

Do you write unputdownable fiction?
We love to hear from new voices.
Find out how to submit your novel at
<u>www.onemorechapter.com/submissions</u>